AF669732

Sunil Gangopadhyay

Soiled Clothes

Translated from the Bengali original *Dhulibasan*
by
Sujal Bhattacharya

NIYOGI
BOOKS

Published by
NIYOGI BOOKS
D-78, Okhla Industrial Area, Phase-I
New Delhi-110 020, INDIA
Tel: 91-11-26816301, 26813350, 51, 52
Fax: 91-11-26810483, 26813830
email: niyogibooks@gmail.com
website: www.niyogibooks.com

Text © Sunil Gangopadhyay

Cover Design: Nabanita Das
Editor: Sucharita Ghosh

ISBN: 978-81-89738-68-6

Publication: 2010

This is a work of fiction. The names, characters and incidents portrayed in it are the work of the author's imagination. Any resemblance to actual persons, living or dead, events or localities, is entirely coincidental.

All rights are reserved. No part of this publication may be reproduced or transmitted in any form or by any means, electronic or mechanical, including photocopying, recording or by any information storage and retrieval system without prior written permission and consent of the publisher.

Printed at: Niyogi Offset Pvt. Ltd., New Delhi, India.

For

Victoria

and

Bhaskar Dutta

1

A motor car is approaching the house at a fairly good speed. Normally, this area is shunned by vehicles. At this hour of the night, one can hardly hear the sound of cycle-rikshaws. Now surprisingly, it seems as if, storming down the path, crashing through the bushes and demolishing the flower plants, a car is heading towards the house. Standing near the window, Mandira can see the advancing headlights.

Her table is placed beside the latticed window. Though the net covering the window is capable of barring worms and insects, yet unfortunately for Mandira, it does not keep the mosquitoes away. However, she is glad that at least it fortifies the house well against frogs. When she had first arrived in this village, the monsoons had just set in, and then she had often seen frogs squatting on the floor and wriggling through. Instinctively she abhors these apparently harmless creatures as they remind her of the macabre shadows of snakes.

A few scattered trees are visible through the window. A little distance away, lies a pond. Occasionally, the moon shines in its water. Last month, at midnight, Mandira was startled by the sound of something heavy falling from a height into the pond. Later, having realised that it was only a palm fruit which had fallen from one of the three palmyra trees that silhouetted the banks of the pond, she felt ashamed of her timidity.

A frog squatting on the floor of her living room, or the sound of a palm fruit splashing into the deep water of a tank—such mundane experiences are unprecedented for her. They often unsettle her. Does this mean that life still has some surprises in store for her? These unexpected surprises and fears make her body and mind lively, vivacious.

Indeed, life ceases to be worth living in the absence of these sensations.

On the opposite side of the pond, stands a well-built but dilapidated house, that was perhaps built by its owner with many expectations, but now lies deserted; even the legal heirs of the house do not visit any more. The ground floor is occupied by a local family but the upper floor is left high and dry, to be reigned supreme by weeds and unwanted plants. Cracks have appeared on the walls as the mighty roots of a peepal tree are forcing their way through. The surroundings have become a den for scavengers. Sometimes at the dead of night, weird noises, resembling the cry of a baby, shake up the neighbourhood.

Known as Lahiri Villa, this forgotten building is up for sale. A few prospective buyers have already shown interest. Rumour is that a certain Marwari entrepreneur is thinking of setting up a plant here for manufacturing phials and small bottles.

Has anyone come to inspect Lahiri Villa at this hour? wonders Mandira.

The small timepiece on the study table shows the time—a quarter to ten. The room where Mandira lives has no other furniture besides a small table, a chair and a bed. A white bedsheet is spread on the bed and a light blue-coloured mosquito net is rigged up on it. A few important books are stored in a cane basket under the bedstead. Mandira does not like to keep the books on the bare floor as they might absorb the damp from the floor. Nor does she like to make the room cluttered and congested by bringing in almirahs and bookshelves.

From the highway, an almost mile-long, semi-concrete road runs up to Battala. From there five narrow avenues deviate into five different directions like the five fingers of a hand. Hence, at this labyrinthine crossroads, wayfarers new to this place, often get confused.

Like the people of this village, Mandira also tries to make it a habit to go to bed early at night, but in vain. How can she? After all, she cannot forsake her habit of reading till late into the night! With much self-determination, at least, she has been able to cut down her quota of cigarettes—from forty to a bare minimum of three. And that too not in public. A herculian task indeed! She smokes her last cigarette at eleven p.m. While reading at night the urge to inhale the blessed puff becomes so strong that at an interval of every five minutes she feels as if a sitarist is harping on the strings to remind her constantly of the cherished moment.

The car must have lost its way, there's no doubt about it, thinks Mandira. Having been familiar with automobiles of various types, she has the expertise to recognise the brand, make or type of the car from the very sound of its engine. Yet in this remote village, the sound of a car at this obscure hour, drowning the drone of crickets, is most ill-becoming and incongruous.

The car stops near her house. The headlights are switched off. The door of the car opens and then slams shut with a bang. At least more than one person alight from the car and engage in a conversation among themselves. Meanwhile, the sound of the car engine has attracted a few folks from the neighbourhood who flock around it. The news of the proposed new factory at Lahiri Villa has caused tremendous excitement amongst the villagers who are speculating on the job opportunities that would open up for the local youths.

'So Lahiri Villa has finally been sold out!' Mandira mutters to herself. It is an old-fashioned mansion with two life-sized lions sculpted in concrete (one of them being headless). Such a dilapidated old building matches well with an obscure landscape like this, she thinks; but if a factory comes up in its place, the village will undergo a sea-change.

'Didi, some visitors have come to meet you,' says Shanti peering through the door. Shanti is in her teens, fifteen or sixteen years old, though she herself doesn't know her age. Her young body hasn't yet started its journey towards womanhood. Though thinly built and tall, she has a handsome face and an unkempt natural beauty. Her complexion resembles the colour of the silt left behind on the sandbank immediately after the tide. Because of her large eyes, she bears an expression of awestruck wonder about this mundane world.

'To meet me?' asks Mandira in amazement.

With her head lowered, Shanti replies, 'Yes, they are mentioning your name.'

Rising up from her bed, she adjusts the pallu of the blue sari, wipes off the perspiration on her face with a tissue paper and, wearing her pair of rubber sandals, comes out on the veranda. Jasmine and China rose shrubs, in full bloom, line both sides of the front courtyard. There has been a mild shower in the evening. The fragrance of hashnuhana is still lingering in the air. In spite of being a moonlit night, the moon lies hidden behind thin layers of clouds.

As the courtyard is small, the car is parked outside the fences surrounding the courtyard. A few men, standing near the car, are talking amongst themselves. Right at the centre of the courtyard is standing a man.

'Who's there?' asks Mandira.

The man remains quiet.

Taking the lantern from Shanti's hand, Mandira holds it aloft and stands on the edge of the porch.

A middle-aged, well-built man, with slightly grey hair around the temples, clad in a grey suit with the necktie loosened, stands staring at Mandira. The man's eyes appear to be drowsy.

His face bears a blank expression, as though sculptured. His hands are folded crosswise on his chest in Swami Vivekananda's posture.

Mandira stands dumbstruck for a while.

A classic scene indeed! A man and a woman keep gazing at each other, spellbound. They are meeting each other today after as long as twenty-seven years. Well, they met twice for a brief spell in those twenty-seven years but that was immaterial. The duration of their separation is twenty-seven years, but it seems to be a millennium now.

Mandira breaks the ice, by addressing him in a normal tone, 'Biman!'

The man's voice, like that of a thespian, trembles, 'Mani are you really ... in this faraway, remote place!'

He is clearly in an intoxicated state. Which is why he sounds so emotional. His glazed eyes, his slightly dramatic manner of speech, though genuine, are nevertheless the result of an excitement induced by a hangover.

'Who gave you my address? It must be Prabir!' she exclaims.

The man immediately retorts in a hurt tone, 'Why? Am I not welcome here? Have I done anything wrong by coming here ... Should I leave at once?'

Mandira steps down from the veranda and clasping Biman's hand, says warmly, 'You're most welcome. Please do come inside.'

Biman takes away his hand and enfolding Mandira, presses his cheek against hers. He breaks into tears like a child. 'Mani, my dear Mani ... you've been staying here for the last two months, yet I didn't know. Why, Mani, why?'

His cry seems to be a heart-rending lament.

At a little distance, the other person is standing quietly in the dark. From a tree an owl cries out in a melancholy note. Mandira is still holding the lantern. She may be singed by the way Biman is holding her.

Biman's arrival is unexpected. Yet she shouldn't have told him that. He has been hurt, so he is repeatedly saying the same things in a weeping voice.

Mandira knows that there is no point in arguing with a drunkard. In a mollycoddling tone, patting his back, she says, 'No, of course it isn't like that. I can never think of avoiding you, can I? Come along inside, Biman. I've a lot of things to tell you.'

A small crowd has in the meanwhile gathered around the fence. Releasing herself from Biman's arms, she casts a glance at them while calling out, 'Prabir, do come in.'

Prabir, tall and slim, below forty, is clad in a batik print shirt. He is Mandira's cousin. Two days back she had a chance meeting with Prabir at Bagdi Market, Calcutta, where she had gone to buy some toiletries. Initially, Prabir could not believe that it was really Mandira, shopping, all by herself, at Bagdi market.

Evidently Prabir is suffering from a sense of guilt for accompanying Biman to his sister's house without prior notice.

'Biman da insisted on coming. You had asked me not to inform our relatives, but I suppose telling Biman da about you was alright?'

Though there are some chairs on the veranda, Mandira leads them into the room as a curious crowd is still standing on the compound. She instructs Shanti to tell the crowd, waiting inquisitively out there, that the visitors are her guests: her brother and his friend.

By this time a light drizzle has turned into a heavy downpour. Rain drops are pattering heavily on the tin shed and sounding like an orchestra.

Mandira offers them two chairs. Biman has in the meanwhile relaxed a bit and the early signs of agitation are gone. Wiping his face with a handkerchief reveals a different countenance: a man with a strong personality, affluent and immensely successful in life.

The flashlight on Mandira's study table has made the room partially bright.

Seeing her, standing with a lantern in her hand, Biman at first casts a searching glance all over the room and then says, 'So you're staying here! Will you live here for good?'

'What makes you say so? Do you think it's not worth living here? This twelve by eighteen feet room is spacious enough, isn't it?' asks Mandira.

'But it's too hot, you don't have fans here,' says Biman.

'Yes, I'll arrange for fans. I'm going to have an electric connection soon. Right now, I hope you won't have much trouble since it has been raining for a couple of days.'

'But it's too sultry and humid.'

'You may be feeling very uncomfortable but I don't,' says Mandira with an impish smile.

That makes Biman rather angry. He shouts, 'But tell me, why must you be living in this godforsaken village, that too under tin sheds? Why!'

Mandira, with that same smile lingering on her lips, says, 'In English the answer to your question is just a 'because', in French *parce que* and in Bengali *emni*. Some personal questions have no answers, Biman.'

'Mani di has left England bag and baggage. She has even sold her house there ... am I correct Mandira di?' asks Prabir.

Mandira, evading this question, asks, 'You've come at this late hour of the night; have you two had any dinner?'

Biman replies brusquely, 'You don't have to worry about our dinner. We've got plenty of chapattis and also some cooked meat. Prabir, fetch them from the car.'

'Not now. It's still raining,' says Prabir.

Lighting a cigarette, Biman brings out a bottle of whisky from his coat's pocket and says, 'Help me with a glass. So who else lives with you here?'

'That little girl Shanti lives with me. By the way, I request you not to drink here.'

'Why not?' asks Biman in a sudden outburst of rage. 'Am I sitting in a temple? Have you set up some kind of a religious institution, that I can't drink here?'

'Oh no. It's just that we happen to be in the heart of a village and the folks here are unaccustomed to it,' Mandira says very politely.

'Do you think they don't drink? Spurious liquor dens have sprouted up at every nook and corner. I don't care a damn about them. I'll have my drinks here. If you don't give me a glass, I'll drink neat from the bottle.'

'Biman da has already drained a bottle down his throat while travelling in the car,' adds Prabir.

'So what?' says Biman, haughtily, 'I can stand more than twenty pegs.'

'Then don't drink it raw. Wait. I'm giving you a glass and water.'

Every night Shanti unfailingly keeps a jug of water and a glass under Mandira's bed. She gives that glass and water to Biman.

'Prabir is a teetotaller. Won't you give me company though, Mandira? Fetch two glasses. I hope you have not given up drinking and become a sanyasini!'

'But when did I ever drink? Occasionally, I had a few pegs of wine.'

'Come on, Mandira, I had seen you drinking at Dr Sen's party at Belsize Park in err ... 1982,' Biman says, frowning hard.

'No, not in 1982, that was in March 1983,' rectifies Mandira. 'I remember having a glimpse of you there. That day I had tasted champagne. Hard drinks like whisky have never been my cup of tea.'

Biman pours whisky in one glass only. After a loud sip, he says, 'I was visiting a doctor's surgery at Harley Street ... I met Dr Sen accidentally. He is a distant relative from my in-laws' side. He had invited me to the party. Had I known you were coming there, I wouldn't have gone to the party. I understood you were avoiding me there because your husband was with you—am I right? So, I never tried to look you up, never tried to intrude ...'

'My husband would be too busy talking to other people at those parties. He wouldn't have time to bother about me. That day I was ...' saying this much Mandira breaks off. She feels it is redundant to give an explanation for an incident that occurred so long ago; though Biman is waiting, curious.

He is still staring at her.

'By the way, when did you start from Calcutta?' asks Mandira, cleverly changing the topic. 'What about your return journey tonight? I'm afraid you'll be very late.'

'That means you want to get rid of us as soon as possible ... am I right, Mani?' asks Biman.

'Chhordi, I don't drive. It's Biman da who drove all the way from Calcutta. So, it's risky for him to drive back this late at night. We should halt at your place tonight.'

'Here? How can you?' asks Mandira, unnerved. 'There's only one room.'

'I'll sleep inside the car,' suggests Prabir.

Casting a glance at the blue mosquito net, Biman says, 'Are you sure that you've divorced your husband? Divorce or separation?'

'Divorce' says Prabir, 'I heard that before. But I didn't know that you had left Europe for good.'

'But I still don't understand you, Mani. You may have been forced to leave England, but that doesn't mean that you have to live in a remote village like this one,' rebuffs Biman, concern lurking in his voice. 'Have you taken it for granted that you have no friend or relation in India? Can't Calcutta provide you shelter?'

'Who will be kind enough to give me shelter?' smiles Mandira. 'I've become quite old, after all. My husband has deserted me. I'm not wealthy. So I'll be looked upon as a burden by all.'

Mandira is exaggerating. Like the setting sun, her youth is beginning to wane, but for this very reason she now looks more lustrous. The signs of ageing are yet to leave their impression on her body. When she stares unmindfully, three creases appear on her forehead. Her skin is taut and her hair is still black. She has never been a paragon of beauty, but she's good-looking and when she talks, she becomes more attractive.

Her husband had not abandoned her. But, surprising her friends in London, one fine morning, she herself took the decision of leaving him and staying alone; practically for no real reason; in everybody's eyes it was for no rhyme or reason.

Mandira's husband, Thomas Brockway was the nephew of Feinner Brockway, the famous MP from the Labour Party, who was once a genuine supporter of India. Mandira had gone to England to pursue further studies in political studies and got involved with an ultra-socialist group of students there. Thomas Brockway or Tom was the leader of that group. It was love at first sight for Tom. He took Mandira for granted, never waiting for her to reciprocate, as if rejection from her side was quite out of the question. He somewhat forced her to accompany him on his frequent political tours across the country—Cambridge, Sheffield, Liverpool, meetings at London School of Economics, etc., and put up at the same hotels sharing twin rooms. On one occasion, Tom had wanted to sleep with Mandira, but she, feeling embarrassed, had declined with entreaties. At this, standing on the bed, Tom had declaimed, 'Oh, despite being a socialist, you're a Hindu, after all; you do not agree to that thing before marriage. But comrade, that very thing is essential for our bodies and minds. Therefore tomorrow we'll be wedded. First thing in the morning ... After that you'll cease to be a Hindu, I, a Christian. We'll be atheists.'

Mandira couldn't seek her parents' consent. Nor did she personally intimate Biman about her decision. Later, her parents couldn't accept the marriage. So she decided to sever all ties with India instead. In the last twenty-six years she had been to India twice. On one visit she didn't even visit Calcutta, but had gone back from Delhi itself. Meanwhile, she had had two children—both of them were quite grown up now. Her husband had been elected to the parliament twice. She also had been working as a copy editor in a well-known publication house.

In spite of all this, after twenty-six years of marriage, she sought separation from Tom. After the divorce she could have stayed back comfortably in London. She was solvent enough to support herself. Her son, residing in the United States, had already volunteered to help her financially. But she couldn't adjust herself to that alien land. She left England for good.

Actually, she was confused—some seminal questions about the very nature of life had suddenly cropped up in her mind. During the early stages of her youth, life seemed to be full of potential. After their marriage she and Tom used to daydream about political revolutions. They believed that in the near future, socialism would be the new world order and that they would take part in those revolutions. The students' movement of 1968 in France made them fancy that it was going to spell the fall of the French government and pave the path for the second French revolution. They believed that it would certainly make quite an impact on the politics of England and that Tom and Mandira would lead the rebels here.

But nothing as such happened. Grandiloquence, without armed movement, never brings about a change in the political system of a country. Tom, an advocate of extremism, gradually leaned towards the parliamentary form of democracy. He had occupied a very important position in the Labour Party. The Conservative Party under Margaret Thatcher had been enjoying majority in the British Parliament for some consecutive terms. But how long? A day must come when the Iron Lady would have to quit. Then the Labour Party would be in power enabling Tom a ministerial position. By this time, he had already secured a berth in the shadow cabinet.

After her marriage, apart from severing ties with her parents, Mandira somewhat detached herself from the local Bengali community as well, barring a handful of close college friends. She was conscious of her post-marital status. Her husband was an aristocratic British citizen, her children were also British. So, it was quite obvious that she'd mingle with the British socialites. She couldn't change her complexion but she was happy that her children were white. Initially, she had to face some awkward situations because of her brown skin, but she never minded that.

With Tom, Mandira had often been invited to parties in the British elite society where she happened to be the only non-white member. A lady, clad in a sari, would warrant special attention there. Misbehaviour with her there was out of the question—rather she was treated with superfluous British courtesy; as though she was a princess. Everyone present there would wait upon her every word and gesture; if she even raised her hand a little, a great many people would rush to ask her, 'May I help you?' Nevertheless, Mandira was not sure about their attitude towards her. Under the surface of pseudo-courtesy, she could sense an air of hypocrisy. For instance, the clumsy chuckle of some ladies or the abrupt and uneasy silence for a few moments, if she happened to intrude into their bonhomie, didn't escape her attention. She knew this distance would not wither away so easily. This was not due to the colour of her skin or the colonial background—the British society never feels at home with any foreigner. They never allow an outsider to break the bastion of their class. Tom's cousin, Martha had married a Greek. She never got social acceptance for that. Mandira heard them saying behind Martha's back that the Greeks had no moral scruples; they're dirty and so on. So they must have said similar things behind Mandira's back also.

But Mandira would not get much time to ponder over these things as long as she was drowned in the ecstasy and abundance of Tom's love. Tom, she earnestly believed, was ignorant of such racial or caste barriers.

At Kensington, Tom owned an apartment but after their marriage, for a couple of years, they couldn't settle down properly. Tom was primarily a bohemian by nature.

With him, she too toured a lot and visited France, Italy, Spain and even Cambodia, North Vietnam, etc. Tom was moved by the extremist movements that were breaking out all over the world. Even the Naxalite movement in West Bengal had a strong influence on his ideology. Some Bengali students had returned to the country to join the movement. Mary Tilor, one of Tom's acquaintances, who had married a Bengali, also came to India to take active part in the socialist revolution. One fine morning, Tom, accompanying Mandira, had come to North Bengal and met the Naxalite leader Charu Majumder. They had then put up at an ordinary hotel in Siliguri.

That was Tom's first and last visit to India. The Taj Mahal or the beauty of Kashmir didn't fascinate him. He was more interested in the political scenario than the nature or history of India. He was only eager to rescue this country from its current state of oppression. One day he caught the attention of the police. He was not a member of the British Parliament then. He had to quit the country on the request of the British High Commission.

During that visit, Mandira had however got an opportunity to spend a few days in Calcutta.

Her mother was then bed-ridden. Her father had passed away a year ago. Nobody had bothered to send a telegram to her though her three sisters were present at his deathbed. Mandira was left out. Why? Mandira, as if, was ostracised. Did they think that she wouldn't come down from London? Or was it that her father had not wished to see her face? Did he instruct them not to inform Mani?

Jagat Dutta, Mandira's father, was basically a liberal-minded man. A science graduate, he was a chemist at Bengal Chemicals. He did not have a son but he educated his four daughters. He gave them unlimited freedom. Mandira was a student of Calcutta University. He never objected to her involvement in campus politics. Rather he often enjoyed sharing his political views with her. Once Mandira, along with some union leaders, was arrested and remanded in police custody on charges of road blocking. Many eyebrows were raised then. But Jagat Dutta took it sportingly even though he had heard from her the minute details of her harrowing experience in the cell which she had shared with antisocial elements like whores and pickpockets. His daughters must share their experiences with their parents—that was all he wanted. He wouldn't have opposed Mandira's decision to marry a foreigner. What hurt him the most was her studied reticence about her relationship with Tom. They had been going around for as long as seven months before their marriage, yet he had been kept in the dark. In his eyes she had become licentious, ungrateful. She had shown utter contempt for her parents' sentiments, so he broke all filial ties with her in utter shock and rage. He had said, 'What's the point of keeping ties with the child who doesn't respect her parents' sentiments? I'm not going to take any financial help from her for the rest of my life. Let her grease the palm of white people!'

The news of her father's death had reached her some days later. Neither her mother nor her uncle had sent any intimation. It was her elder sister who had informed her a couple of days before the shradh ceremony. Mandira didn't come home. Didn't she have any feelings? She was aggrieved, awfully upset, but she never blamed her mother for this. But she couldn't forgive her sisters and their husbands, particularly Sankar da, her elder sister's husband, who on his visits to London, used to put up at Mandira's apartment and thereby saved his hotel expenses. Through Sankar da, Mandira had sent expensive gifts such as perfumes, toiletries, wrist watches for their daughter. Her two younger sisters also kept in touch with her through mail. Now, how could she forgive them when they deprived Mandira of having at least a glimpse of her father on his deathbed? She didn't believe in the rituals of the shradh ceremony. So, there was no chance of her attending it. She felt depressed, especially for her mother, but the latter also didn't ask her to come.

When Tom, during that visit, was asked to leave India on political grounds, Mandira had stayed back and spent some days with her mother. She had suddenly fallen ill. In the beginning, her mother also wasn't on good terms with her. But Mandira wasn't hurt by this and was constantly by the side of her ailing mother, as though she went back to the days of her childhood. Her mother lying on the bed appeared to her like a child and she herself felt like a mother, caressing her young daughter. Her mother used to say, 'Mani, do you remember when you were a kid, you used to hit your head against the wall to express your anger?' Hearing this Mandira would feel like becoming a child once again. Bending down beside her mother's bed, she would say childishly, 'Ma, do you remember how one day I was furious and cut my locks with a pair of scissors? Who was the cause of my anger that day?' Her mother laughed and replied, 'It was me!'

She was glad that her mother spent more time with her than she did with the other daughters. Talking about the old days had made her feel quite nostalgic. Her childhood flashed before her eyes.

The news of Mandira's marriage had shocked her mother more than her father. Her heart had been torn into pieces and she had wept pathetically. She couldn't accept the fact that her dearest Mani, whom she bore in her womb, gave birth to, nourished, did everything for her education, could forget them so easily.

When Mandira heard this from her sisters, she lowered her head in shame. She had realised her fault. Tom was unwilling to wait, yet she should have tarried a little. She wouldn't have listened to her parents' objections, yet she wouldn't have suffered from a sense of guilt had she informed her parents before her marriage.

Overwhelmed by Tom's love, Mandira had forgotten everything else. But she loved her parents no less. At that critical juncture of her life, she had forcefully tried to erase the memory of her parents. But it's not possible to do that; Mandira couldn't. Reunited with her mother after so many years, Mandira had realised how the grievous wounds had accumulated over the years in her mother's heart on account of the separation. Her mother, too, held her close to her bosom, forgetting the bitterness of the past, as though she was eager to compensate for the lost days.

But the happy days didn't last long. In the meanwhile, her mother had recovered from pneumonia and come back to normal life. Mandira would prepare special fish curry for her and she would eat it with relish. That day at lunch, she had even asked for details about her son-in-law's favourite dishes—whether he was fond of Bengali cuisine or not—and on the same afternoon, she had a massive heart attack and passed away.

After her mother's death it occurred to Mandira that she had lost her ties with her motherland as well. Why should she feel attached to Calcutta or India, any more? What was there to bring her back to Calcutta again? The memories of her life before marriage were also effaced to a great extent.

Even at that point she didn't remember Biman for a single instance.

2

Mandira's children shunned politics. Traditionally, sons of the Brockway family studied economics, mathematics or political science and took active part in campus politics. During their student lives, members of the Brockway family, generation after generation, dominated the students' unions at college. Tom's father and uncle were secretaries of Oxford Students' Union. In later days, Brockways became parliamentarians, professors or journalists. This was the trend in their family.

Robin, Mandira's son, studied medicine. The militant students' movements of the 1960s and 1970s subsided in the 1980s. The new generation of boys and girls stayed aloof from politics as they had learnt a lesson from their parents' bohemian lifestyles, failures and disillusionments. They were witness to the utter chaos and uncertainties in the family as a consequence of their parents' involvement in politics. So they, unlike their parents, were career-conscious and selfish with all their activities centering around building a career. They believed that in the wake of rapid mechanisation, the only thing that would ensure social security was a bright career. Naturally, the dream of a social revolution and establishment of a new social order was totally shattered. Bidding farewell to the culture of wearing dirty, unkempt clothes and growing long, dishevelled hair, the boys preferred more formal haircuts and attire such as wearing ties with matching socks. The bras, once out of fashion with the mothers and aunts, now returned to their accustomed place with their daughters; the hemlines of their skirts went down below the knees.

Robin was basically a bright scholar. He passed the final medical examination with flying colours. But after graduating, he understood that private practice wasn't an easy task. Unless one boasted of a genealogical background in medicine, it was impossible for someone to click in the profession in London. The boys and girls passing out of the medical colleges occupied the surgeries of their forefathers and easily got the old patients by way of inheritance. Robin lacked such a background. Mandira personally knew a couple of Indian doctors doing roaring practice in Harley Street. She wanted to introduce Robin to them and ask them to back him. But he promptly turned down his mother's proposal. And why not? He had not learnt Bengali, nor did he know his mother's country. There was nothing Indian in the colour of his skin and hair. His friends were Europeans; he had never been to India. So, it was beneath his dignity to approach an Indian doctor seeking a favour. Robin, however, loved his mother, though this love was slightly laced with a kind of selfishness.

Tom was so busy that he had no time to think about Robin's career and future prospects. That was also an election year. One fine morning Robin joined the National Health Service. He was posted in Glasgow; his workplace was in a dirty, conjested ghetto. His work was somewhat monotonous, but he was bent on getting acclimatised to it.

After the completion of his first year, Robin, accompanied by his girlfriend, visited USA where he had a few acquaintances. One of his friends referred him to a middle-aged doctor in Buffalo. Robin and his sweetheart stayed with this doctor during their visit to the Niagara Falls. He was amazed to see the doctor's swanky bungalow, swimming pool, tennis lawn, four cars, of which two were BMWs, one a Mercedes and the other was a Cadillac. This was just the tip of the iceberg. Robin's girlfriend Hilda, coming out of the bathroom, said, 'Robin did you see the gilded taps?' He couldn't believe it to begin with, then he confirmed—yes, those were made of pure gold. This made Robin's head turn—how could it be possible? The doctor, as far as he knew, saw patients till noon. In the evenings he relaxed playing tennis or doing something else. Still such a huge income? Incredible!

Robin made up his mind. He wrote to his mother, 'Mom, you didn't like my Glasgow job; you'll be glad to know that I've got an opportunity here to work as a junior to Dr Paul Arnold. There's a bright future ahead. I hope to buy an apartment within a year. I wish you will come over here and spend some time with me. You must come, Mom.'

The question of taking permission from his father did not arise since Robin's links with his father had already become fragile.

Robin never returned from America.

Robin was not an exception. The National Health Service couldn't attract the British doctors. For lucrative income, many of them migrated to the States. The British hospitals filled up the vacancies by appointing doctors from the third world countries. These immigrants, in spite of being highly meritorious, were willing to work at low wages and the government made a clever use of the situation. The obsession of the British youths for America is no less than that of the youths of Karachi–Dhaka–Manila for England.

Lizzi, Mandira's daughter, had been overactive right from her childhood. Fidgety, restless, she never walked at a normal pace—always bouncing up and down the stairs. She had inherited her blue eyes and blonde hair from her grandmother who lived in Dover. It was she who named her Elizabeth though both Tom and Mandira hadn't liked the name. The British names lacked variety. From a limited range of names, the entire English populace christened itself. After her son's birth, Mandira carefully chose a name for him that would be commensurate with either an English or Indian name. But she couldn't apply this tactic in the case of her daughter.

By the time Elizabeth was two years old, Tom had become a very active member of the Labour Party. Mandira used to accompany him during his political visits to small towns. She had to leave Elizabeth in the care of the nanny, who shortened her name further. Now she was known to everybody as Liz. Lack of parental care and too much dependence on nannies made her wayward and obstinate.

Liz was basically intelligent but inattentive at studies. At the O Level, she fared so poorly that the school authorities called her guardians. Tom couldn't go. Mandira met the principal alone, who was shocked to meet a woman with black hair, clad in a sari. For her fair complexion Mandira was often mistaken for a Spanish. But what about her thickly set black hair? Normally she wore jeans and shirts but that day she was wearing a sari. The principal, being a confirmed racist, muttered, 'No wonder that girl is doing so badly! She is particularly weak in English language and literature!'

Returning home, Liz said to her mother, 'Mom, I won't go to school, I don't like studies.'

Mandira was exasperated. She rebuffed angrily, 'Well, don't go to school if you don't wish to. What can I do? You're too old to be compelled to stay at home and study. Your father doesn't bother to look into your studies. As if this is my headache alone!'

After her anger ebbed away, Mandira tried to counsel her child, 'Liz, honey, what will you do then?'

Clasping her arms round her mother's neck, Liz had said, 'Mom, I want to travel! I'll visit India. I'll take lots of snaps of Calcutta. Mom, Calcutta is so dirty, isn't it?'

There was no question of Tom taking a break from his busy schedule and visiting India for his daughter. Mandira knew that she was not likely to get leave from her office. So she hesitantly replied, 'Well dear, I'll take you to India, this winter. The streets there may be dirty, but you'll find meat and vegetables that are far more fresh than what you get here.'

With a quizzical look in her eyes, Liz exclaimed, 'Are you sure, Mom?'

'Oh! Sure darling.' But ultimately she couldn't keep her promise.

Liz had started dating right from the age of sixteen. Every weekend she would go out on a date, usually with different boyfriends. Often, it so happened that she didn't return home on many Friday nights. The first time this happened, Mandira couldn't sleep a wink, tossing and turning all night. Tom was out of town, in Sussex. Twice, first at midnight and again at dawn, she felt that she ought to talk to Tom over the telephone. But she restrained herself from doing so at the last moment.

Next morning, Liz was back home at eleven. Mandira had forgotten that she and her family belonged to the British way of living. Like a typical Indian mother, she had furiously demanded an explanation.

Liz had replied excitedly, 'Don't forget, Mummy, I've already celebrated my eighteenth birthday. Do you think I'm still a baby? Do you want me to get married like an Indian girl and be thrown into a harem?'

Mandira didn't know what she should say now. She, after all, could not impose her thoughts upon an adult. She restrained herself, realising that she was interfering in one's personal freedom.

A little later, Liz drew close to Mandira and said in an impish tone, 'Mom, you know my friend Peggy—her parents have gone to Spain. We spent the night in her house; there were eight of us, five girls and three boys. We danced and sang and had lots of fun till three in the morning. Then we were all lying down in bed in the living room. I wanted to call you up but they all taunted me, saying, 'Mother's baby, come on baby, have a candy!' Suzanne whispered into my ears, 'Try and find out your mother's reactions—is she worried at all? Look, my mom's too liberal about me; it makes no difference to her—whether I come home or not. Next morning she goes out for shopping before I return ... it hurts me.'

After this incident, Liz went away to Paris that summer. The custom of exchange prevalent between the families in London and Paris help the two countries cement cultural ties in many forms. For instance, a girl from a French family spent her vacation with an English family in London. During this stay, she could improve upon her knowledge of English language and customs. Again, the French family made a reciprocal arrangement for an English girl in Paris. She in turn learnt to adore French perfumes and clothes.

In the beginning of that year, a French girl, who was translating Shakespeare in French, had come from Paris to London and spent a month with the Brockways. She had, however, put up at the apartment of Tom's elder brother, who was a professor. The latter had no children. So Liz, representing the Brockways, went to Paris that autumn and spent some weeks with that French family.

Liz came back from Paris in tow with an English boy. The fellow was an ill-paid reporter of a tabloid. He was without hearth and home. Son of an affluent man, he was detached from the family. He lived in the attic of a house in Golders Green. Liz, hardly nineteen then, was so madly in love with him that she couldn't think of even a moment's separation from her beloved. So she left home to live together with him.

Mandira had been alarmed, well in advance, by her daughter's wayward tendencies, wilful nature, and had been contemplating to send her to a hostel. But Tom didn't approve of the idea. One day the children will have to bid farewell to their home and parents. Let the childhood memories be the cherished possession of their life. This was Tom's firm conviction. Though he stood in the way of sending Liz to a hostel, he never gave time to the children. He was too preoccupied with his career to look after Liz and Robin. Sometimes he took a break from his hectic schedule to spend time with the family. He was partial in his affection to Liz and, during his occasional homecomings, used to spend some quality time with her. Thereafter, he would disappear for two or three months at a stretch.

When Liz left for Golders Green, Tom didn't stop her, for he knew that there was no use in doing so. He was, however, upset. He had said to Mandira, sighing, 'Our daughter has become an adult and that indicates we're getting old, aren't we?'

He had believed that Liz would return in a few days, but she didn't. Gradually he drowned himself in his work and the thoughts of his daughter seemed to have blurred.

But Mandira found herself in a void.

Her day-to-day life had not altogether centered round her children, for she knew that the kids would not live with her forever. One day, they would grow up, be self-sufficient citizens free from parental control. Then they would independently take decisions about their own future. In England, she had seen adults taking decisions about their own lives. They were all independent citizens here. But in India, Mandira knew that adulthood would never ensure self-sufficiency. India boasts of a huge population; but how many of them have the privilege to live life on their own terms? Sixteen- or eighteen-year-old Indian boys are treated as juveniles; nobody pays heed to their views. And Indian girls? The less said about them, the better. Parents are scared of sending them out of home after sunset, as if they will be devoured by tigers. Mandira's father was a bit different from the average Bengali father, yet he had to give in to the pressure of near and distant relatives and neighbours, who were constantly ready with pieces of advice for Jagat Dutta: 'Look, your daughter is getting derailed, take care immediately or else you'll repent later.'

Staying in England for over two decades had taught her to be practical about children. Filial affection must not overstep boundaries, otherwise both will suffer. Parents must be slightly detached in showering love and affection on their children. They should ensure a certain amount of freedom and privacy for their children. After a certain age parents should give importance to the opinions of their children. Otherwise they begin to disrespect their parents. Consequently, filial bonds begin to weaken after a certain stage.

Mandira, however, was prepared for the inevitable—the children would leave home and settle elsewhere—this was the order of the society. But she had made a mistake. She had not chalked out her future plans after the children's departure from home.

Mandira's husband, had by then, become a high-flying politician—career was more precious to him than family. Moreover, Tom was basically apathetic to family life. When he would come home, he would be accompanied by a band of political friends and party members and their animated talks and debates would continue till late into the night.

Tom was broad-minded, idealistic and generous. The society, the nation and, of course, his own party occupied the largest share of his heart. His attachment towards his wife and children was comparatively less. He should not really be blamed for that—in fact, not everyone is destined to be a devoted householder. And Mandira, sadly enough, had noticed that Tom was not giving her more than two or three minutes at a stretch. Their conversations centered round some trifles: giving some instructions over telephone from the office or at best asking her to accompany him to a theatre. It was Tom who always showed some interest in the theatre although these were all perfunctory attempts. But he was always reticent about his party affairs and personal troubles. He never divulged his personal secrets to Mandira. If she showed a little curiosity about him, he dexterously sidetracked, left the place on the plea of a telephone call or an urgent appointment. Tom had another bad habit—he spent no less than an hour or more in the toilet. How many of his fans and colleagues, Mandira wondered, knew this?

No one could claim that their marriage was under any apparent strain. But Mandira, for quite some time, began to believe that their relationship lacked marital bliss. She was Tom's wife but not life partner. It was not that a third person had intruded into their life. Mandira worked in a male-dominated office. She had a lot of interaction with other men there. She had to sometimes stay back at office even after office hours. Occasionally, she had to visit her director's house to take briefs on important issues. She was personally close to many male colleagues but she always maintained a respectable distance from them. She abhorred casual sex and for that reason was ridiculed as a moralist and a prude.

Tom's nature of work allowed him to come in close proximity with many female colleagues and coworkers. But he too was very cautious about his interactions with them, for he knew that a public figure like him was easily vulnerable to scandals. When he had become a MP, he had to engage the services of a private secretary. As usual, there was no dearth of public who were fond of sensationalising a public figure's attachment to a good-looking private secretary. Tom's secretary was Linda; Mandira was fond of that simple-natured girl. She knew that Linda had a lover. Nevertheless, she couldn't rule out the possibility of a physical relationship between her husband and Linda. Still Mandira would not tax her mind about this, for it was alien to her nature to be a suspicious, nagging wife, who, she had seen from her real-life experiences, made her husband's life a misery. She hated the idea of doubting her husband on the basis of sheer suspicion.

Tom had to visit his constituency in Sussex quite frequently. He had a rented apartment there; it was less expensive than a hotel. The rumour had it that one or two girls frequented that house during Tom's stay there. Mandira never raised the issue before Tom. She knew that he was not against casual sex, and had had a couple of affairs before marriage. But she accepted this reality. She might not support casual sex but that didn't mean that everyone would follow her ideals. Perhaps there's no harm in casual sex—Mandira tried to comfort herself. Perhaps it's also a kind of freedom, license. The society doesn't crumble because of this though the ego of some men and women are assuaged by it.

Then what ailed her? It was Tom's subtle indifference towards her. She noticed that he was gradually moving away from her. In the past, Mandira used to accompany him on his political tours. The reason behind this was to help him in taking stock of his personal possessions. For a couple of years now, he had stopped asking her to accompany him. Did it mean that he was unwilling to bring his Indian wife to the forefront? She knew that the orthodox members of the National Front had by then begun to spew venom against the immigrants—had that made Tom alert beforehand? Then, as a representative of the liberal Labour Party, he should have all the more flaunted his Indian wife with due honour before them.

Or it might be that Tom was not thinking on these lines. He perhaps had taken it for granted that, the honeymoon being long over, Mandira, now a middle-aged woman, should be confined within the four walls of her home busy raising her children. But when the children left, leaving her alone, he never felt it necessary to give some time to her. Even when his friends and associates paid visits, Mandira hesitated to appear before them. But there was a time when she had spontaneously taken part in the bonhomie. She had felt no inhibition in asserting herself. But now she recoiled herself into a cocoon—as if she was an outsider, with no right to share her husband's seasoned political world. She had occasionally tried to take part in their discussions; they gave her a patient hearing, then cleverly changed the topic. Sometimes one of them would be more courteous, saying, 'Let's hear what Mani has to say about this,' then someone in the middle of her speech, would say, 'How nice! Oh really! Isn't it something? How very clever of you, Mani!'

But Mani was not so naive—she knew that these were empty exclamations without any sincerity. She could easily read Tom's looks—he was, as though, trying to say, 'You're a novice about the mine workers' strike in England, I think you've more urgent business to attend to.'

But was it true? She had been living in this country for a quarter of a century. So how was it that she was still in the dark about the problems of the mine workers or the European Common Market? She had no right to say anything about British interests. Should she be deemed an outsider? They preferred reticence in her presence regarding India. If she mentioned anything about India, they'd invariably smile and change the topic. One day, she recalled Tom's close friend, Edwin, saying, 'Mani, do you know what happened that day after the India–England test match? By chance, India won the match at the last moment and a group of spectators, with Indian flags in hand, ran into the ground and began to dance. These people were of Indian origin but British passport holders!'

Mandira had been upset to hear this and had rebuffed with suppressed indignation, 'Edwin, I agree those people were over-enthusiastic, nevertheless, do you think that India won the match by sheer chance? Don't you think that India played well and displayed its superiority over England? I know that India played a very good match at Lords. What a fantastic batting line-up right upto the ninth wicket!'

Edwin laughingly said, 'I see Mani, you're an Indian supporter at heart even today!'

So Mani knew what's what. She stopped taking part in their gossip sessions. Even if she happened to be present in their company, she either kept quiet or retired to her room and watched films on VCR. She felt unwanted.

Robin's departure from home didn't make Mandira as lonely as Liz's absence did. Her daughter was wayward, naughty, yet she had occupied a most special place in her heart. Liz had never been to India then, yet when Mandira chided her in Bengali now and then, she would say, swinging her hair, 'Oh! Understood Mummy, I understood what you meant.' In fact, she knew that Liz was proud of her mother's Indian origin. Once she had gone to a party wearing a sari. She shared her experiences with her mother. Now in her absence, Mandira's life was a vacuum.

Liz lived together with her boyfriend in an attic at Golders Green. Not once did she come back home during that period. Though she talked with Mandira over telephone, she never showed much interest about her father. Most of their telephonic conversations revolved round her experiences at a new party she had attended. Mandira, sometimes, felt an urge to visit Liz's home but she desisted from doing so: how could she unless they invited her, at least perfunctorily? Liz was no good at cooking. They, like others of their age group, dined out; but what about breakfast? Who prepared that? Mandira was inquisitive about such household matters.

The problem with Mandira was that she had never anticipated the impending challenge of solitude in middle age, ignored by the grown-up kids and a busy, workaholic husband. She had never mingled with the Bengali society in London. In fact, she had never wanted to do so for she wanted to remain a British citizen in the true sense of the term. Tom was not interested in Indian culture. Political affairs of India attracted him a bit but he was apathetic to Indian culture. Even Indian cuisine, except fish curry and papad, did not fascinate him.

Mandira never invited her Indian colleagues home to dinner because she was apprehensive of Tom's brusque behaviour with them. Tom was basically haughty and insolent. Those who could not carve a niche in political discussions with him, were nonentities, misfits in his opinion. Besides, he avoided guests on his to-be-home days. She knew this well.

Mandira used to be back from office by six in the evening. The first duty was to prepare dinner for the kids. But now she had no hurry. Most of the evenings, Tom skipped dinner at home, specially on the eve of the elections. So, Mandira felt no urge to cook for herself. She had never been a gourmet; most of the evenings she ate sandwiches. Back from office she would take a bath, wear a housecoat and sit before the TV. But she could not keep her eyes glued to the screen. She had not made a habit of watching serials; only a few selected movies and musical programmes lured her to the TV set. One day, while watching a TV programme, she was startled to see her husband there. He was being interviewed and the programme was pre-recorded. Strange! Tom had told her nothing about the interview! He must have forgotten or it might be that he did not think it was worth mentioning to her. Mandira was hurt, for she believed that nothing should be kept secret between a husband and wife.

Mandira was fond of Rabindra Sangeet, even after so many years of living abroad. She had a formidable collection of cassettes. Tom never objected to this habit of hers. Once, Satyajit Ray's *Pather Panchali* was being shown on channel 4. Mandira somewhat forced Tom to see the film. He obliged her and after the film, had said, 'Very authentic. The film exposes how the British left the Empire in tatters. They left India so many years ago, yet India, till today couldn't stand on her feet. But look at China ...'

'Tom,' protested Mandira, 'the film portrays the condition of rural India that existed seventy years ago. Now the situation has changed a lot.'

'Really?' asked Tom sarcastically. Apart from this, he had nothing to say about this world-famous film.

Sometimes, her TV viewing got interrupted by odd phone calls. Out of every ten calls, nine were for Tom. Only one would be from Liz. She telephoned either in the morning or on holidays in the afternoon. Liz and her partner never stayed at home in the evening. Mandira had tried to contact them over telephone in the evening on several occasions.

Tom was a public figure and it was quite natural that he would be the recipient of many phone calls. But what about her? Couldn't she expect a phone call? What had she got from life?

London was perpetually busy. Streets dazzled with lights, thousands came out of the tube, theatres, restaurants, cinema halls, etc. But Mandira was alone. She had no one to accompany her to these rendezvous. She accompanied Tom to some formal parties. She had to, rather, for husbands without wives at parties were vulnerable to scandals. So Mandira, all decked up, had to attend these parties with an artificial smile on her lips. Sometimes, she felt like crying out loud.

Of late, she had started feeling that life had become meaningless to her. She was employed but was she indispensable at the office? She was no longer that important to her children. But what about love? Was their love for her on the wane? But how could it be? Love surpassed mundane needs of one's life. So, probably she was still loved by her husband and children. But their love seemed to be covered in a veil of stiff formalities as well as some indifference that left her feeling desolate.

So, did she feel that her life had lost its significance? She never wanted to call it a day. She wanted to live, but not at the cost of this monotonous life. She must find an objective worth living for—an elixir of life. She must, for she could not let herself get exhausted, so soon.

3

That day was eleventh January. It had been snowing incessantly since early morning. Christmas had passed away without any snowfall. On the thirty-first there was a little spell of snowfall but that was negligible. But for the last three or four days heavy snowfall had been going on. It was causing traffic disruptions. Mandira had not gone to office. She had been lying in bed. Rarely did such luxury come one's way on weekdays. Tom had not come back home the previous night as the winter session in the parliament was going on. The session ran till ten-thirty p.m. After that he spent quite some time with his party colleagues and made up their next day's strategy. When the parliamentary session was in progress, Tom normally did not return home. He, along with his colleagues, put up at hotels near the party office. He would be equipped with two sets of changes with him.

Liz and Bob were on a visit to Greece. So no phone call from Liz was expected. Mandira could have spent the whole day lolling in bed. Suffering from an inexplicable restlessness she prepared coffee for herself. Again and again. She had not done her shopping this weekend. Tom never did the shopping. All these years she had done the shopping by driving down once a week to replenish stocks. She found the stock of milk and vegetables to be negligible. But today she would not go out to fetch them, even if she had to go without lunch. Rather she would spend the day sipping lots of coffee. After the third cup of coffee she lit a cigarette and stood by the window. Drawing the curtain aside she could watch continuous snowfall. The snow covered the trees outside like white flowers. The motorcars passed by but without any noise. During snowfall there prevailed an uneasy calm.

Suddenly Mandira wanted to break open the glass window and jump out of the room. But the very next moment she herself was puzzled. What made her long for this? Why should she die now? So early? It would mean a colossal waste of life!

She felt her head reeling. The two sides of the forehead were throbbing. She had all along enjoyed a sound health except for the last hospitalisation for treating a kidney stone. Both her deliveries were normal. Maybe the heat generated by the continuous running of the room heater was making her feel sick? Men and women were walking down the street, wearing three to four layers of clothing, that too, under the heavy overcoats. And she? Inside the house she was wearing only a flimsy, almost transparent nightgown. In spite of her long stay in England, she had not yet reconciled herself to these apparently contradictory situations.

She opened the windowpanes and looked out of the window and felt a bit relaxed. She recalled her childhood days in Calcutta when she used to drench her head in the rain by sticking her head out of the window. In their house in Calcutta they didn't have a balcony. Here, too, she did not have one. In fact, most of the houses here don't have balconies. Now flakes of snow seemed to be caressing her face and eyes as she was standing at the open window.

A little later Mandira discovered she was running from one room to another; but why? Was she searching for something? No, nothing as such. She tried to restore her self-composure as she remembered that she was staying indoors that day only to relax.

She poured some red wine in a glass and placed it on a side table. She switched off the heater to let the room temperature come down. Switching on the TV, she took a book and got back to bed. Then she lit another cigarette. She hoped that the book, cigarette, TV and the snug feeling of the bed would come together and compensate for the loneliness within her.

A little later the telephone rang. She got out of bed and most expectantly lifted the receiver: 'Hello, could I talk to Mr Thomas Brockway please?' She knew it was natural that the call was for Tom. Who would call her at this hour? And how would Liz know that Mandira had not gone to office today? Still, couldn't she expect a call? Even if the caller was someone whom she didn't like, she wouldn't have minded perhaps. The phone book was lying there, she could have called a friend or acquaintance, but she desisted. She felt ashamed to pick out one at random and make a call.

She did not get back to bed; she started keeping things in order. Things were at sixes and sevens. Hers was a fairly large apartment with three bedrooms. Tom was never in favour of buying a house; he always preferred an apartment. Mandira went on dusting the rooms, putting the books back on the shelves. Beads of sweat covered her forehead.

But why was she doing all this and for whom? Tom never cared for such things; she was doing a thankless job.

Mandira went into the bathroom. She thought that lying in the bathtub might help her relax. She mixed hot and cold water proportionately and then dropped some bath salts in it. Then undressing herself she lay in the tub. One could read books or talk on the telephone here as there was a receiver beside the bathtub.

Once in the bathtub, Mandira began to rub her body with a sponge, as though she was anxious to take a quick bath. In her early youth she had a habit of reading books, lying in the bathtub. A little while ago she was contemplating doing this again but it would not perhaps be commensurate with her present age. Even if she ever had had plenty of time at her disposal, she never spent much time in bathing. If she ever happened to spend a little more time bathing, she felt she was being summoned by her household obligations. She was also conscious of her self-imposed duties. So then, she was really beginning to feel her age. Nearing fifty, she still possessed an attractive figure. Mentally also she never felt that she was growing old. Physically and mentally, she failed to notice any difference in her own self—between the present and the past, say ten years ago. Yet it was a fact that she had grown in years and become older than before.

Sitting in the bathtub, and leaning her head against the blue wall, Mandira cried her heart out for sometime. Tears trickled down on the foam.

A little later she wiped her body and hair and came out of the bathroom. While wearing a sari, she wondered: what went wrong in her life? Did she expect too much? Was this kind of frustration common to all women of her age?

The Bengali residents in London had expressed their apprehension that her marriage would hardly last three or four years. Thomas Brockway, hailing from an aristocratic British family, had a bright future in British politics. Why should he rot all his life with an Indian wife? The oriental, exotic glamour associated with marrying an Indian woman would vanish soon. Mandira, too, very soon after her arrival in London, married into a British family without being familiar with the British code of conduct and etiquettes. When the English people would say, 'How nice!', 'Beautiful!', 'Wonderful!', 'I like it!' to express admiration or approval for someone or something, it took five to seven years for Mandira to understand which one of those exclamations was fake and which one genuine.

But quite contrary to these predictions, the marriage did not break. She spent twenty-six years being Tom's wife. There had been no noteworthy incident that could bring their marriage to peril. There had been once a minor misunderstanding. Then Robin was only four years old.

Tom's friend, David Andrew was obsessed with India. He was a divorcee. His Irish wife had left him recently and he was consequently depressed. He used to visit Mandira off and on and was very familiar with her. David's obsession was India—its music, fashion, food—everything was his favourite. He had even worked in India for some time. That was the starting point of his obsession with India. During his two years tenure as an employee of the British Council, he even stayed for six months in Calcutta. At that time, one of his friends, whose name was also David, David Mccachion, was teaching at Jadavpur University and doing research on the temple sculptures of Bengal and Orissa. David Andrew had travelled extensively with that fellow through the rural areas of Bengal. Returning home he could not forget Indian culture and way of living. He could be seen wearing kurtas, his home was decorated with the icons of Nataraj, he hung a sitar on the wall. He would request his visitors to listen to the music of Bismillah Khan and the flute of Pannalal Ghosh. His wife had no reservations about David's obsession with India; the cause of their divorce lay elsewhere.

After the divorce, David's mental state was disastrous. Tom and Mandira often invited him to dinner. During those visits he used to discuss India with Mandira; interestingly enough, he used to praise India profusely but she would love to counter him—she used to be critical in her attitude towards India. David seemed to be extravagant in his praises. According to him, Shantiniketan is more fascinating than Oxford, the streets of Calcutta, though full of potholes and puddles, are safer than those of London.

He was full of praise for the hospitality of Indians, however poor they might be.

During those conversations about India, Tom felt bored. Either he kept mum, or yawned or slipped into the bathroom. This pattern continued for a while. David stayed for hours after dinner. Tom used to feel, that it was Mandira who forced David to stay back. She at first could not sense this. She didn't like the fact that India should be dragged into all discussions. Her country of origin may be India, but in her mind she believed she was a global citizen. She still believed that socialism would soon become a great leveller for mankind. She favoured David because he was very gentle in his demeanour. He always spoke in a low voice and never imposed his opinions on others. Even when opposed and proved wrong he always wore a smile on his face and proposed, 'Let's go to Southall tomorrow evening and I'll host an Indian dinner in your honour.' Once Tom had gone to Sussex for a two-day tour. But he didn't return even after a week. Mandira spoke to him on the telephone day after day, everyday and Tom, on the pretext of urgent business, deferred his date of return. On the seventh day, she said, 'If you can't be back soon, then let me go there and be with you.'

Tom replied, 'No, I'm too busy here ... you needn't come now ... have fun with David ...'

Except for this last remark, Tom didn't say anything against her interaction with David, who had perhaps just been seeking his dream 'India' in Mandira. And Tom, with wounded pride and jealousy, was trying to derive sadistic pleasure by making allowances for them in his preplanned absence.

Her relations with David ended there. She couldn't directly ask him not come anymore. But she cancelled two consecutive appointments for dinner with him. She stopped attending to the phone herself. David had once managed to get expensive tickets for a musical concert by the sitar maestro Ravi Shankar and invited Mandira to accompany him, which she declined at the last moment. David recognised the hint. He used to visit their house in search of some solace for his broken heart, but he had never imagined that he could be the cause of breaking his friend's home.

That was the only occasion when Tom had misunderstood Mandira. After that episode years rolled by but they never had any confrontation to speak of. Tom was sensitive to Mandira's background—she had to bid adieu to her parents, home, country after getting married to him. So he must not push her away, though he was aware of the growing rate of divorces in English society. Marriages in general did not last—the divorce rate was as good as sixty-five per cent. Hence their long-lasting, married life raised many eyebrows.

Then what was bothering Mandira? Though basically indifferent to family affairs, Tom left no stone unturned to make her happy. Their sex lives had lost much of its charms—they rarely had sex in recent years. It was quite natural for a couple married for a quarter of a century. Often Mandira felt tempted to discuss this with a woman of her age. But she felt embarrassed. In fact, she had no female friend with whom she was on intimate terms. She was a bit close to Martha, Tom's cousin, who was of her age. Martha had divorced her Greek husband long ago. Her second marriage too did not last. Recently she had married again. Mandira often wondered whether she really enjoyed sex at this age or not. She never got a chance to talk to Martha in private; for she lived in West Berlin; and one could hardly share these thoughts over the telephone.

Mandira was still sexually responsive. And Tom? She recalled how over-enthusiastic Tom was in the initial years of their marriage. Now was it that his tremendous work load had stifled his sexual urges? Should everyone take it for granted after so many years of wedlock? Mandira was not sure about it. She had seen many middle-aged wives, with awfully disgusting figures, bullying their husbands into having sex. In fact, they derived some sadistic pleasure out of this bullying—a kind of perverse substitute for normal sex!

This was the peak period in Tom's political career. If his party came to power, he would find himself in the cabinet. Their children had grown up and become self-sufficient. So it was a situation where Mandira should share her fate with some other married women of her age; she should while away her leisure hours shopping, maintaining the house, looking after her husband's well-being. She could even accompany Tom on his tours and he would also gladly give his consent if she desired to visit India for a couple of months.

So what actually went wrong in her life? Why couldn't she hold back her tears? Why did she feel restive? Had there been nothing else for her to look forward to? That was eleventh January. Mandira had tried to commit suicide three times. If she called it a day, would there be any loss to this world?

In the afternoon snowfall had ceased; by evening a storm raged. She had forgotten to close the windows. She was startled by the sound of the shutters banging against the window. The television was on but Mandira paid no attention to it.

Sharp at eight o'clock she rang up Tom.

Tom was then attending a dinner along with his party colleagues. His wife's phone call made him anxious.

In an unusually quiet tone, Mandira said, 'Tom, would you please come home, right now ... within half an hour?'

'Why Mani, what's wrong with you? Are you feeling sick? Have you called the doctor?'

'No, nothing as such. I just want to see you once, Tom. That's all.'

'Oh, come on Mani! Feel free and tell me what has happened to you. You know the kind of pressure I have to withstand. Just a while ago there was a news break ... haven't you watched TV today? Even today's newspapers have already made a coverage of the incident.'

'Tom, won't you come?'

'Listen darling, several thousands of contaminated tins of HP Foods baked beans have been seized at Yorkshire. You know the plant is situated in Norfolk, which is a stronghold of the Conservatives. They are bound to make an issue out of this.'

'Tom, I'm hell-bent on seeing you today.'

'You seem to be incorrigible, Mani. Listen, I promise to take you to Bolshoi Ballet this week. I have got the tickets. Now there is a storm raging outside ... how can I come in this weather? If you feel bad, please have a sleeping pill and go to bed.'

'Tom, if you don't come today, you won't be able to see me again.' Saying this Mandira disconnected the call and sighed deeply.

This was a kind of blackmail, which Mandira had never indulged in before. In fact, this kind of behaviour had always been alien to her nature.

A minute later she felt she should ring up Tom and apologise. Or she could say that she was just joking. He needn't come. He should not risk his work to come home to his wife just for the sake of meeting her. She was not a newly-married bride, after all.

But she couldn't do that. The arrow once shot couldn't be called back again.

She came to the living room and sat in the grandfather chair. The *Guardian* was lying beside her. She picked it up and glanced through the pages. She had not even read the day's newspaper. Yes, the HP Foods news was covered on the first page. Mandira was never fond of baked beans though she knew it was a staple food for breakfast in almost all households in Britain. It was quite natural that there would be chaos and consternation at the news of the contamination of baked beans. Some days ago there was a rumour that a certain brand of German wine was adulterated causing hospitalisation of some people after consumption. This created a stir and the government immediately prohibited the sale of German wine. The demand for French and Italian wine shot up, for England did not manufacture wine; it imported wine from the continent. Tom had said that it was just a rumour, suspected to be a conspiracy by some French and Italian wine manufacturers who aimed at capturing the wine market in England. Smiths Crisps was also a very popular brand in the biscuit manufacturing industry. One fine morning it so happened that pieces of glass and wood were found in the tins. This too created an upheaval in the market. The company tried to defend it as a calculated sabotage—some rival groups contaminated their products at the factory at Lincoln in eastern England.

In a bid to earn unlimited dividends these business houses had lost all sense of moral scruples. They were always up in arms to strangle their opponents and business rivals to death. Who cared if a couple of children died after eating the baked beans?

Mandira's eyes fell on another piece of news on the third page. She reread it but couldn't believe in its contents. It was about the visit of a seven-member team to Cuba. Thomas Brockway was one of the members. What shocked Mandira was that she was in the dark about it. Strange! Mary Web was also in the team. Mary's nickname was Tomboy—yes, she was an aggressive lady with strong oratorial skills. After her divorce from her first husband she had been single for several years. These days Mandira knew that she regularly accompanied Tom during his tours. Perhaps they were just good friends, thought

Mandira, though Tom never invited her to dinner. The date of departure was reportedly five days later—the next Monday. She was stunned. Tom was bluffing when he had said that he would take her to the Bolshoi Ballet in the weekend.

Just twenty-nine minutes after her phone call, she could hear the front door being unlocked. Tom came in a taxi; he never drove a car though he possessed a driving license. Mandira drove the family car. Tom enjoyed a nap sitting beside the driver. This was one of his eccentricities.

He entered the room after rubbing his snow-smeared feet on the doormat outside. His shoes tapped on the floor. He hung his overcoat on top of the hatrack. He calmly looked into her eyes and in a soft voice said, 'Hello, Mani.'

Mandira didn't leave the chair she was sitting on. She was also staring into his eyes. Tom drew near her and pressed his lips coldly on hers. Just a formal kiss.

Then resting both hands on Mandira's shoulders he asked seriously, 'Any bad news? Come on, Mani, don't try to hide it from me. Tell me right now, is it—Robin or Lizzi?'

Mandira smiled dryly. Only if their children were in trouble would it be deemed bad news. She had not fallen ill, and there was no question of her having some personal trouble. After all, Robin and Liz were quite well.

She merely said, 'Sit on that chair. I have something to tell you.'

Like an obedient boy, Tom pulling the chair, sat on it, one leg crossed over the other. He was wearing a brown suit. He was looking awfully tired, and his eyes revealed signs of sleepless nights. His lips promised high ambitions; over the years he had gained some extra fat on his body though it was commensurate with his age.

Tom was a male chauvinist; he had the last word in all family affairs. But today things looked different. Mandira seemed to be calling the shots.

He was staring at Mandira who continued to be silent. He broke the ice like a typical Englishman, 'What ghastly weather today. The roads are under two or three feet of snow. From tomorrow there is a bus strike. The weather forecast says this kind of weather will continue for a few days more; you can't see the sun from this side of the Suez.'

Glum-faced, Mandira kept staring at her husband.

'I am seeing you in a sari after a long time. Any engagement outside?'

She shook her head saying, 'No. I'm not well.'

In a sympathetic tone Tom asked, 'What's your problem, dear? Tell me.'

'I have no problem as such. But I feel terrible.'

Tom nodded as though he had understood what Mandira meant to say. Then very gently he said, 'You called me just to say this?'

As though he wanted to clarify that her capriciousness was not a justifiable cause to call him home. They were not a young couple; they were mature enough to have something concrete, tangible to state when they would meet.

Seeing Mandira clam up once again, Tom suddenly erupted, 'Don't be ridiculous, Mani, you know well how busy I am! You've made me brave this ghastly weather to come to you just because of your whim. What nonsense is this cruel joke of yours? I told you that the baked beans controversy was going to be blown out of proportion.'

In a calm voice Mandira said, 'I'm sorry, Tom. I shouldn't have called you home this way. I'm really sorry. But I just want to tell you something in person. I'll leave this home. I want you to divorce me.'

'What!'

'I seek a divorce from you.'

'You've gone out of your head? Are you sure of what you are saying?'

'Perhaps I have gone insane. I seek your indulgence to carry on with my insanity.'

'What do you mean? Do you want to go back to India?'

'You seem to forget that I've no one left in India. I do not maintain any ties with India now. Why should I want to go back there?'

'Then? What do you want to do?'

'I want to stay alone. Don't be mad at me; let me go. You don't need me any longer. I'm just a burden in your life. After my exit, you'll enjoy greater freedom and concentrate better in your job.'

Tom almost sprang up from the chair. His face had turned red in rage and fury. Flinging up his two arms, he said, 'How could you say all this? Who said that you're a burden to me? Have I ever made you feel that? Have I never sacrificed even a little for you? Have I ever misbehaved with you?'

Shaking her head, Mandira said, 'No, you have never misbehaved with me. But I think I have lost all charms for you. You don't need me.'

'Need! What an ... ugly word! Our relationship has never been based on needs. There's something called love. I thought it was never lost between us.'

'Our middle-aged love has become too old. It has accumulated rust. It doesn't resemble the ardour of our youthful days.'

'Do you think, Mani, that we should cuddle each other like a newly married couple and whisper sweet nothings into each others' ears? What nonsense are you gripped with? You have never been devoid of reasoning and logic! I believe today's foul weather has wreaked havoc on your mood. If I were free today, I would have given you company. Please, I beg your pardon just for today; I've a very urgent piece of business to attend to.'

'Tom, I have requested you to divorce me.'

'Oh come on, you're harping on the same string, Mani. Can't you understand how awfully insulting all of this is for me? What's you ground? I have always honoured you as my dear wife. I repeat, it's a sheer temporary whimsicality on your part. If you enjoy sound sleep, you'll overcome this stress.'

'Perhaps it is the outcome of my delirious state of mind. But I request you to let me indulge in my lunacy.'

'We can discuss all this later. Now I'm too busy. I'm going out. Good night.'

Tom turned towards the door. Mandira, leaving the chair, ran towards him to catch hold of one of his arms.

Her face had taken on an eerie lustre and her flashing eyes bespoke a tremendous excitement.

She imploringly said, 'Tom, please tarry a while. Do you ever remember me talking like this? Today I long to say all this from the core of my heart; please allow me to say what I wish. Please spend a little more time with me now.'

Extricating his hand from Mandira's grip, he said disdainfully, 'Now I am losing my patience. I'll just wait two minutes more. So tell me—has a second man entered your life?'

With tearful eyes she replied, 'No, no, no! You are the only man in my life, rather had been, till this evening.'

'Mani, you are not making sense.'

'Men do not want to admit the fact that many marriages are based on needs after a certain period of their marriage. Since you became a public figure you desperately needed a public image of your being happily married, of having a decent family life. You're a busy man, unable to afford sufficient time for your children. So you needed a wife to look after your family. Wherever you go, you're aware that someone is looking after your family.'

'Don't you belong to this family? Are not they your children as well? Are you not happy with my fame, success? Sorry, I couldn't understand all this before.'

'I also didn't understand it before. Previously I used to believe that the family, household, children—everything belonged equally to both of us. We shared our responsibilities, joys, sorrows, failures, everything. You are brilliant; it's quite obvious that you'll be in the public limelight. I must look after the family; this is a kind of sharing. Shall I not rejoice at your achievements? You're after all my husband. But one fine morning I realised that I'm exhausted. I'm absolutely alone. The family no longer depends on me; our children are self-sufficient and I have no contribution towards my husband's achievements. I'm superfluous in the family. I have to depend on the newspapers to find out that you are going to Cuba leading a delegation of parliamentarians.'

Tom now felt a bit uncomfortable. He was going to tell a lie but restrained himself. At the top of his voice, he said, 'Oh, it's a trivial matter. So this is what is really bothering you! I was so busy that I forget to tell you. I would have told you later. The news is not absolutely correct. All MPs are not being accompanied by their spouses. Only two of them ... that old Gilbert ... the condition of his heart is not good, so Catherine is accompanying him and the other one is Oliver; you know Jenny never leaves Oliver alone ... He is such a henpecked husband ... it was finalised at the eleventh hour. And by the way, I'm sure you would not get leave from your office now.'

'You never even asked me once.'

'Oh, alright, if this is the cause of all your accusations against me, you are most welcome to come with me. It will not be very difficult to make travel arrangements for you.'

Mandira moved a little away from Tom. Then turning her face towards the wall, she said, 'No, Tom. I don't want to take anything forcefully from you. I have realised that I'm of no worth to you. I just want to see whether I'm of any worth to myself or not. Please Tom, bid me farewell.'

He bitterly said, 'It's a highly crucial time in my life now. Do you want to spread a scandal by seeking divorce from me? Are you really that ungrateful?'

In a grief-stricken tone, Mandira said, 'No, Tom, I won't slander you. I'll silently walk away from your life. No one will have an inkling of what is happening in our private lives. Some will come to know later but they, too, will forget in due course.'

When Tom was touring Cuba, Mandira regularly followed the newspaper ads, in search of an apartment. At last she really liked one at Harrow on the Hill in north London. It was small but pretty nice—a semi-detached bungalow, with a small plot of garden in the front and a patch of open space at the back, ideal for a kitchen garden. The price was within her reach. Mandira used to spend half of her earnings for the household expenditures. Tom had instructed likewise. She saved the rest of the amount. She however required more money to buy the house. Her bank readily agreed to give her a loan against mortgage.

4

After the property deed was finalised, Mandira beamed like a teenager. Though not in proper London, the house was in Greater London. It was her own property. She would tend a garden here. Tom was always reluctant to buy a house. When Mandira would wistfully speak of a garden he would suggest to her to go to Dover and spend a couple of days with his mother there.

Mandira had shifted to her new home before Tom returned from Cuba. She broke the news to none except her daughter. Liz was very happy and volunteered to help her mother in the interior decoration of the house. She even went to the extent of saying, 'Mom, you have taken a right step. Had you stayed longer in that large, three-room apartment, you would have gone mad out of solitude. Why should you keep on sacrificing so much for Dad? Father can engage a housekeeper for himself. Besides, he is having an affair with Mary Web … this is common knowledge.'

Mandira did not like the last remark. She rebuked her daughter, 'Don't talk rot. I warn you, don't make a single adverse comment against your father. And you talk of a love affair? It's not so easy. You people of this generation mistake intimacy for love. Moreover, I think it will be a nice thing if Mary and your father are on very good terms.'

Liz jokingly said, 'You have ensured lots of freedom for Dad. Now what will you do with your life? Look for an Indian boyfriend for yourself.'

Tom came back from Cuba but they could not meet. On the telephone he berated Mandira. He firmly believed that she was ungrateful, selfish. He had never interfered in her personal freedom and other privileges. Yet she was audacious enough to leave him. Tom was under the impression that only a man, a male chauvinist, had the right to desert his wife. He could not accept the reality that Mandira had taken the upper hand.

Far away from London, at a small town, they secretly signed their divorce papers. Even the press was kept in the dark about it.

Mandira brought nothing except her garments and some important papers from the Kensington apartment. And the car. Tom normally did not use the car. But Mandira could not move an inch without her car. Tom had gifted that car to her. It would have been an insensitive act on her part, had she returned it to him while leaving.

Mandira was used to being lonely. But unlike in the former apartment, here the solitude did not trouble her. She did not have to wait in vain for her husband to return home. Here she was as comfortable as fish in water.

She had to face one discomfort. Her office was at quite a distance from her apartment. For some days, she went to office in her own Volvo car. She did not have to bother about suitable parking space since there was a spacious one inside the office compound. But she felt tired after driving all that way. On her way back home she would invariably be disgusted by traffic snarls. Traffic bottlenecks had become the order of the day. Even the Ring road was not immune from its curse.

So Mandira decided to keep her car in the parking lot at the nearest tube station and then travel by train upto the office. After a pretty long time she directly experienced the lot of the commuters. Jostling, elbowing, pushing among the passengers was a common sight ... Many trod on others' feet but never apologised even perfunctorily. The commuters were busy levelling allegations against the government. They spared no opportunity to condemn the opposition party as well. Occasionally she happened to hear the name of Thomas Brockway on the lips of her fellow commuters. She was aware of the rumour about Tom and Mary Web's relationship. One day she overheard an interesting comment by a commuter.

Most of the tube rail passengers owned cars but travelled by tube to save expenses. Moreover, the road conditions often discouraged them to travel by cars. One day a fellow passenger commented, 'Roads are not being mended, so vast potholes lurk in every street, ready to bend wheels and sprain ankles—worse than anything you ever encountered in Calcutta.'

The word 'Calcutta' made her reminiscent of her city. She thought, Ah, my poor Calcutta! At the slightest opportunity every Tom, Dick and Harry take potshots at it. To the British in the past it was the Calcutta of the Black Hole tragedy. Now it is the city of potholes. Anything that is inferior, dingy, sordid in any part of the world is compared to Calcutta. Some days ago she was reading an American novel; there she read a line: 'The electricity production in Los Angeles is under such wrong planning that in the near future it will plunge into darkness, like Calcutta.' In fact, nobody seems to forget Calcutta. For quite a long time a play titled 'Oh, Calcutta' had been on show. It was really an obscene piece of drama, the subject matter of which was in no way connected with Calcutta. Still the name circulated among the people. The caption itself was something vilifying.

But millions of Calcuttans led normal lives, having their share of fun, happiness, music and other cultural activities. Some people there lived in misery, true, but where do some people not live in misery?

Mandira had completely severed her ties with the Bengalis living in London. But she now resumed her contacts with some of them. Almost everyday she bumped into one or two Indians. It was not civil to overlook them, so she would exchange pleasantries which later developed into some kind of friendship. Many of them were new arrivals there, staying for about five, ten or at best fifteen years at a stretch in London. They did not know Mandira personally but had heard about her. The wife of a British parliamentarian is an Indian—it was quite obviously a topic of hot discussion among many. They were under the impression that Mandira was too proud to keep in touch with fellow Indians. The rumour in the Bengali circle was that she was adamant on erasing her original identity. She allegedly kept away from Durga Puja and other cultural fests organised by the Indians residing in London.

Gradually the news spread that Mandira Brockway had divorced her husband and was now living in a separate apartment all by herself; it had become a hot topic for the scandal-mongers.

One day in the tube, Mandira came across an Indian girl sitting opposite her. Mandira deduced her Indian identity from the way she had draped her sari. After eye contact on a couple of occasions, Mandira smiled at her. The compartment was so crowded that it was not feasible to talk. The lady was in her mid-thirties, fair-complexioned, with a face resembling the female portraits painted by Botticelli. It seemed she had seen the face before. Was it because of her resemblance with the portraits?

With Mandira she also got down at Kings Cross station. During office hours, everybody was in a hurry. None could afford to spare a moment to talk to an acquaintance. It was an uphill task to push one's way through the crowd. At the escalator, the lady stood just beside Mandira. Hesitating a little, she asked, 'Excuse me, by any chance are you Mandira Dutta?'

Mandira had not heard anyone using her paternal surname for a pretty long time. It was almost two years since she had heard someone speak Bengali. When she went to Southall for shopping, a Punjabi shopkeeper would address her, 'Didi, namaskar. How're you?' That Sardarji once lived in Calcutta.

Now in response to the lady's question, Mandira, curious, nodded her head.

The lady said, 'Namaskar, you do not know me, but I know you, rather I knew you. In Calcutta you lived at Manoharpukur road, didn't you? My elder sister studied in the same college with you.'

Lifting her hand, Mandira stopped the lady and said, 'Yes, Arpita Majumdar of Mahanirban road ... your face resembles Arpita.'

'I'm Prarthana. You used to visit our house quite often then.'

'You're Chini right?'

'Oh, you remember that also?'

Mandira had a sharp memory. She could remember the minute details of an episode that might have occurred say twenty-six or twenty-seven years ago. She could remember any telephone number and recall any face she might have come across even once in her life.

'I might not have recognised you, for I had seen you long ago when I was too young. But yesterday in the train one of my acquaintances told me that you're Mandira Brockway. It then struck me that one of my elder sister's friends was Mandira ...'

'Where does your didi live now?'

'Didi lives in Durgapur. She may visit me this year. I've asked her so many times to come over here, you know.'

'How long have you been here?'

'More than eight years.'

The escalator stopped. Now Mandira would have to take a right turn. Prarthana brought out a notebook and scribbled something hurriedly. Then she said, 'Look, this is my address. I'll be glad if you drop in some day.'

For courtesy's sake Mandira should also have given her address. She had the visiting card with her, printed by her office but the address written on it was the old one. She wrote her new address, striking off the old one on a card, and gave it to Prarthana.

Coming out on the street, Mandira began to feel a kind of satisfaction after speaking to Chini. She got the impression that even today, after so many years, the rhythm of the Bengali language found an echo within her soul. She was thinking about Chini, an eight- or ten-year-old kid then, cute and naughty. Mandira had been fond of her. She had a good singing voice even at that age. That Chini was now a slightly obese, married woman. Now she could apprehend her own age.

All these years, she had shunned close contact with her Indian friends. Her children, husband—were all British. What if she had maintained an identity of her own? Tom had married her for who she was. Her nationality didn't matter to him. But after her marriage, she was against the idea of bringing the whole of India in tow with her. She had no friends of her own. But why? Sankar da had visited their Kensington apartment a couple of times. During his visits Tom had gone to Sussex. Mandira never entertained any distant relative from India seeking her hospitality.

In London during winter, evenings fell so soon that Mandira could hardly experience what afternoons were like. Getting down from the train, as she came to the parking lot, she would find her car wrapped in snow. Even the yard in front of her house would be covered with a sheet of ice. Before parking the car she had to remove some of the ice sheets. She enjoyed doing that. Now she didn't feel bored to cook for her own self. For a long while now she hadn't had her favourite Bengali dishes like onion in masur daal, loughanta (a dish prepared from gourd) and brinjal fries. Amazingly, she couldn't forget the taste of these dishes even though she had not had them for years. She wouldn't confine her lunch to sandwiches only.

On returning from office she would enjoy a cup of coffee while watching news on TV. Then she would have a bath. Thereafter would begin the dinner preparations.

The kitchen was small but compact. Putting something on the oven, she read books.

Robin rang twice in one week from America. He was urging her to visit him. Mandira was yet to fly across the Atlantic. Once she had been eager to tour across the Latin American countries. Now she never liked to leave home. She simply wanted to enjoy her newly acquired freedom to her heart's content. Even today when the telephone rang in the evening, she thought of Robin. But lo and behold! A woman's voice in lucid Bengali said, 'Good evening, this is Prarthana. How do you do, Mandira di? I'm inviting some of my acquaintances to my home this weekend. Will you please come and join us? Truly, I'll be very glad if you come. There are a number of Bengali families in my neighbourhood. They are eager to meet you.'

Mandira hesitated before giving a reply. She was not sure whether she would be quite at home in the presence of a group of Bengali families, after so many years. She was no longer confident of her Bengali pronunciations. Why were they so eager to meet her? She was not a celebrity. Were they inquisitive about her private life?

Mandira told a lie. 'No, I'm sorry, I can't keep your invitation this weekend. I would rather invite you to come one day to my house.'

The very next day she received a call from another Bengali—Mr Probodh Sengupta. He introduced himself saying, 'I'm the secretary of the local Sunday school. I hope you've heard the name of our Sunday school?'

'No, I'm sorry. I haven't heard of it; I'm new to your locality,' said Mandira a bit hesitantly.

The Bengalis living in England discovered that their offspring were becoming rootless. They did not know the Bengali language; many of them hadn't even heard Tagore's name. They were reluctant to respect great men like Lord Ramakrishna, let alone the question of visiting India. All these things inspired the Bengalis to set up Sunday schools in each borough. The Sunday schools, usually located at a community centre or a church, aimed at giving lessons in the mother tongue, native culture, etc., to the young generation whose parents hailed from Bengal. At the outset, Greater London Council extended some financial assistance to the Sunday schools.

Probodh Sengupta was the secretary of one such Sunday school. He invited Mandira to deliver a lecture on the coming Sunday at his school.

Mandira was amazed at the invitation. 'Are you asking me to deliver a speech? How can I do that? I'm not that fluent in Bengali! Besides ...'

The gentleman insisted but Mandira firmly declined the offer saying, 'I'm sorry, I can't help. But I'll definitely visit your school one day, not this Sunday ... well some other Sunday ...'

Mandira felt a bit emotional at the thought that the Bengali community was curious about her; she liked this. She was fond of socialising yet she couldn't get over a kind of inhibition. She was apprehensive that people would trespass into her private life and try to dig into her past.

She enjoyed her freedom in a life of detachment. This joy was visible on her countenance. Yet she knew, somewhere in the deepest core of her heart, there was a wound which remained invisible on the surface. The decision to leave Tom had been a harrowing experience for her. She was reluctant to share this trauma with anyone.

Prarthana seemed to be a popular figure. She had given Mandira's phone number to several others. Late in the evenings, Mandira had to attend many phone calls. One day, a girl from the other end of the receiver said that she was her distant cousin and that she wanted to meet her. Dr Sen from Belsize Park called and said in a tone of mock anger, 'You didn't inform us before shifting to a separate apartment. You didn't keep in touch with us. It's a pity that I came to know your whereabouts from Prarthana. I'll be glad if you visit us one day. The sooner will be the better.'

At office, one day, she bumped into Ed, one of Tom's friends. Author of three books on economics, he had come to discuss his latest book with his publisher.

Ed came to Mandira's chamber. 'Mani, I'd love to be treated to a cup of coffee,' he said.

Ed knew everything about her private life. But he carefully avoided the issue. Some time later, he said, 'What are you doing on the twenty-fifth of this month? There's a get-together at my residence. Why don't you join us?'

Casting a glance at the desk calendar, she said, 'Well ... twenty-fifth, I'm afraid I can't keep your invitation.'

'Why? Do you have any other appointment that day, Mani?'

Mandira hesitantly nodded her head and admitted, 'Yes, I've another engagement.'

In a sharp tone, Ed said, 'Mani, you might have distanced yourself from Tom but will you do the same with us? Are we not your friends? Why do you feel uncomfortable to visit my home?'

Mandira had to tell a lie. She told him that she really had another prior appointment.

Mandira was in a fix. She was sure Tom would be present at the party. She couldn't face him right at that moment. Besides, she feared that David might also be present there.

They had had a mutual separation. There was no harm in sharing jokes with ex-husbands, if they happened to bump into each other. But she was reluctant to meet him right then. She was still weak. Tom's rage was yet to ebb. He hadn't telephoned her even once.

She declined the offer to attend the party on the twenty-fifth at Ed's house but she was sure Ed would invite her some day again. Ed's wife, Stella was a very good hostess. She threw frequent parties. Besides Ed, there were a host of other acquaintances of Tom's who were likely to invite Mandira. What would she do then? Would she turn down all the offers? She had mingled with the British society for a quarter of a century. Would she sever all ties with it so easily? Again she had been detached from the Bengali community over the years. Now should she renew her contacts with it? Or should she keep an equal distance from both the communities? She couldn't come to a decision.

The weather had been bright and sunny for a pretty long time. But since the middle of March, the weather turned for the worse. The mercury dipped so low that out on the streets, the tip of the nose would turn red. Every evening, there must invariably be snowfall. The driveway in front of her residence would also plunge into one-and-half-feet layer of snow. She didn't like to sit at the steering during those days. But she was compelled to go out. Marks and Spencer was having a sale. She had to buy some wollens from there.

The whole of Europe now went under the grip of a cold wave.

Today Mandira decided to skip cooking. She was content with a glass of milk. Now it was fifteen minutes past ten. She had brought some manuscripts from her office. She was glancing through them while waiting for the live telecast of the Winter Olympics from Calgary, Canada, to be shown at eleven p.m.

All at once the doorbell rang. At first she thought it must be an auditory hallucination or perhaps a sound on the TV. But it was repeated. Yet she couldn't quite believe it. Who could be visiting her on this cold night, without an appointment? Her next-door neighbours were an old couple with whom Mandira shared a cordial relationship.

But that was limited to tête-à-têtes on gardening or weather. On holidays they occasionally visited her by ringing the doorbell. They would normally go to bed by nine. Were they in some kind of trouble and seeking Mandira's help?

Through the magic eye on the door, she indistinctly saw the tall figure of a man. The man raised one of his arms.

Having opened the door Mandira turned speechless for a while.

Wearing a heavy overcoat under a raincoat and a hat stood Tom. Always busy, famous, holder of important posts at different times, Thomas Brockway had come to Mandira braving snowstorms and that too without prior appointment. Incredible!

Mandira felt her heart pounding like a hammer. Like that eleventh of January when Tom had become apprehensive of some trouble befalling Robin or Liz, Mandira was also today apprehensive of a similar kind of ill omen. Was anything wrong with Robin or Liz? Children, wherever they might be, are intuitively connected with their parents. Was Tom's visit portentous of some bad news related to them? Had he come to break the news personally to her?

In a serious tone, he said, 'Hello Mani, are you expecting guests tonight?'

Mandira was puzzled. She shook her head to say no.

'May I come in then?'

Mandira made way for him to come in. Tom entered the room and took off his raincoat and kept it on a stool.

There was no question of kissing. He didn't even kiss her formally on the cheeks. Looking this and that way, Tom said, 'I have come to see you. Your house is quite nice.'

Mandira hadn't uttered a single word yet. She knew Tom would take time if he had any bad news to break.

Tom said, 'May I see the rest of your house?'

When a guest drops in it is courtesy to let him look around the house.

Mandira's apartment consisted of a drawing room, a bedroom, a kitchen and a bathroom. The drawing room, however, was spacious.

Having surveyed the rooms, Tom pulled a kitchen chair and sat on it.

'Very cosy and compact. Quite comfortable for a single person. Are you well, Mani?'

Tom was speaking very casually but Mandira was feeling uneasy. Her countenance revealed that she was suffering from a sense of guilt. She lit a cigarette.

'The children keep in touch with you. They don't do that with me. Robin had once telephoned me from Buffalo. But I don't know how Liz is. Is she alright? Did she come to meet you?'

'Yes,' replied Mandira. 'She has been here on a couple of occasions.'

'I was busy all day and was feeling tired. I returned home late in the evening. Do you know what happened then? I had forgotten that you no longer lived in the Kensington apartment. Opening the door, I was expecting you to be watching TV in the living room. I was almost on the verge of calling out to you by your name.'

They beheld each other for a few seconds. Then Tom in a mild tone said, 'I miss you, Mani.'

Mandira slowly said, 'I miss you too. It's true!'

They had been overwhelmed for a few moments. They soon overcame it.

'I hope I haven't bothered you by coming this way without prior intimation. I know I shouldn't have come like this. Normally I'm not as impulsive as is evident from today's behaviour.'

'Tom, I don't keep any hard drinks or alcohol at home; shall I make coffee for you?'

'I would like tea rather ... do you have the Darjeeling tea that I am so fond of?'

'Yes, I have ...'

'Will you please write down for me the name of the shop from where you used to buy Darjeeling tea? Actually I don't remember its name.'

Mandira lit the gas stove and put the kettle on. Then coming back to Tom she asked, 'Who prepares your breakfast? Have you engaged any housekeeper?'

'No. I do it myself. It's quite alright.'

Mandira smiled faintly. Let alone toasting a piece of bread, she had never seen Tom enter the kitchen.

'I'm however eating out for my lunch and dinner.'

'That is not good for your health. Tom, you work so hard, you should take care of your health.'

'I find you've become a chain-smoker, Mani.'

Tom used to be a chain-smoker in his college days. A new trend had begun in the 1960s when smokers used to stuff ganja inside cigars and puff. But Tom gave up smoking when he was contesting elections for the first time. Now he was one of the pioneers of the anti-smoking campaigns. But he couldn't make his wife give up smoking ... Many men had given up the cancer stick but their partners continued smoking.

Mandira poured boiled water into the cup and dropped in a tea bag. Then she asked, 'You are not taking sugar, are you? Your blood sugar had once crossed the permitted level. You don't do any physical exercise either.'

'I'm growing old, Mani. I had started jogging but I get tired soon.'

'Why can't Linda come and prepare your breakfast?'

'Linda ... well, I don't like Linda coming to my home off and on. She helps me in the party office.'

'Then somebody else might do that for you.'

'Are you talking about Mary Web? Do you want her to come over and prepare my breakfast?'

'No, I'm not talking about anyone in particular. Someone should take care of you.'

'Robin was asking me on the telephone whether I'm going to marry Mary Web. He seemed to be very annoyed with me. The children are on your side, as though I'm the culprit, as if I've driven you away from home, as if I've broken the marriage!'

'But I've never said anything of that sort to anybody. I have never complained against you, believe me.'

'Listen Mani, I know that a rumour has been spread about my relationship with Mary Web. In fact, there is no dearth of rumour mongers. The fact is, you know that I'm a confirmed MCP but Mary is a radical feminist. Can we ever reconcile? We often quarrel. Many people take these fights to be the basis of an amorous relationship.

Mandira remained silent. She had heard lots of things meanwhile about Mary Web. Whatever be the relation between Tom and Mary, why should it bother her? Even a feminist is not out of reach. A case in point would be a noted feminist writer whom many people considered to be a lesbian because of her ultra feminist views. But lo! When it came in the open that she was pregnant, people realised that she didn't hate men altogether. She had become the stuff of gossip mills and butt of ridicule for some time. Perhaps feminists are reluctant to marry but they are not against affairs.

'Mani,' said Tom, 'I've a piece of news for you. There is a vacancy in the Far Eastern Manuscript section at the British Museum. Are you interested in accepting the position? You'll have better prospects there. Previously I had some inhibition in recommending your name as you were my wife. But now I don't have any problem as such. Can I send your name? You're undoubtedly qualified for the post.'

'Thank you, Tom. I'm happy that you thought of me. But I'm sorry I won't accept the offer; I'm quite happy with my present job.'

'Alright. If I come of any use, please feel free.'

'Okay.'

'If I visit you occasionally, of course, when you're free, will you treat me with papad fry and fish curry?'

'Oh, sure! I'm sorry, today I don't have papad at home.'

'Some other time. Good night,' said Tom, getting up.

'How will you go now in the midst of snowfall?' asked Mandira anxiously, 'wait a bit, I'll drop you at the tube station.'

'No need of that. My taxi is waiting for me outside. Thanks for the tea.'

Having gone up to the door, Tom put on the raincoat and then looking around, stretched out his hands. Mandira reciprocated. Both of them remained in each others' embrace for a while.

Tom whispered, 'I care for you, Mani. I'll never forget you. I wish you all the best.'

'The days of our love shall never be belied,' replied Mandira. 'Believe me, I have no allegations against you. All the best.'

After Tom's departure, Mandira stood at the door, nonplussed. She had felt slightly aroused in Tom's embrace. She was longing to remain embraced in his bosom. The body seeks the warmth of another body. Her body was still young, responding.

How splendidly Tom behaved today! But Mandira knew it was his affected weakness. Lasting for an evening only. It was a kind of sudden emotional change. Had they been mutually separated and had Mandira returned to him, she knew he would have started behaving as before, after a couple of days only. He would have taken his wife for granted as usual. The husband's mindset is that his wife will look after him like a slave. In this regard there's a striking similarity between the British society and the Bengali society. This is why the rate of divorce in English society is so high. The wife is as though bound to make a lot of sacrifices for her husband's career, fame and success. For the sake of courtesy the British husbands pretend to be very nice to their wives at parties but back home they have no time to spare for them.

No, this distance is fine. It's quite sufficient to live in the sweet memory of the past. Tom would feel embarrassed later for being so emotional before Mandira. Men are cautious enough not to repeat their mistakes. He would never visit her to have papad fries and fish curry.

Some days later on an afternoon, an incident brought about a sea-change in Mandira's life.

That was a holiday. It was springtime and Mandira had toiled hard for a pretty long time in the garden. She made a row of roses. Her next-door neighbours, the old couple, were away to Belgium. Mandira was looking after their garden in their absence. Many of the plants had broken out into blossoms meanwhile. Many cute-looking, red-haired kids were playing on the street. The sight brought back memories of Liz's childhood days.

After tending the garden, she had her bath. Being refreshed she prepared a couple of cheese sandwiches for lunch. After eating them she lay on the bed.

Normally she wouldn't sleep in the afternoons. But that day she was very tired and soon fell asleep.

She didn't know how long she slept.

All at once she felt like being jerked out of bed. She ran towards the bathroom. She felt pain in her abdomen and with it nausea. She was feeling extremely ill with excruciating pain in her stomach and chest. She had never felt like this before.

She started throwing up in the sink but before she was done she started reeling and collapsed on the bathroom floor. She had a nasty bump on her head. While keeling over, one particular thought flashed through her mind: she had eaten three pieces of cheese sandwiches. She had read in the newspaper that one particular brand of cheese had been found poisoned. Did she buy that brand? Some of it was in an unsealed lunch box. She shouldn't have stored that stuff.

Though she lived alone, it was her habit to lock the bathroom door after entering it.

Now her whole body was smeared with vomit. She was unable to stand straight. She tottered towards the bathroom door and tried to reach the telephone receiver.

But suppose she died before help reached her? She felt like her eyes were drawing to a close. Was it death?

If she lay dying in the bathroom, there would be faint chances of her being traced before at least four or five days. Elderly people living alone rot in this way. The police arrive only after a stinking smell comes out of the house. That is why single septuagenarians here opt for marriage, just to get a companion. Mandira had craved for an independent life. Was this the kind of life she had actually longed for? Now it could be that she was going to die, unattended. Had she fallen sick at the dead of night, whom could she have called out to? Her former husband? She was not sure whether she would be able to contact her daughter over telephone. Her elderly neighbours were also out of station. Had they been present, it wouldn't have helped much. Mandira had no close friend, no relative whom she could have called for immediate help. Now she was unable to reach the bathroom door.

5

The rain has stopped. Prabir fetches the meat and chapattis from the car. Biman has downed a couple of pegs of whisky. In a sottish tone, he says, 'Please heat the meat. I can't eat cold stuff.'

There is a small storeroom attached to the kitchen. Shanti sleeps in it. She has fallen asleep. Meanwhile, Mandira lights the stove and puts the pan over it. She pours the meat into the pan. It's a red broth with some oil floating over it. She feels nauseous at the mere sight of it and can't think of having such rich food.

Biman used to win bets eating lots of hot curries. At College Square, they would throng around an alukabli vendor and Biman would demand, 'Add more chilli powder, some more, a little more ...' He would have tears in his eyes, yet he would finish the stuff with great pleasure. As if it was a great feat on his part.

Despite putting his digestive system through such tortures in his youth, Biman is today drinking whisky to his heart's content. This proves that his liver hasn't been damaged yet. People living in tropical countries can digest lots of chillis. Mandira has seen Shanti eating green chillies effortlessly.

When Mandira comes back with the heated meat, she finds Biman lying on the floor. She tries to rouse him and push a morsel into his mouth but he spits it out on the floor. She stares sadly at the floor.

Prabir has eaten some meat and chapatti. Still, there is much left. Mandira has no refrigerator.

'We must leave,' says Prabir, 'I don't know how Biman da will drive the car all the way back to Calcutta.'

Biman defiantly shouts from his reclining posture, 'Of course, I'll drive the car. Your sister wants to turn us out.'

'Prabir, why don't you learn driving?' asks Mandira with annoyance.

'Why should I? Do I own a car?'

In this situation, Mandira won't let them go. But where will they stay? She has only one bedroom with a single bed in it.

She says, 'Come, let's sleep. Biman will lie on the bed. You'll have to share the mat on the floor with me. You can't sleep throughout the night because of mosquitoes.'

'No, I'll sleep inside the car. It must not be left uncared for; you don't know the local people. They will vanish with parts like the headlight or even the wheels,' says Prabir. Then he rushes out. Perhaps, his actual intention is to leave his sister alone with her former lover, rather than to guard the car.

Mandira smiles a bit. In a room, she is now alone with Biman, after twenty-seven years and a few months. Nevertheless, the gap between the two periods doesn't appear too long.

The door must be shut to keep away stray dogs. Besides, she is scared of frogs and snakes. The village folks are curious about Mandira's house. Have they fallen asleep? Forget it. There's no other way right now.

Having risen, Biman is now sitting, leaning his back on a leg of the cot. His eyes look grey. He lights a cigarette.

'Now, I'll smoke,' says Mandira.

Stroking the floor beside him, Biman urges her, 'Come, sit here.'

Mandira doesn't oblige him. Puffing the cigarette with great satisfaction, she says, 'You have stayed back ultimately. Have you told your wife that you are not returning tonight? Won't she be worried for you?'

'You seem very concerned about my wife! Forget about her. I often stay out of station on office tours.'

'Biman, please sleep on the bed. I'll lie on the floor mat.'

'No, I hope this bed is spacious enough for both of us. Mani, come close to me, very close to me.'

'No, I can't sleep pressed close to each other in this narrow bed.'

'Oh, come on, Mani! You're still a prude, though you have been in Europe for so many years.'

'You people are under the impression, gathered mainly from movies, that all foreign-returned people become promiscuous overnight.'

'Mani, do you remember the night that we spent in our Padmapukur residence?'

Mandira doesn't forget anything so easily. She recalls even the faintest event from millions of memory cells stored in her brain. That was the marriage ceremony of one of Biman's cousin sisters. Urmila was Mandira's bosom friend. They sat up late chatting with the bride and the bridegroom amidst music and merry-making. It was a large building, rented for the occasion at Bhawanipur. At around three o'clock in the night, when most of the revellers were dozing, when Biman suggested, 'Let's go for a stroll on the street,' Mandira didn't object. It never occurred to her that it was unsafe for a woman to be out on the streets at that hour of night. In fact, she had great confidence in Biman. She would feel safe in his company. Besides, she was in her early twenties then; that was an age when people hardly cared for dangers.

That night, she didn't face any danger. In fact, that was her maiden experience of being out in the middle of the night. The street looked like a river. Lampposts stood on either side but there was no sign of human beings. They were walking down the middle of the road; clasping each others' hands, they were singing as if it was a scene in a film. That was a moonlit night, a bit of blue moon had let loose the floodgates of moonlight on their faces.

They had walked upto Biman's house in Padmapukur. There was no one in his house, for everyone had gone to attend the wedding. Biman had opened the lock and stepped into the house, keeping his hand around Mandira's shoulder. Going up to the first floor of his house, he had said, 'Come, let's lie down here and get back before dawn. No one will have an inkling about it.'

Why didn't Mandira agree that day? There really was no obstacle. They were intensely attracted to each other. Biman was a subtle dialectician, well-versed in literature; he was well-abreast of the contemporary global situation. So, when he spoke Mandira used to stare at him, spellbound. Still why couldn't she agree? It was not that there was a big moral barrier; she was just feeling that the time wasn't ripe. Not in this way.

'No, not in this way!' She had said this repeatedly while refraining Biman.

Biman had tried to force her a bit but soon gave up. In fact, it was very difficult to disobey Mandira. Her clear, determined 'no' was enough for submission.

Had there been physical intimacy between them that night, Mandira's life would have taken a different course. Probably, she wouldn't have gone abroad and even if she had gone, there would have been no question of marrying Tom.

In a room of that empty house, Biman and Mandira sat close to each other for an hour. While speaking to her, Biman had kissed her finger just a few times. In fact, he too didn't want to belittle himself in her eyes by lacking self-restraint. As if he also was convinced that the time was not ripe.

Tonight, a similar scenario recurs after a span of twenty-seven years.

Leaning over and gripping Mandira's hand, he says with a passion accentuated by drunkenness, 'Why have our lives become like this? In six months or so, after reaching London, how did you forget me?'

'I didn't forget. I merely chose a different life. Biman, it sounds odd, typical of old people, to lament over the past. In fact, I don't have any regrets. Your life too didn't take a wrong course.'

'I have been waiting for you for so many years. I was sure that you'd come back one day, Mani ... Mani, I didn't forget you for a single day of my life!'

Mandira smiles. Had Biman been in his senses, he wouldn't have said such melodramatic things. He is basically very intelligent. If someone chants the name of his former lover ritually for twenty-seven years, it should be taken for granted that he is a psycho-neurotic patient. Actually Biman must not have done any such thing. After one and a half years of Mandira's marriage, he also married a girl hailing from a renowned family in Calcutta. He is now the father of three children and owner of a construction company. So, in no way is his life unsuccessful. He might have thought of Mandira occasionally—that was par for the course. But she is sure, with the passage of time, her memory must have faded from his mind. Actually, what has hurt Biman is the fact that she has not contacted him after returning to Calcutta.

'You've come after a marathon gap of decades ... single, and still you insist that it's not high time ...?' sulks Biman. 'I want you, I want you!'

Mandira gets up at once, saying, 'Wait a little, I'm coming.'

'Where are you going?'

'To the bathroom. Just a minute.'

Taking a torch, Mandira walks towards the bathroom.

The bathroom is very small. There is no running water there. Water fetched from a tubewell nearby is stored in a big drum. A commode has been fitted but buckets of water have to be poured into it. To avoid the stinking smell, Mandira repeatedly washes it with phenyl and bleaching powder and drops some eucalyptus oil on the floor after every wash. She can't tolerate foul smell.

At one corner of the bathroom, there is a spider's web. Mandira has repeatedly destroyed it, yet the creature comes back to rebuild the web. Mandira is not scared of cockroaches and lizards but she dreads spiders. In London, she had seen cockroaches and house lizards but not a single spider. She lights the torch to locate the spider. Yes, it's not there now.

She shuts the door and stands leaning her back against it.

Thomas Brockway is not an alcohol addict. Normally, the English don't revel in drinking. They hate boozing. But there are exceptions. Initially when Tom and Mandira held parties at their house, she had seen a couple of Tom's friends who were reckless drunkards. One of them was Ed, the economist, who had never touched wine but was fond of scotch. At a certain stage, he'd start breaking glasses. Another one was an Irish fellow, whom everybody called a wine barrel. In an intoxicated state, he'd try to dance with Mandira. So, she was quite adept at tackling drunkards. She knew, some minutes of silence would make them fall asleep.

Mandira did not contact Biman. That's true. But his sudden arrival has not made her unhappy today. She was on intimate terms with him during her college days. Their courtship lasted for a couple of years. In England, when she dated Tom, often a sense of guilt used to prick her about Biman. But the attraction for Tom was also irresistible. She was undeniably dazzled by the opportunity of coming in close contact with the English society. But she was after all not betrothed to Biman. So, she did not break any promise by marrying Tom.

Still, she hates the idea of sleeping beside Biman today, when he has appeared twenty-seven years later in her life, just like a comet. He is married and has children. She will not allow Biman to seek sexual favours from her tonight. She is a divorcee but that doesn't mean that she is cheap and readily available. Is he willing to divorce his wife and desert his children right at this moment and come to her? If she should ask this of Biman, what would be his reaction? Mandira cannot suppress her smile. She had posed this question to Mike, Tom's Irish friend, who had once tried to kiss Mandira, secretly. Hearing her question, he had almost fleed from her. They were Catholic and hence there was no question of divorce.

About half an hour later, Mandira comes back to Biman and finds him fast asleep on the floor. Now, there is no point in rousing him to send him to bed. She sits close to him with her face over his. He is senior to her by two years yet he still looks young because he has a baby face. Now, asleep, he looks like a perfectly innocent child. The lips reveal his wounded sentiments.

With a tissue paper she delicately wipes Biman's mouth which is smeared with food. Then she cleans the floor littered with the leftovers of food, bones, etc. Mandira is very particular about cleanliness. She removes the shoes from his feet. Then she starts applying the mosquito repellant cream all over his face. She has not touched a man for a long time. Her heart aches. She is a human being, after all. All humans need a companion. But Biman can't be her companion. He'll at best seek to make Mandira his mistress!

She then applies the cream all over her body and decides to spend the night reading at the table. She will not go to bed while Biman is lying on the floor. And Prabir must be fantasising that his sister is sleeping in the arms of her former lover. Idiot! He should never have brought Biman here in such a condition.

The book, *Landlessness in Bengal,* has been brought from Calcutta. She has been reading the book to understand the lot of the landless peasants in rural areas. In India, the problem is absurdly high. Take the case of landless labourers or educated unemployed youths—all the figures are astronomical. The day before yesterday, she was reading a news item that said that the Reserve Bank of India was recruiting six hundred and fifty clerks while the number of applicants reached three-and-a-half lakhs!

She can't concentrate on the book now; she never desired to involve herself in Himalayan problems plaguing Indian society. She just wants to live in a small, obscure place, keep in touch with the folks and share their joys and sorrows. This is not possible in European countries. People there don't like to interfere in other people's problems.

She is nearly dozing off at the table but the mosquitoes, buzzing near her ears, make her jerk into wakefulness.

As the dawn breaks over the horizon, she opens the door and comes out on the veranda.

The night was refreshed with one or two brief spells of showers. The morning is glowing with a beautiful sunshine. The red China roses in the courtyard are sparkling. The ten or twelve brinjal plants that Mandira has sown have also burst into blossoms.

Mandira washes her face and mouth in the water from the tubewell and perambulates for a while in the courtyard. There are not many houses near her residence. But she can hear noises of several kinds indicating that the villagers have already arisen from bed and started their day's work.

She draws a cane chair and sits on it. She remembers that she is supposed to visit the Lakhapur weekly market with Shanti. A little later, she will bid farewell to Biman and Prabir.

Shanti comes out sleepy-eyed; rubbing her eyes she asks, 'Didi, shall I make tea now? How many cups?'

'Boil a pretty large quantity of water; I'll prepare tea. Before that, wash your face and mouth and brush your teeth. You'll find a pot with cooked meat in it. Don't eat it, give it away to the dogs straying near the pond. Perhaps lured by the smell of the meat a dog has already been here in the courtyard wagging its tail ...'

Mandira is brewing a sufficient quantity of tea ... Right then Prabir turns up.

Instead of scolding him, Mandira smiles at him. She had not given him the mosquito repellant cream. His face, as though, has been swollen by mosquito bites. Can anyone escape from the attack of mosquitoes by barely pulling up the car windows? He has got the punishment he deserves.

'Oh! I couldn't sleep a wink. When I raised the windowpanes I felt so hot, and when I rolled them down, huge mosquitoes, as big as birds, swarmed into the car.'

Mandira laughs and says, 'Don't worry. The large-sized mosquitoes don't cause malaria.'

Looking this and that way, Prabir asks, 'Where's Biman da?'

'He's inside. Go and call him here.'

Shanti comes back with only two cups. There are no more cups in the house. There are two glasses though. Shanti has already washed them but Mandira isn't reassured. She's very fastidious about cleanliness. She goes to wash them with her own hands.

The cups have been given to Biman and Prabir while Mandira and Shanti take the glasses.

'There's no biscuit in stock. You may have puffed rice,' says Mandira.

Biman looks quite different now. His face is now coated with a film of shame and surprise.

Taking a sip from the cup, he says, 'I don't take biscuits with tea. I slept on the floor last night.'

To test Biman, Mandira says, 'You fell asleep while chatting with me.'

'Really?'

Mandira realises that Biman has forgotten many incidents of the previous night. Amnesia. It is the result of a regular habit of consuming alcohol. Now if she tells him that he had a nasty fall on the ground, he will not be able to refute it with confidence.

With the cup in hand, Biman comes down to the courtyard and looks around. 'You'll live in this house forever, under a tin roof and that too alone?'

'Isn't the house beautiful? It's very calm and quiet. So what if it's under a tin shed? Rainwater doesn't seep through it. The village is also nice. Will you have a look?'

'No. I'm least interested. Now we must leave. Before that, Mani, I reiterate, you can't live permanently in this village. You've no idea of rural Bengal. At best you can come over and spend your weekends here. But give up the romantic notion of living here. I'm in the construction business, engaged in the building of multi-storeyed apartments. Recently, we have finished a project at Salt Lake. I want to book one flat for you there.'

'Two flats are yet to be booked,' adds Prabir.

Mandira emphatically says, 'I'll never live in a flat in future. I've decided not to live in a flat, eat tinned food, frozen food and use a fridge.'

'Your long stay in Europe has made you phobic. You don't know how dangerous it can be for a lady like you to stay in these areas. Rape, murder are common affairs. I can't let you live like this. Moreover, you own a British passport. So, I think it's illegal on your part to stay here. Had you been in Calcutta, we could have at least manipulated things for you.'

'No, I have an Indian passport. I have not changed my citizenship yet. So I don't find any trouble.'

'How did you get to know about this place? Did you come here straight from London?'

'No, how could I do that? First I came to the New Alipore house. There I met Tagar, Shanti's elder sister who was a maidservant at my sister's house. Tagar was talking about her native village which was near the Sunderbans. She was telling me how the menfolk ventured into the forests to collect honey. I was thrilled to hear all this and decided to visit the place. On one of my visits, I heard that this particular house was on sale. Another bigger one was there, but that was more expensive. So, I chose this one. This small house is quite snug for me.'

Meanwhile locals have started passing by her house. A group of urchins are standing around the car.

Biman keeps on insisting that Mandira should accompany him to Calcutta. But she doesn't agree. With a smile, she says, 'Look I've not become a rustic altogether. I occasionally visit Calcutta and I hope we'll meet there.'

Last night Biman travelled that long distance from Calcutta on the spur of the moment. But today he has to attend an important lunch meeting with a business party and some government representatives. He's obliged to go there. It'll take at least three hours to reach Calcutta. The road conditions are very bad. So he can't afford a delay.

The car was left in the open throughout the night. It has been exposed to rainwater. So the engine is not starting. The battery has been weakened; perhaps the carburettor has gathered dust.

In India most of the drivers do not understand the machinery of a car. Even when they have to replace a tyre they seek the help of a mechanic. Whereas in Europe, a small repair work entails a pretty good expenditure. Therefore most car owners there try to pick up some working knowledge of car repairing. Having failed to get the car started, Biman says in despair, 'Prabir, do go to the petrol pump on the main road and fetch a mechanic. You must get someone.'

'Let me try once,' says Mandira.

Perhaps it's a sheer coincidence! As soon as Mandira sits at the steering and pumps the clutch a few times, the engine starts.

'There is magic in your touch, for sure, Mani,' marvels Biman.

'Even if I don't get anything else to do, I think I can at least get a driver's job—don't you think so?'

'A woman driver!' says Prabir. 'Well, why don't they try to be drivers? No manual strength is required to drive a car.'

Again once the engine is switched off, it doesn't restart. There must be a genuine problem somewhere.

'Come, I'll accompany you up to the main road,' says Mandira, 'I'll do some shopping there. Shanti, do come with the bag and sit in the back seat.'

The car moves along the zigzag course while a band of kids run after it. Mandira feels thrilled. In London no one can imagine that some people are still excited at the mere sight of a vehicle.

'Chordi, do you go to the market daily?' asks Prabir.

'Yes I buy fresh fish only. I can get a very good variety of fish here. I've not seen such large prawns somersaulting before as the ones I get here.'

'Both of you have come out without locking the door; are you not scared of thieves?' asks Prabir.

'Who'll steal in broad daylight?' retorts Mandira.

'One day you'll have to pay for your blind faith. Do you think the village thieves have any sense of propriety?' chides Prabir.

Reaching the main road, Mandira and Shanti get off the car. Biman is sitting at the steering. The engine is still making some noise.

Before leaving, Biman says, 'Mani, I'll always be anxious for you. Why are you behaving so whimsically? I hope there will be no dearth of accommodation for you in Calcutta.'

Mandira's parting words are, 'What if I do behave a bit whimsically?'

6

The adulterated cheese spread had not made Mandira so much ill as it had frightened her. For some time she was gripped by the fear of death. A terrible stomach-ache had made her faint in the bathroom. She was saved but she could not help thinking that it could have been fatal. That day, she fully realised that her solitary existence had turned out to be a curse for her. From that day she was cured of her fascination to live alone. Every night she would be plunged into a pall of fear.

Since that incident, she had constantly been suffering from a fear psychosis. She had purchased a cordless phone which she used to carry to the bathroom. But this couldn't be a permanent solution. She couldn't be mentally relaxed and lost her love for her new home. She had woven a fantasy around an independent, carefree life as though it would be like living on an untrodden virgin island, or beside the river Yarrow. In fact, Mandira never possessed the mental make-up to live alone. In the midst of many people, in times of fun and festivals, some people sometimes feel lonely, but that is just a kind of feeling only; there's an intense pain in that loneliness but that's not a reality. That's the malady of civilisation. Again it's a fact that one can't live in isolation from the civilised world. Togetherness is the very spirit of civilisation.

At that critical juncture of her life, Mandira had planned to visit India for some days. She had spoken to Liz over the telephone to find out whether she was willing to accompany her. Liz had said, 'Alas, Mom, you are now asking me to accompany you! I'm so crazy about visiting India! Bob, too, is willing to cover India, but he's contemplating to go next year. By the way, Mom, I can't go now. I've conceived. I haven't yet decided whether I should keep it or not.'

Mandira was startled. 'You've conceived? The baby ... can I give any suggestion?'

Liz said, 'I've understood from your tone what you'll have to say. Everyone of your generation will opine that we should get married soon and make the baby a legitimate one—am I not right?'

'No, I was not going to say that. As a matter of fact, you're too young to take this huge responsibility. You're so restless, how can you take care of a baby? If the parents are not willing, the baby should not be brought into this world.'

'But Mom, a part of me wants to have the baby. The problem is that Bob is not at all willing. He's saying that we can marry soon, if we're eager to do so, but on the condition that we should not have kids within the next three years.'

Both Liz and her boyfriend had come to Heathrow Airport to see her off.

Mandira hadn't decided then how long she would stay in India. She had taken six weeks' leave from office. But she was soon disillusioned with Calcutta. In close to three decades, the city had undergone a sea-change. It was no longer the city she knew in her youth. It was almost next to impossible to get back the city she had left behind twenty-seven years ago. Except for her elder sister and brother-in-law, the attitude of the two or three acquaintances, whom she bumped into, seemed to be very unsettling; as if, they intended to say that Mandira had come back to do penance for marrying an European! But that was not true. She hadn't committed any mistake by marrying Tom. Mandira's other two sisters lived in Durgapur and Poona respectively. They were asking her to stay with them.

One fine morning, she decided to visit Sukhchar with Tagar, the maid working at her sister's home. She loved the village at first sight. Her decision to settle down here was taken on the spur of the moment.

To others, it was a sort of madness. Mandira knew this yet for once in her life she wanted to indulge in this kind of madness.

Once some affluent landowners had lived at Sukhchar. That is why there were several concrete buildings, many of which were large and meticulously built. Some of the landowners possessed even four to five hundred bighas of land. They might have led their lives in luxury and affluence. But with the dissolution of the zamindari system and advent of sharecroppers, the condition of the landowners became miserable. Their descendants migrated to cities in search of livelihood. The buildings lying uncared, unattended have become dilapidated and uninhabitable over the years.

The main occupation of most of the folks is fishing and growing green vegetables. They also raise paddy once a year. The village boasts of a school and a boys' club. Some educated youths work as clerks or group D staff in offices in the towns and commute daily from and to this distant village.

The villagers have accepted Mandira. At least, that is what it seems so far. Somebody from the city wants to live in the village—there isn't anything wrong in that. What has raised some eyebrows is that the person in question is a single woman. Through Tagar, they have come to know that Mandira isn't just a city-bred lady; she is from a far-off land called England, though by virtue of TV and of course the ubiquitous newspapers, England is no longer outlandish for these folks.

Mandira has voluntarily got herself acquainted with the ladies of the neighbourhood and told them how she was tired of living in the city. So, she has come to live in the village to recover her ruined health, especially to recuperate from her asthmatic problems. Unassumingly, she maintains a low profile. She has told them that her children are married. Her husband is a very busy person. So, she has to live alone. These things have aroused some sympathy among the village women. They occasionally offer her vegetables growing in their kitchen garden. Mandira too reciprocates by treating them to tea at her place.

Mandira's house isn't elaborately furnished; she deliberately avoids expensive furniture that may attract the attention of the villagers.

As Mandira's constant companion, Shanti is extremely helpful. She is always at her beck and call and runs errands for her. Her only drawback is that she's extremely casual about cleanliness. She wipes her hands on her sari, blows her nose, but never washes her hands. She carelessly rinses the utensils instead of scrubbing them first. That is why Mandira has to keep constant watch over Shanti. For no rhyme or reason, she'll tell her to wash her hands time and again. This has made Shanti think that her foreign-returned mistress has a mania for cleanliness. She chuckles at Mandira's fastidious ways.

Shanti is around fifteen or sixteen years of age. At that age, Mandira's daughter, Liz was well-developed as though she were an accomplished young woman. She had already started going out on dates. In comparison to that, Shanti appears like a child. The signs of feminine grace are yet to blossom in her. She is flat-chested. Where lies the cause of this difference? Is it because Liz was well-nourished?

Shanti's father is a landless labourer. He doesn't have any permanent source of income. Nevertheless, he runs a family comprising of his wife, a widowed sister and six children—almost like the family of cats and dogs. All parasites surviving on the leftovers. Now, however, Shanti and her elder sister Tagar are earning a bit by working in others' households. Despite living in penury, Shanti's parents are trying to get Tagar married.

It's a fact that during her childhood Shanti didn't get nutritious food. But now she's being well-fed—plenty of rice, besides fish, curry, curd, etc. Mandira has always been accustomed to having yoghurt. But now where can she get that sweetly flavoured yoghurt mixed with a variety of fruits, a common delicacy in Europe? Here she eats her own homemade curd sweetened by a little bit of molasses or sugar. Shanti eats whatever else Mandira eats. Yet why has her health not improved even a little in these two months?

Why single out Shanti alone? Mandira has noticed that the health of ninety-nine per cent of the women of the village is abysmal. So she feels embarrassed in the company of the womenfolk, as she possesses an attractive figure. The women of her village have breasts, either as swollen as gourds or as flat as bread. Most of their faces are scarred with freckles. Mandira knows that the root of these deformities lies in a damaged liver. Excessive use of vermilion causes lead poisoning that makes the parting of their hair as wide as highways.

Mandira isn't fastidious about her make-up or attire. Lipstick is out of the question. She has had her eyebrows plucked but now she lets them grow. Her cropped hair also has grown long by now though when going out, she covers her head with the free end of her sari. She doesn't wear sleeveless blouses and all her gorgeous and costly saris are now at her elder sister's house. Usually she wears white saris with blue borders. Yet she can never be mistaken for a village woman. How can she hide the original charms and loveliness of her shape? Her face reflects her Western upbringing.

Shanti's first duty in the morning is to boil water. For that purpose, a cauldron has been bought. Then the boiled water is cooled and poured into two pitchers. Initially Shanti was so amazed that she'd roll about in laughter. She couldn't understand the need of boiling water if it was to be cooled again for drinking. 'Do they do this in your England?' she asked Mandira one day.

'No, little one, nobody drinks boiled water there. In fact, they consume very little water,' Mandira smilingly replied.

'My God, don't they drink water even when they're thirsty? Do they never feel thirsty?'

'They normally prefer tea, coffee, soft drinks like your lemonade, ice-cream, etc. They rarely drink water.'

Mandira uses firewood for cooking. Coal is readily available in the village. But firewood is very cheap. She is astonished at this, for everything else in the village is dear. What is the secret that has made firewood so damn cheap when other articles are so expensive? A student of economics and political science, Mandira is quite obviously curious to know more about this. She has a fairly good idea about the relation between socio-economic conditions and the prices of commodities, and the control of the administration over the rural areas of the third world countries.

On investigation, she has come to know that the Sunderbans is on the other side of the river Raymangal. Wood is smuggled from there and supplied to towns via this village. Large logs of wood are carried in boats to this village for cutting and chiselling. The barks and outgrowths are used as firewood by the locals.

One day Mandira went on a visit to the Sunderbans. She wasn't allowed to dismount from the boat. She had a glimpse of the forests, canals and riverbeds from the boat. To her great concern she had seen how the forest areas were fast depleting. She has heard the name of Sajnekhali before but the way deforestation is being carried on, the day isn't far away when this world-famous forest reserve will disappear.

There is a brick kiln on the outskirts of the village. Mandira hasn't seen a kiln before. Around one lakh bricks, quite big in size, are burnt on a vast stretch of land. A large number of labourers are at work. On one side, one can see huge piles of logs of wood, resembling a small hillock, to be used as fuel for burning the bricks. She is shocked to learn that such a large amount of firewood is required for burning bricks. With rapid urbanisation the demand for bricks is growing. But shouldn't they give a serious thought to the fact that for the very survival of human civilisation, they should nourish forests?

Nobody seems to pay any heed to Mandira's protestations. She is just a silent spectator to the harm inflicted on nature and environment.

On getting past the Battala crossing, and walking some distance along the road to its right, one will come across a narrow canal. A dilapidated foot bridge is used to cross it. Motor cars don't ply on this bridge. So nobody bothers to repair it. Or probably it can't be repaired because of a scarcity of wood. When a passer-by walks on it or a bicycle runs over it, the bridge shakes as though it is going to cave in. Mandira, while walking on it, feels thrilled at the thought of an impending crash into the canal. The canal water swells in times of high tide and during low tide it is reduced to a muddy bed. Standing on the bridge, she can watch a strange shoal of fish, tiny creatures that move along the slushy bed, leaning on their heads and even climbing on the edges of the canal. Mandira stands gawking at the creatures for she hasn't seen a fish walking before.

At the end of the bridge stand a couple of shacks housing a tea stall and two groceries and a rice-grain stockist. On either side of the road are spread marshy lands, thickly infested with scum and filth of all kinds.

At the tea stall, Mandira comes upon a gang of local youths gathering every afternoon for their 'adda'. In comparison to their urban counterparts, the village youths speak in a louder tone. When Mandira walks past them quietly, she has noticed that the boys break off in the middle of their raucous conversations. One day she overheard one of them saying to his friends, 'Look, the haughty memsahib is coming.'

Mandira is yet to personally know any male resident of this village. She knows that these men are too shy to introduce themselves to the fairer sex. The unhealthy distance between the two sexes instigate the young men to derive perverse pleasure by passing lewd comments on women walking by. But this trend is relatively low in a small village like this as the eve-teasers here run the risk of being apprehended by their own kinsmen; still Mandira is sure that she is the target of their gossip mongering.

One day, having crossed the bridge, Mandira pauses at the tea stall and says with a smile, 'Good afternoon, I am a newcomer at Sukhchar. Would you please tell me one thing—do you have a library in your village?'

The boys look blankly at one another. Then one of them says, 'Yes we have one. It's called Rabindra Pathagar.'

'Can I find it open right now?'

They take some time discussing among themselves and then two of them accompany Mandira to the library.

Mandira has earlier heard that the village boasts of a library. She could have visited it with Shanti. But she has now approached the local chaps with a purpose: to make friends with them. On her way to the library she makes light conversation with them and slowly the initial awkwardness passes. One of them is called Shasthi and the other one Sahadev. They're in their early twenties, as old as Mandira's son. Yet secretly they're glancing at Mandira's figure.

Having walked half a mile, they arrive at the library building—a shack with a tin shed. The library door is locked.

Keeping Mandira standing there, both Shasthi and Sahadev walk towards the back of the library, evidently intending to fetch somebody. The sky is cloudless and darkness is yet to descend. She is eager to get back home before the evening stars start shining brightly in the west; she is after all scared of snakes.

A little later, a tall middle-aged man, clad in lungi and a loose shirt, with dishevelled hair, emerges with Shasthi and Sahadev.

'Good evening, may I become a member of your library?' Mandira asks.

The man doesn't reply. He is busy unlocking the library door and glances at Mandira with curiosity writ large on his face.

Inside the library hall stand two long benches on one side and a table and a few chairs on the other side. Against the wall are placed three almirahs made of very cheap wood. They're full of books, while some books are piled on the floor as well. A pretty large portrait of Tagore is hung on the wall. On the opposite wall is a charcoal sketch of Karl Marx. The face is more or less recognisable at a glance.

Dusting a chair with his towel, the man beckons to Mandira, saying, 'Please sit down.'

Below Tagore's portrait is a notice board inside a frame. It says: 'The library remains open everyday except Sunday, from seven a.m. to nine a.m. and four p.m. to seven p.m.'

It's evident that any visitor intending to borrow books from this library, during the working hours, is supposed to call the librarian from his house located behind the library.

The man goes to the table and tries to open a drawer. Then lifting his face he says, 'Shasthi, fetch some tea.'

'I won't have tea. Thanks,' says Mandira.

Paying no heed to her, he casts a meaningful glance at Shasthi.

Sahadev says, 'This madam resides near Lahiri Villa. She has bought the house that once belonged to Gadai da.'

The man says, 'Did you live in London before coming to our village?'

Does the information spread through wireless? thinks Mandira to herself. Everyone here seems to know that she once lived in London.

Mandira smiles, 'Yes, I have lived there for a pretty long time.'

'Then what will you read here? We've altogether five hundred and eighty books in our stock. All are Bengali books. Not a single book in English. And the stocks aren't upgraded.'

'It has been long since I've read any Bengali book. So I'm eager to read them again.'

With much difficulty he opens a drawer and fishes out a cigarette packet. Then lighting one he occupies a chair and says, 'The subscription is two rupees only. If you wish you can be a member. Before that please have a cursory glance through the books. Otherwise why should you pay the subscription?'

'Only two rupees? How do you manage to run the library with this meagre subscription?'

'Even this sum is too much for them. We've only eighty-three members. Hardly ten or twelve of them subscribe regularly. We can't even meet the expenses for buying kerosene oil to light the lamp.'

'Does this library belong to you then?' Mandira asks naively.

'Why should it? It belongs to the village. I just set it rolling. These furnitures, books—everything is donated. The benches were donated by the Garais, the rice-grain dealers. Two of the almirahs were given away by Suleman sahib and the table by Chandi da.'

'And the books?' asks Mandira.

'Some of them were my father's. The rest I collected from the local residents. There were several of them with the Lahiris. Quite a large number of books had been damaged.'

Shasthi returns with four glasses of tea placed on an enamel tray.

Mandira falls into a dilemma. She dislikes having poor quality tea. Apart from the cheap brand, the smell of the fume is most distasteful. Also she suspects that the glasses aren't cleaned properly before being reused. They have yellow stains.

Most reluctantly she takes a sip.

Mandira is impressed by this gentleman. His name is Sajjad Jahir. Basically outspoken and a primary school teacher by profession, he runs the library by dint of his personal initiatives. He has written to the government for assistance, but in vain. In fact, the government doesn't feel obliged to extend financial assistance to a library that attracts hardly ten to twelve readers per day.

A committee comprising some prominent and influential persons of the village has been formed but none of the committee members seems to have any headache for the improvement of the library now.

Yet why is Sajjad continuing with it, braving all odds? If asked this, he replies with some air of ire, 'I'm carrying on simply because I like doing it. How can a village go without a library? I open it daily and on days when there's no visitor to the library, I just spend the time dusting the books and perhaps going through one or two of them myself.'

Sajjad is a married man with two children; with him lives his mother, a widow. Though he has a full-time job, he loves to spend his time in creative pursuits. That is why he's different from the rest of the villagers.

In a couple of days Mandira develops a good sense of camaraderie with Sajjad.

He is the only intellectual living in this village. Armed with a BSc. degree, he has a schoolmaster's job, besides running the village library. But above all, his discourses on any topic gives the impression that he's able to think on a broader spectrum—the world beyond the narrow confines of his village life. He has an opinion of his own.

The neighbourhood to the west of Sukhchar is chiefly populated by Muslims. Though the village takes pride in the communal harmony existing between Hindus and Muslims, it's not difficult for an outsider like Mandira to sense the subtle dividing line between the two communities. Even though the Muslims outnumber the Hindus in terms of the population of Sukhchar, the former are poignantly conscious of their minority status.

Among the Hindus the rate of literacy is low. The educated youths migrate to towns in search of jobs. But the Muslim youths have stayed back, for their prospect of getting jobs in large establishments, owned by Hindus, is obviously bleak. But Sajjad shouldn't be compared with the other members of his community. He's an exception.

Mandira never frequents the library alone. She brings along Shanti and another local girl called Bina who lives close to Mandira's house. Having passed the higher secondary examination, she's waiting to be married off.

For further studies she has to attend the college at Basirhat, where she must stay at a hostel. But her parents will not allow that. Even Bina herself is not ambitious enough to override her parents' diktat. Her father is a fishmonger who supplies prawns, rohu, katla to big markets. He's more or less affluent. He has sent off his son to town to study in a college but doesn't do the same for his daughter. Investment for a son means rich dividends; as the future bread earner of the family, he'll also look after his old and infirm parents. But the daughter is meant for someone else's family and thus her parents should be armed with a lump sum amount to send her off to her in-laws' house.

Mandira cannot but dwell on Bina. In her youth in Calcutta, she had seen several girls like her. These girls were encouraged to drop out in the middle of their education and keep on waiting till it was time for their marriage. The girls who lacked in feminine grace and charms had to wait year after year to get married. What a colossal waste of human resources! These girls cannot even utilise whatever education they've already received. Bina's brother, who is elder than her by only two years, looks after their fish trade. But she is not given any job. They've appointed three more employees to assist them in their business. Bina could have replaced any one of those employees. But it is quite out of the question in her family. She, however, is fond of reading story books.

Sajjad Jahir is younger than Mandira by around fifteen years. Yet, afraid of a scandal, she never comes alone to the library, usually manned by a solitary Sajjad. Bina and

Shanti are always with her during her visits to the library. This gives them an opportunity for a small adda session at the library. The tea-stall gossip-mongers, who had never stepped into the library premises before, have also taken to dropping in occasionally now.

Mandira, however, doesn't pay more than the membership subscription of two rupees a month. She hasn't made any commitment to donate, say an almirah or bench. She is just an ordinary member.

Though she tries to project herself as an ordinary member, her presence has rejuvenated the library atmosphere. Even the president of the library, Serajuddin Ahmed, who had shied away from visiting the library for a long while, one day, out of sheer curiosity, paid a surprise visit. Incidentally, there was a heavy shower and water was seeping through the tin sheds.

That day, in the midst of the rain, they could hear the sound of the loudspeaker from a distance. Mandira was asking them, 'What are they blaring the mike for? Is it for a jatra? I haven't seen one in many years.'

'It's for the festival of Bakr-Id,' said Sajjad. 'Nowadays they use a loudspeaker on any pretext—Id, Sabebarat, Milad Mehfil or anything on earth. They even use a loudspeaker for azan in the mosque.'

Ahmed sahib, evidently annoyed with Sajjad, hurled back the question, 'Why do you say that? Don't they use loudspeakers during Hindu festivals? Durga puja, Kali puja, Lakshmi puja—there's a long list of them.'

'You're right,' said Sajjad. 'The list of festivals is getting longer with each passing day.' Then turning to

Shasthi he said, 'They even observe a puja in your name, isn't it, Shasthi?'

Shasthi gave a toothy smile to say, 'One can earn much these days from the microphone business ...'

'Yes, mikes are used in meetings also,' said Sajjad. 'Madam, nowadays two types of festivals are in vogue—political and religious. In the recent past, the area was under the hold of the Congress party. Since the last election the Congress have been vanquished. Now the Marxists are in power. This Ahmed sahib himself is a Marxist.

'Interestingly enough, the more the Marxists are out to hold their sway over everything, the more you can see the popularity of religious ceremonies.'

Ahmed sahib in a grave tone countered, 'What else is there for the folks to rejoice in? These festivals give them a chance to indulge in some kind of revelry, fun and frolic. We shouldn't be interfering in it.' Saying this he rose to leave; perhaps he didn't want to drag the conversation further.

While leaving he turned to Mandira to say, 'I'm going to invite a jatra troupe to Sukhchar soon. This is not a matter of the panchayat. I'll do this on my own initiative.'

Mandira too got up taking along Shanti and Bina with her. She too didn't want to get embroiled in the middle of a religious discussion. Personal opinion of any kind might land her in trouble.

'Madam, you're borrowing books for Shanti; can she read?' asked Sajjad.

'Oh yes, I can. I can read. I can read all the books,' said Shanti at once.

Mandira smiled and said, 'I don't force her to read. I just select some books according to her reading level. I had seen her reading the book written by Dakshinaranjan Majumder. In fact, I leave it to her own discretion.'

'Of course, I'll read. I'll read many more books. You must lend me good books,' insisted Shanti.

Shanti's juvenile enthusiasm made everyone smile.

The village has a primary school. Many girls drop out of the school after standard four or five. None of them have developed any reading habit, though there is a library at their doorstep. A reading habit at least enriches the mind and enlarges one's vision. Why don't the village elders counsel the village girls to develop this particular habit?

Mandira, however, doesn't try to advise them. She is very conscious of her outsider status and doesn't want to do anything to attract adverse attention. She hasn't come to the village to do social work, let alone the question of getting involved in politics. She has come in search of her own happiness, absolutely her own. She isn't sure how long she will stay here. If she leaves abruptly one fine morning, having instigated a whole lot of rural people into activity, they'll term her actions as the whims and caprices of a lady of the elite society. Even she herself will suffer from a guilty conscience.

As Mandira, along with her companions, was about to leave the library, she saw a youth dismounting from the bicycle. Mandira had seen the fellow on one or two occasions with Sajjad. One day, she saw the man spewing venom at Sajjad. Seeing Mandira, he had, in embarrassment, toned down at once.

He is Javed, as black as ebony, strong and sturdy and near about thirty years of age. Almost regularly, he wears a distastefully dazzling green vest and has the habit of applying so much oil to his hair that even his forehead glistens. Mandira has observed that most of these people lack a sense of colour coordination. Initially, Mandira had felt quite out of sorts with it, but now she has adjusted herself to this.

Sajjad has introduced Javed to Mandira, but the latter has a tendency to keep shy of her company. The sight of Javed causes an errie sensation all over her body. The fellow keeps quiet yet looks at her quaintly. The glance as though, pierces through her body.

One day, soon after Javed's departure, Bina says, 'Sajjad da, why do you allow Javed here? He's a rogue!'

'How can I stop someone from coming to the library? It belongs to everybody.'

'What will he do with books? His job is to pick fights with people. That day he had come to raid our fish depot ... he was paid back in the same coin. That's why he was hurling angry glances at me today. Phew! I'm not frightened.'

'Why should you be frightened? A rogue deserves to be thrashed,' replies Sajjad.

'Now he has enlisted with the Jamate–Islami to become a fundamentalist. Don't you know he walks in their processions?'

'I see! But only a while back he was a cadre of Ahmed sahib's Marxist party. These people change colours like a chamaeleon!'

'But Sajjad da why are you putting up with his antics? What an audacity he had that day when I saw him hurling angry invectives at you! Why didn't you throw him out?'

He's a bona fide member. He pays subscriptions regularly. The library is not my father's property, after all,' argues Sajjad.

'Fie your membership! Return his subscriptions. If ruffians like Javed visit your library my father won't let me come here.'

Heaving a sigh, Sajjad turns to Mandira, 'Well, madam, I know the guy since his birth. He was not so rotten before. He was actually quite obedient to me. I'm not in politics; so how can I help them? But he won't try to understand my limitations. That's why I often become the target of his temper tantrums. People use his sturdy robust build, for notorious acts like looting bheris or squandering other people's crops. Youths like Javed are used for these illegal acts.'

Mandira wants to leave.

But Sajjad continues, saying, 'Madam, you didn't live in this country for a pretty long period of time. So you don't know the ground realities here. On the surface, India is recognised as a secular country. But where's the secularism? Are you aware of the Vishva Hindu Parishad and RSS making inroads into the villages? They are trying to rename Mamudpur, a village in our neighbourhood, as Maheshpur. Most of the Hindus have their consent in it. At Bechu babu's estate, they're determined to capture the land, once belonging to the factory, and set up a temple of Lord Shiva there. If things go on like this, will a Muslim ever feel secure? One fine morning, I may have to face a situation like this: "Hey, you're no longer Sajjad Jahir; you'll henceforth be known as Sajani Mondal."'

Bina giggles and says, 'Why don't you be so? Sajani Mondal is after all a very good name. I can't commit Muslim names to my memory. The name of the village adjacent to Mamudpur is Kalikapur. Then don't you think that Maheshpur rhymes with Kalikapur?'

Sajjad says, 'See madam, how Hindu zealotry has already penetrated deep into the society. Things were quite different even in the recent past.'

'Is that so!' says Bina. 'Then how will you view the enthusiasm of Javed and his cronies while collecting subscriptions for the mosque? They block the highway and extort money from the truck drivers.'

'It's always a vicious cycle,' admits Sajjad. Then turning to the wall he says in an oddly perplexed voice, 'I'm afraid perhaps a day will come when I'll also join Jamate-Islami.'

Mandira feels sorry for Sajjad but she can't comfort him. In fact, while staying in England, she had heard that in India, the communal forces were strongly rearing their ugly heads. All the newspapers in London had published in detail the story of Ramjanmabhoomi–Babri Masjid conflict. The special correspondent of the *Times* had personally visited the spot and taken many snapshots. On one hand, unlimited financial assistance is coming from the Arab countries to stoke the fires of Muslim fundamentalism and on the other hand, among the Hindus, some megalomaniac gurus are sprouting up every now and then to bully people across the world with a show of their self-styled authority. Even at the fag end of this twentieth century religion is used as an instrument of factionalism, cessation and feuds.

The erstwhile Indian subcontinent is now broken into three fragments. The western and eastern segments of it have been declared Islamic states. Ninety-nine per cent of the Turkish population is Muslim; nevertheless it is a secular state. Whereas Bangladesh and Pakistan had to profess their constitutional allegiance to Islam. Most of the Hindus once living in Pakistan have been thrown out of the country. The very few who still live there have no voice of their own. Seceding from Pakistan, a new country called Bangladesh was born with some new ideals. But a few years after its inception, the word secularism was stricken out from its constitution. The minorities there are treated as second-class citizens. In such a situation, they are bound to suffer from a state of fear psychosis as well as an inferiority complex.

Placed between these two Islamic states, India is trying to survive as a secular nation. The task is not at all an enviable one. Stimulated by the examples of Pakistan and Bangladesh, a section of Indian Hindus intend to convert India into a Hindu state. The voices of these fanatics are getting stronger day by day, particularly in the north and west. Like the Hindu minorities in Bangladesh, the Muslim minorities in India are also living in fear and resentment. Wherever possible, they try to unite under the aegis of international Islamic fraternity. It's obvious that the seeds of fundamentalism are easily sown in their minds.

Though in theory, the Government of India has adopted the policy of secularism, in reality it doesn't or can't strictly adhere to its ideals. The state has not been able to uphold the actual meaning of secularism to the masses. The masses have seen how time and again the political parties openly appease the religious communities to win elections. Till date the state has not enacted a uniform civil code relating to marriage and right to property. Jawaharlal Nehru couldn't show the courage and audacity of Kemal Ataturk, not a single Marxist leader equals to a tiny fraction of Lenin. They can't tell the masses, 'Keep your religion indoors; don't come out with your dogmas and creeds on the streets. Religion advocates peace, not conflicts and feuds.' Till today the state hasn't set an example by giving exemplary punishment to the people inciting communal tensions, riots, etc.

Mandira had seen her husband and his friends smiling contemptuously at the news of communal riots in the subcontinent. They were reluctant to admit that the British imperialists had sown the seeds of communalism in the subcontinent. Reacting to Mandira's protest, once Tom's friend, Ed said, 'Well, well, even if we admit to our guilt, still why couldn't you resolve it in as long as forty years? Why couldn't you educate your countrymen? Forty years is not a matter of joke indeed! Have you ever witnessed a strong movement across the country protesting against religious superstitions?'

The controversy over Ramjanmabhoomi–Babri Masjid turned out to be the butt of ridicule for Tom's friends. They looked upon it as a medieval issue. They couldn't believe how sensible persons of the twentieth century indulged in quarrels over a mosque, built in the name of an emperor who lived five hundred years from now, and a temple built in the name of an epic hero who belongs to ancient folklores and legends. Tom's friends asked her if Indians were aware of the story of Hagia Sophia at Istanbul? It's around one thousand and six hundred years old. In the entire Roman Empire there was no other church as big and splendid as this one. Here over one thousand years the Christian devotees had been offering prayers to Jesus. Later as the Byzantine Empire was destroyed at the hands of the Ottoman, that church was converted to a mosque. For over five hundred years Muslims had been taking part in the namaaz at this mosque. But at present Hagia Sophia is neither a mosque nor a church. It's now a rendezvous of all sorts of people from all over the world, irrespective of caste, creed and religion. It is a historic monument. 'What does your temple–mosque at Ayodha look like? Is it worthy of Hagia Sophia? Then turn it into a museum. Or if it looks ugly, or if the structure is devoid of any historic value, then build a hospital or a college there. Tell the people engaged in the feud, hailing from both the communities, that temples and mosques are already aplenty in India, so there's no need of any more. But there is still a dearth of hospitals and colleges in the country. Doesn't your government have the guts to state this patent fact to them?'

Mandira, however, personally believes that had India been able to set an example of secularism, worth emulating, its neighbouring states of Bangladesh and Pakistan would have been at a certain stage influenced by India's ethos. It's not so easy to keep the common people in the dark for long. Had the masses of Bangladesh and Pakistan witnessed the victory of secularism in India, they would have also shrugged aside their religious excesses. As the largest and major nation in this subcontinent India should have taken up this responsibility.

Religion is deemed as so sacred a thing in India's neighbouring states that nobody dares to question its position. The ruling party in India is increasingly being dominated by people steeped in corruption and nepotism. The opposition and the progressive parties like the Marxists avoid interfering in a sensitive issue like religion. They publicly condemn the communal forces but secretly form alliances with these forces to win elections.

In a precarious situation like this only the people with some lofty ideals are hurt. They comprise a microscopic minority whose voice is drowned in the dark recesses of irrationality.

The difference between people like Sajjad and Javed is strikingly clear—Sajjad suffers from a state of mental anguish, while Javed is desperate for self-defence and resistance.

Getting off the cycle, Javed casts a sly look at Mandira and her two women companions. Mandira smiles at him, but he ignores her and slips into the library hall.

Having advanced a little, Bina rudely says, 'If that rogue Javed comes here regularly, I'll stop coming to this place. My father can't tolerate him.'

Mandira says, 'Alright, don't come. After all, one can survive without reading books.'

7

At times, Mandira feels bored with the rustic life and is tempted to return to the city. She is after all a city-bred person. After spending her childhood and adolescence in a rented house in Calcutta, she went off to London. Her experience of the countryside is just confined to her glimpses through the windows of running trains.

At Sukhchar, she likes the fresh vegetables, fish and a pollution-free environment. She is also fascinated by the attitude of the people, who, unlike their urban counterparts, have not become self-centered. Though they sometimes quarrel, they love and care for each other. Even the local gossip extends a hand to help a neighbour in distress.

Nevertheless, Mandira occasionally suffers from a sense of claustrophobia. She sometimes longs to be in the city.

From the courtyard, Shanti is calling out to someone in a loud voice. Mandira is startled, as she happens to find a similarity between Shanti's voice and that of her daughter Liz. Her heart aches in filial affection. How is Liz? She had only once spoken to her, on the telephone from Calcutta, that too after a great many attempts. She told Mandira that she had aborted the foetus. They did what they considered to be right for them. But has the abortion affected Liz's health? Mandira is troubled with anxiety for her daughter.

Also, she thinks of Robin at once. He is basically shy. In the presence of strangers, he has a habit of biting his nails, with his head bowed down. Mandira has heard that in America, the introvert kinds don't make much headway with their career. One has to blow one's own trumpet and flaunt one's own abilities there. Meanwhile, Robin's girlfriend has left him. Is he living alone now? Mandira is sieged by a number of thoughts concerning her children. She's a mother, after all, and filial affections aren't just instinctive—something more than that.

Nowadays, the young generation considers letter writing to be a backdated means of communication. Especially in the Western countries, the practice of writing letters is on the wane. Telephone has considerably lessened the importance of letters. Introduction of a device, called audio-tape has tolled the death knell for letters in countries like Sweden, where cassettes are sold instead of postage stamps at post offices.

In London, she was able to speak to her children occasionally. But here it has been long since she has heard from them.

Mandira says to Shanti, 'I'll go on a short trip to Calcutta. Will you accompany me?'

Shanti readily agrees. She has never been to Calcutta though she has heard about the fantastic things in the city from her elder sister. Calcutta is just seventy kilometres away from Sukhchar, but most of the people of this village have never been there.

'Will they allow me into the city if I travel wearing this sari?'

Mandira smiles and says, 'Is there any gateway to Calcutta where the janitor will stop you?'

'Didi, you must this time buy me a nice blouse.'

Shanti is so thin and rickety that she'll look better in a frock rather than a sari. Here the affluent ones wear frocks but it's a taboo for the poor. If she tries to make Shanti wear a frock it'll perhaps be a little excessive. But Mandira's blouse will be too large for her.

Giving one of her own saris to Shanti, she says, 'Come, I'll buy you a nice blouse from Calcutta.'

Jagu, a person who works in Bina's house, agrees to sleep on Mandira's veranda and guard the house.

After lunch, they set out for Calcutta. They take the express bus on the highway and reach Esplanade in the evening after a journey of two and a half hours. Calcutta's roads are badly maintained; full of potholes and the air is heavy and cloying with smog and grime; yet the city's bustle is very familiar to her, almost in her blood.

Alighting from the bus, she dashes to the CTO and rings up Robin. She is hopeful of getting Robin at home now since it is early morning in America.

Robin pretends to be very anxious for his mother and asks if she's in need of money, assuring her of all kinds of assistance. He'll send open tickets for her if she longs to return to England. But he can't give any information about his sister.

Next, Mandira rings up Liz but the phone goes on ringing. Mandira feels upset. The extravagant couple must have taken a sudden break from their schedule and gone off on a vacation. She decides to try later. She is more concerned about Liz than Robin.

Mandira at first contemplates to put up at a hotel but changes her mind. Her elder sister and brother-in-law, Sankar da will be hurt at this. Having done some shopping, she says to Shanti, 'Come, let's have tea first.'

Hailing a taxi, they come to Park Street. Most of the hotels here are bar-cum-restaurants. She decides upon Flurys. As she steps inside, the delicious aroma of cake and pastry reaches her nostrils. The tables are covered with spick and span white cloths; visitors are talking in low tones. Mandira has long been accustomed to this kind of cultured ambience.

Mandira treats Shanti to some chicken sandwich and fruitcake; the latter devours them ravenously, her eyes expressing a divine experience, unique in her life.

Mandira pities her. Refreshments looked upon as very ordinary, commonplace in some countries, are beyond the reach of billions of people living in some other countries. Her daughter, Liz would have scornfully turned up her nose at the sight of this ordinary fruitcake.

Mandira makes a phone call to her didi. Sankar da answers the call. He is a bit puzzled to hear her on the other end. 'Where are you speaking from?' he enquires.

'From Park Street. Is your house full of guests? Are Tusu, Mantu also there?'

'Where are you exactly at Park Street? Wait there till I come. I'll pick you up in twenty odd minutes.'

Mandira tries to convince him that she can reach his place in a taxi but he doesn't listen to her and disconnects the line.

Mandira orders another cup of tea. Nowhere else has she tasted such excellent quality of tea as in Calcutta. Not even in England. One can get a very expensive brand of tea in London; but why can't its taste and aroma be the same? Is it because the tea leaves lose their flavour after being shipped through such a long distance? Or it may be that the tea cannot bear the protein fortified and extremely pure milk of their country. Shanti is wearing a pair of rubber slippers. Though her sari is not inexpensive, yet from her appearance, it is quite apparent that she is Mandira's domestic help or someone of that category. People from other tables are casting curious glances at them. Mandira is aware of this kind of snobbery, typical of Calcuttans. She's mentally prepared to give a fitting rebuff in fluent English to anybody who raises an objection for bringing Shanti here. The snobs here are silenced by English. But no one has said anything as such. One can't of course raise objections because someone is merely staring!

Sankar da too raises his eyebrows and says, 'You brought this girl with you here?'

With Shanti in the back seat and Mandira beside him, he is driving the car.

'So, your experiment failed! Phew! I knew well enough you wouldn't stick to this serving-the-poor-villagers posture … All these are fantastic notions, easier said than done. I hope you haven't invested much into them. In fact, you can't make an inch of progress with those people,' Sankar da banters.

Mandira smiles and says, 'Don't you know how parsimonious I am? Attracted by the low cost of living, I've settled in the countryside.'

'I hope you've sold the house and I'm sure you've been cheated in the process.'

'I haven't sold it.'

'Don't worry. I'll arrange for its disposal. London is the ideal place for you. Stay in my house as long as you wish. Then go back to London. I hope you haven't resigned from your service? It's a pensionable service, isn't it?'

Mandira has observed that not only Sankar da but all of her sisters are of the opinion that she must go back to London. In that case, they could put up at Mandira's London residence during their overseas tours. Apart from this selfish end, they also believe that it was a foolish thing to forsake one's job and property in London to live in an uninhabitable country like India.

Sankar da is near about sixty, lean and handsome, with a face revealing an aristocratic background. He has already suffered a mild heart attack, which nowadays has become a status symbol for all successful men. Once Sankar Majumdar's ancestors owned tea gardens. Now, these were sold out. Sankar da is the top executive of a tea board.

'Mani, today we'll dine out. Where do you want to go?'

'Why should we dine out?' asks Mandira in surprise.

'I want to treat you to a sumptuous dinner. Would you like to go to Tangra for Chinese?'

'Won't didi come with us?'

Sankar da's smile is laced with mystery. He says, 'No, your didi won't join us. Come, let's first have our dinner.'

'Wait, wait,' counters Mandira, 'We have just had tea and pastry a while ago. Now, I can't eat anything more. Come, let's first go home.'

'Then we can do one thing. It's a lovely evening. What about having a couple of drinks at a place of our choice? Where can we go I wonder? Well, would you like the open air lawn at the New Kenilworth?'

Having parked their car near the hotel, Sankar da tells Shanti to keep waiting in the car till they come back.

Mandira guesses from his deportment that he is eager to tell her something in private, before going home.

Occupying an empty table on the open lawn, he orders scotch for himself. Mandira refuses to have anything.

Lighting a cigarette, he says, 'Now tell me about your experience in the village. Name the persons who duped you.'

Taking a cigarette out of Sankar da's packet, Mandira asks, 'Why didn't you bring didi today?'

'Your didi is out of station. She went to Durgapur the day before yesterday. It was an urgent call from Tusu who was running a high fever. Her daughter's exams are around the corner. Ajay alone can't manage all this. So your didi has gone to look after them. I'm alone here.'

'Didi went away leaving you alone!'

'Why? You think I'm a little boy!'

'You once fell ill with a serious heart ailment.'

'That wasn't serious. My heart is in a perfectly good condition now. It is still young and wants to get as well as give something ... Papun and Jayeeta were expected to come down to Calcutta tomorrow from New Delhi. But they've called and informed that they're not coming before Monday. I haven't passed this information to your didi. She still knows that they're coming to stay with me.'

'Why didn't you go to Durgapur?'

'Do you think I've no preoccupations of my own? Your didi has now taken up the role of your mother. If any of your sisters are in trouble, she rushes to help them. She has no time to look after her husband—a very old husband after all!'

'In didi's absence, you seem to have become a chain-smoker, Sankar da.'

'I smoke only while drinking. I wish you would not talk like my guardian. Now listen Mani, your didi is out of station. I'm alone at home. Do you have any reservations about staying with me? Of course, I'd love to have your company. God knows what will be your didi's reaction though! Tuni isn't unaware of my special liking for you.'

Mandira looks at him with disbelieving eyes, as though she never heard of a thing like that before. Why should her didi take it otherwise, if she spends the night in the same house with Sankar da? He visited her twice at her Kensington apartment in London. On both occasions, Tom was away from home. She had chatted with him till late into the night in his bedroom. She had herself driven him around in her car to several places. As Sankar da badly wanted to watch a Shakespearean play, they had spent the night at a Stratford hotel. Tom would never bother to question the propriety of the bonhomie and camaraderie between Mandira and her brother-in-law. Didn't Sankar da narrate his exotic experiences to his wife after returning from abroad?

'Next month you're scheduled to visit London again. Had I been in Harrow, wouldn't you have put up at my residence? I lived alone there,' reminds Mandira.

'Can I think of any other place other than your residence in London? But things are quite different here, you know. By the way, we can do one thing to avoid complications. Your didi isn't coming back before a week. Papun and Jayeeta are arriving on Monday. You'll tell them that you've also come on Monday.'

'Shall I tell a lie to didi?'

'Just a white lie, to keep your didi in good humour,' he tries to rationalise.

Mandira hates this kind of hypocrisy. She, however, hides her contempt by wearing a smile on her lips. She had initially thought of spending the night at a hotel but now she makes up her mind to stay at her sister's place.

'Now, get up please,' she urges him, 'I'll cook your dinner tonight.'

Having cast a passionate glance at Mandira's face, he says, 'Let's go!'

Sankar Majumdar's house is in the old-fashioned mould; these kinds of buildings are fast disappearing from

Calcutta. Entering through the large iron gate, one steps onto an untrammelled garden. Out of the two garages, one has been rented out for a kiosk. On the ground floor, in addition to the drawing room, there are two more rooms lying unused. There is an outhouse at the back which is used as a cook and servants' quarter. The five rooms on the upper floor were once upon a time bustling with the members of a joint family.

After the death of Sankar Majumdar's elder brother, his son has settled in Jodhpur Park.

Sankar Majumdar has three children—the eldest, Papun lives in New Delhi, the daughter is settled in Abu Dhabi after her marriage and the younger son is pursuing higher studies at IIT, Kanpur. The upper floor now wears a deserted look.

Mandira doesn't have to cook. The old cook arranges their dinner. Shanti has been sent off to her elder sister on the ground floor.

The dinner is over, yet they are sitting at the table, finding nothing interesting to drag the conversation further. Sankar da looks at Mandira admiringly, and rests his hand on her shoulders on flimsy pretexts. On one occasion, he leans over Mandira's face and lightly presses his cheeks against hers. His lips are thirsting for kisses.

Mandira is stunned at Sankar da's strange deportment. Is it simply because didi is away from home? But at the London apartment, they were alone. At the Stratford hotel, they had booked two adjacent rooms. Mandira had stayed in Sankar da's room, till two o'clock at night. He was quite normal then. Was it because, then Mandira had a husband? Now the house is empty, but more than that she is now an unattached woman. So he can easily take advantage of the situation. These things are very common in the West. In our country this is well and good provided it's not made public.

But men don't notice one particular thing—whether the woman is willing or not. They take it for granted that a divorced woman or a widow is always craving for physical intimacy and has no will of her own.

He draws nearer to Mandira and nestling close to her, says, 'Your long stay in the countryside has largely benefited you in one particular aspect; your sunburnt figure doesn't betray your age. You appear to be in your mid-thirties. You could easily marry again.'

Rising from the chair, and shifting her seat a little away from him, Mandira replies with the same lingering smile on her lips, 'Yes, I want to marry again. Would you please do me a favour by finding a suitable match for me?'

She washes her hands at the washbasin. Then she says, 'I am feeling sleepy now. I think you should also go to bed. Good night.'

Mandira comes into her room and bolts the door. She changes into her nightgown and while she is applying moisturiser on her face, she clearly feels the presence of Sankar da outside her room. She can hear his short excited breaths. Basing her judgement on purely feminine intuition, she knows that he doesn't have the guts to knock at the door. There is a limit to the manifestation of lust in such men. They cannot so easily cross the forbidden 'laxman rekha'. Their sense of propriety stops them short.

Sankar da is basically a perfect gentleman. Today, he has fallen prey to some emotional weakness. Tomorrow morning, he'll be ashamed of his conduct.

Mandira turns off the lights.

Mandira is sure of one thing; Sankar da's overtures didn't arouse her at all. But had she been aroused, what would have been the fallout? No, she would never allow herself to be seduced, thus betraying her didi.

8

Next morning Sankar da has been trying to impress upon her that he is awfully busy. He has said that he has an urgent official appointment and must start for office by nine a.m. He has little time to spare for Mandira as he is busy flipping through the office files. She, however, is freely talking to him. She brings another cup of tea for him and says, 'Sankar da, I think you have to work very hard in your office; shouldn't you retire now?'

'They shall not release me even when I reach the age of superannuation,' says he. 'By the way, Mani, as I'm very busy today, I won't be able to give you any time. I can send the car for you, if you want to go somewhere.'

'No, thank you, Sankar da, I don't want a car today. I'll talk to didi on the telephone. I've never been to Durgapur. I'm planning to pay a visit to Tusu.'

Just as Sankar da is about to leave for office, Prabir turns up. He is astonished to see Mandira. 'Mani di, when did you come? Have you bid farewell to your rustic life?'

Seeing Prabir, it occurs to Mandira that she should telephone Biman.

'Prabir, can you give me Biman's phone number?' asks Mandira.

'That contractor Biman? Have you met him in the meanwhile?' Asks Sankar da in a jealous tone, as though Biman is his rival.

In around forty-five minutes after Sankar da's departure, Biman turns up. Though Sankar da has ridiculed him as a contractor, actually Biman owns a large construction firm. Quite a few architects and engineers work in his firm. Biman is a student of statistics though he didn't opt for employment. In collaboration with some German and British firms he is engaged in the construction of large bridges and plants. He is a busy person now.

Nevertheless he has taken a break from his busy schedule to attend to Mandira. 'Get ready, Mani,' he says, 'today I'll take you on a pleasure trip.'

Today Biman looks quite reserved. During the daytime he is a man of business.

He hasn't asked Prabir to come with them. He is not driving the car; there is a Bengali chauffeur at the wheels. With Mandira he sits in the back seat. Offering a cigarette to Mandira, he says, 'So what have you decided? Won't you return to London?'

This is Mandira's first cigarette of the day. Lighting it she replies, 'I haven't decided anything yet.'

'Do you like to live in the village? Are you not disturbed by anyone there?'

'No. I'm quite happy there. The experience is unique.'

'Well Mani, later it occurred to me that for a person who lived in London for many years, it could be difficult to settle in Calcutta. Comparisons will automatically arise. Calcutta's pollution and dearth of civic amenities ... look how that bus is belching poisonous smoke—carbon monoxide. In comparison to city life, you must be happier in the countryside: lots of things are still fresh there. The only attraction of Calcutta is its people. Provided you have your close relatives living here. I hope you're not feeling lonely in the village, are you?'

'No, the village folks are anything but indifferent.'

'I have some very good news about your Sukhchar. Before that let me tell you another important thing. I know you well. You're the last person to seek help from others even if you are in deep trouble. Suppose you're bored with your life in the village. If you then want to come back to Calcutta, where will you stay? I don't think you're keen on living at your didi's place for an indefinite period. In that case you should have an independent apartment. But if I offer you one, you won't accept it. In such a situation I can arrange a job for you. Good emoluments and perks.'

'Do you want to absorb me in your firm?'

'I would be very happy if you join my firm. There's even a suitable opening in it now. But I know that will hurt your ego. A British firm, working on several projects in India, is going to open an office in Calcutta. It's mainly for liaison work. They'll gladly accept you.'

'No, Biman. I'm not thinking of a job now.'

'But how long? One day your savings will run out. Your pitcher will run dry unless you occasionally refill it.'

'That's why I live in a village. Daily expenses are very low there.'

'Mani, I'm very eager to know one thing which I couldn't ask you that day. Or perhaps you might have told me but I can't recall as I was in a drunken state ... Why did you leave London? Is divorce the only reason? I hope you'll tell me frankly and honestly.'

'No, divorce is not the only reason. In fact, I lost the meaning of life.'

'Please explain what you exactly mean by this.'

'I was constantly haunted by a question. What shall I do with my life? I began to feel that I have no role to play in other people's lives. I've lost my place in the scheme of things whether as a mother, as a wife, as a relation or as a friend and neighbour. I'm superfluous in their lives. Am I redundant even to myself? I've been in search of that answer. It had become unbearable for me to stay in London anymore. So I decided to experiment with my life in this country. Perhaps here also my quest will be in vain.'

Biman instructs the driver to turn left. Then looking out of the window, he mutters carelessly, 'What shall I do with this life?' He seems to have heard the line somewhere before. 'Where did I read this line? In which book?'

Mandira says, 'Are you quoting this line from any book?'

'Yes, seriously, I've read the line in a Bengali book, but I can't remember the name.'

'I've read very few Bengali books,' admits Mandira. 'Though I'm reading some books these days.'

Through the Maidan, leaving the Raj Bhavan on its left, the car is running towards the Ganges. She looks at Biman curiously. The day is hot and sultry, with a blazing sun overhead, not tailormade for a walk on the riverbank.

No sooner do they come halfway along the Eden Gardens, than Biman says, 'Stop the car here.'

The car stops. They walk a little. Biman says, 'This is the Mohunbagan club. Do you remember that tree beside the clubhouse?'

Mandira goes to the sprawling tree and stands under it. In a low voice she says, '1962, most probably August; am I right?'

Biman in a grave voice says, 'Unlike you I can't remember the dates and years with precision. But last week as I was going past it, I at once recalled that day.'

Years ago, a young man and woman were returning through this way from a fair at Eden Gardens. Then they had no car and could not afford the taxi-fare. Aimlessly walking, they incidentally fell prey to a thunderstorm. Drenched to the skin they rushed to this tree for shelter. There was no other creature around them. The man had laid his hand on her shoulder. Their courtship had not yet reached such a stage where it would even permit a kiss. Even if there was no one else around watching them, their sense of propriety would have refrained them from indulging in kissing in a public place.

Frightened by the crashing sound of a thunderbolt, Mandira had sunk her head in Biman's bosom. He had held her tightly in that embrace for a long time. The rain had stopped an hour later. Mandira's slipper had got torn and getting rid of the pair, she walked barefooted for the rest of their journey.

Today Biman stands for a while in the same posture—resting his hand on Mandira's shoulder. Then he says to her, 'Do you know why I ran to your house that day, in that intoxicated, befuddled state? That is because with you is associated my bygone youth. I had wanted to recapture that youth by drawing you close to me, though I know it's never possible in reality. You've come back as a different person and my life too hasn't stood still at that place.'

'Anyway, I've quite enjoyed coming here today.' Then looking into his eyes she says, 'Come, let's go away from here. Passers-by are looking askance at us. It proves that we're misplaced here.'

Then their car reaches College Street. Getting down from the car at the Coffee House, Biman says, 'Come, we'll walk in front of the university building. It has been long since I came here last.'

'I had come one day recently,' says Mandira sadly, 'I didn't like the sight at all. The pavements have been encroached by hawkers, you can't spot the railings of the college square, nor the swimming pool from the street, which seems to have become narrower than ever before. I felt claustrophobic. I prefer to treasure my sweet memories of the College Street of the past.'

'Then wait a minute.' Saying this, Biman slips inside a bookshop. He comes back with a copy of the selected volume of the complete works of Bankim Chandra Chattopadhyay. Getting into the car, he directs the driver, 'Airport.' Then turning to Mandira he says, 'I couldn't rest until I was sure where the line, "what shall I do with this life" occurred. Now I'm quite at peace with myself. It occurs in the eleventh chapter of Bankim's *The Practice of Theology*: 'From a very young age, I was haunted by a question, "What shall I do with this life?" Throughout my life, I sought after a reply to my question."

Then placing the book on Mandira's lap, Biman smilingly adds, 'Bankim, however, has given a very naive answer. Perhaps, you wouldn't like it.'

Mandira goes through the portion of the text and then smiles. Bankim writes:

> *For the answer, man spends his whole life, reading books, seeking other people's opinions but fails to elicit a satisfactory answer. At last, the individual has the self-realisation that it lies in the devotion to God; that without spiritual devotion there exists no humanity. This is the ultimate goal of human life.*

Having read it, Mandira says, 'I'm a layman. This answer won't help me. I've had no self-realisation of bhakti and I don't hope to acquire it in future either. Having spent so many years in Europe, I had forgotten all these lofty thoughts of our philosophy.'

'I too am a very ordinary person. Only the sanyasis can appreciate Bankim's answer. But as an ordinary person, I can give you a suggestion, "Life's worth lies in loving life."'

'Isn't this a kind of selfishness?' retorts Mandira.

'If you're absolutely concerned with your self-interests, it's selfishness. But I'm talking about love for life in a broader perspective that includes deriving pleasure as well as providing happiness to others. If one becomes bitter about life itself then everything appears to be unnecessary.'

Remaining silent for a while, Mandira says, 'Perhaps, you're right. I've gradually begun to love life again.'

'Good,' says Biman, 'Life's after all a seven days' wonder. So given the transitory nature of life, it makes no sense in wasting time in undue brooding. It is wise to squeeze out as much happiness as possible out of it. Some derive happiness from social work while others find happiness by reading poetry at home. The ultimate goal in both the cases is the same.'

'How are you, Biman? I mean, are you happy?'

'Can a person always be happy? Isn't it inappropriate to even expect this? I also have some sorrows and disappointments. The greatest cause of my displeasure is you. How I pine for you even to this day!'

The car is, by this time, out of the city and speeding along the highway. 'Why are we heading towards the airport?' asks Mandira.

'For a long drive this is a fine stretch. Now we can spend our outing in several ways. If we drive a pretty long distance along this road, we can find a couple of swanky guesthouses. Booking a room there, we can spend some time in solitude; lying side by side on a bed we can keep on chatting. Now and again we shall go back to the past, twenty-seven years from hence and again return to the present. Do you like the idea?'

Chuckling, she asks, 'Anything else?'

'Or we might go to the airport hotel and have our lunch quietly,' says Biman.

Still Mandira impishly asks, 'Or?'

'If you want something else,' said Biman, 'we can leave the airport far behind and travel on and on until we stop at a wayside inn where we'll loll on a charpoi and enjoy a lunch of chapatti, tadka and mutton kasa ...'

'There is one other thing that we could do. Suppose we buy two air tickets to Assam and upon reaching there, live in a jungle and enjoy an unfettered life of boundless freedom,' suggests Mandira.

Staring at her, Biman says, 'Can a city-bred person transform overnight into someone accustomed to eking out a living in the forest? Had we been in our youth, say mid-twenties, we could have perhaps done this. Now we're bound by family obligations. You're not so much as I am.' Saying this, he laughs and Mandira too joins him in the laughter.

A little later, Mandira says, 'For the time being, I hope, we'll enjoy a lunch at the airport hotel more than anything else. Today it's so hot that lolling on a roadside charpoi won't be much comfortable. Besides, I've come to taste the joys of city life.'

'I knew this would be your final decision. Having spoken to you on the phone, I at once booked a table there. Listen Mani, I'm scheduled to leave for New Delhi by this afternoon's flight, though I could have cancelled my tour programme had there been a different plan to spend our outing. Now, after the lunch at the restaurant, my car will drop you home.'

'Well, today I'll treat you; when we were young, you had treated me on several occasions,' says Mandira.

'What! You call those treats? I couldn't spend more than two or three rupees for eating out in those days.'

'Don't you think, that amount is more valuable than two or three thousand rupees today? You'd always spend the last penny in your pocket.'

Biman, taking one of Mandira's hands in his own hand, says, 'Mani, you're still as pretty as earlier. It isn't a lie that you were responsible for the major dissatisfaction of my life. But all our desires can't be fulfilled. We also derive a kind of queer pleasure out of the sorrows we bear in our hearts. I will never force you for anything; nor shall I ever hurt your self-esteem. All I want is that I can occasionally meet you.'

'You were saying that you had some good news about Sukhchar. What's that?'

Biman is shocked at this lapse; he apologetically goes on, 'What an idiot I am! I forgot that very thing. It's fantastic news, not only for Sukhchar, but also for me. And for me, it's good in two ways.'

'Please tell me about it in detail.'

'An industrial plant shall be set up in your village. I've got the contract for the construction work. Already, they've bought a large, dilapidated house. They'll have to acquire more lands.'

'What kind of factory? A glass factory?'

Biman laughs. 'A glass factory! Oh no, it's something bigger than that. It's worth twelve crore rupees. It'll have the potential to employ a huge number of local people.'

'That is good news, no doubt; the agricultural lands yield crops once a year. It's not sufficient to provide them succour throughout the year. There's no industry around. Now I hope there'll be some alternative ways of livelihood.'

'I'm very glad to have become a part of this project. After this, I'll have to visit the area frequently. Soon, I'm going to build a bungalow there for my night stays during my visits. Naturally, I can meet you there. I won't have to lie to my wife to justify my reason of visiting Sukhchar.'

Saying this, he holds Mandira's hand and presses it mildly.

9

Negotiations for Bina's marriage have proceeded further; some members of the bridegroom's family will come this afternoon and she will be paraded before the selectors.

This is a novel experience for Mandira. Though her elder sister had an arranged marriage, she was away from home when the groom's family members had come to select her didi. She had gone to Trivandrum to attend the Youth Festival. She was more preoccupied with politics rather than home. On her return, she was told how the delegates from Sankar da's family hadn't asked too many questions; they had just asked her to sing a song. Sankar da hadn't come then. He had first met didi at a wedding party and had had a crush on her.

Bina's mother has personally come to request Mandira to be present at the occasion. The groom's uncle, who is a homoeopath, may hurl a few critical questions at Bina. In that case, Mandira may be able to help her.

Bina lives in a joint family of around fifteen members living in a large house. Adjacent to the house, stands a temple that houses the family deities. On another corner stands the barnyard. The kitchen garden is rich with a variety of vegetables. The fine health of the pair of cows in the shed suggests that it's an affluent man's house.

The groom's family have arrived in a matador. The team consists of two ladies, two elderly gentlemen and the groom. They have been ushered into a well-decorated room, the floor being covered with mats and cushions. The house owner is in the fish trade; therefore there is an unmistakable odour of fish inside the house. To cover it up, perhaps some perfume, albeit of cheap quality, has been sprayed in the sitting room. But for Mandira, the smell of the perfume is more pungent than that of fish.

The bridegroom's family evidently suffer from a superiority complex since, being the judges of today's parade, they have the right to reject Bina. It matters little how much hospitality may be showered on them. Bina's family is now in a subservient position. The bridegroom's father is wearing dhoti and punjabi but the boy is clad in shirt and trousers. The groom, a college drop-out, is now in his early thirties. He works as an assistant in his uncle's dispensary. It is a queer thing that despite being an eligible bachelor, he is still unmarried. He looks glum-faced.

Bina's father, Ghanashyam, with an oily face and flattering tone is supervising the reception of the guests. Basically, a choleric and ill-tempered person, Ghanashyam is trying to masquerade his angry image under an obsequious smile. This is quite natural.

In another room, Bina is being groomed. Her face is caked with extra layers of powder, in an attempt to lighten her dark complexion. Her aunts are giving her some tips to face the interview. But Bina is straightforward. Pouting her lips, she says, 'I know all this stuff. But if they ask me to sing a song, I'll say, I can't.'

Bina's mother says, 'We've told them that our daughter can't sing but does fine embroidery work. If they raise this topic, you must show them the laces. Tell them that you can knit sweaters ...'

Mandira is enjoying these goings-on. She's chewing betel leaves that have turned her lips crimson. Bina's mother is older than her yet she calls her Mandira didi. Again and again, she is seeking tips from Mandira as though she is supposed to know better than them by virtue of having returned from abroad. Mandira tries to allay her fears, 'Don't worry. Bina is an intelligent girl. They'll select her at a glance.'

During her youth, Mandira was strongly against this practice of parading the girls before the groom's families for selection. The very thought of it sickened her. Are women cattle? Women are subjected to humiliation at every stage of the Hindu marriage customs. This marriage, instead of ensuring the union of a man and a woman, in fact, gives a man the licence to savour a woman, who must be decked with ornaments, and must bring with her, furniture, bedding and other accessories at the time of marriage. In accompaniment of the chanting of mantras, the bride is offered to the groom. The bride's father will tell the groom, 'My dearest son-in-law, please accept my daughter for your pleasure but please see to it that she gets proper food and clothing.'

Mandira is now sure that her objections against the practice will make no sense in the conservative Hindu society, that will have to wait for centuries to reform and change its ancient customs. There's no dearth of supporters of the practice of sati even to this day. Widow remarriage is still taboo in society. Dowry demands and bride burning continue unabated. Unless women can select their life partners, this shameful practice of parading oneself before the selectors will go on. The girls helplessly look to their parents to choose life partners for them. If Bina tells her parents that she won't oblige the groom's family by parading before them, then Mandira will lend her some courage. But lo! Bina herself is willing to do her parents' bidding.

The guests have been served luchi and meat. Now it's time for Bina to appear before the selectors. Bina's maternal aunt is giving her some last minute suggestions: 'Don't scurry across the floor; walk at an elegant, gentle pace and keep your head bowed all along in the presence of the groom and his kinsmen.' Bina's mother, with folded hands, touching her own forehead mutters, 'Durga! Durga!'

A gang of neighbouring women have flocked at the door. Mandira stays aloof though Bina's mother is urging her to go inside the guest room where Bina's bridal test is going on.

Instead, Mandira comes to the kitchen garden and pauses under a scaffold built for a climbing vegetable plant. She is admiring the plump, juicy sponge gourds hanging from the platform. Their colour is light green but she can't say that it's bottle green. Even the colour green has a wide range of shades to offer. Had she not been to the countryside, she wouldn't have come to know about this mystery of nature. The green of mango leaves can be distinguished from the green of kadamba flower leaves. Similarly the green of sponge gourd is different from that of chalta.

Mandira has seen these sponge gourds being sown. They're not plants in the true sense of the term. They're creepers that have been later raised on the scaffold. Then they burst into white flowers. Her joy knows no bounds when she first spots a tiny fruit looking like a green chilli. From seeds to plants, from plants to flowers and then to fruits—she hadn't seen this process before. The village folks are familiar with it, so they find nothing unique in it. But Mandira is still thrilled at these experiences.

On the scaffold are sitting three warblers. So small in size, yet what a perfect shape! Mandira has read about these beautiful songbirds in her childhood but never seen one before. She recalls the rhymes, written by Upendra Kishore Roychowdhury. Today she sees the tiny creatures with her own eyes. With pure joy, the birds are somersaulting on the raised platform. Looking at these creatures, Mandira thinks to herself that her decision to leave London was not an exercise in futility after all.

She recalls the line, 'What shall I do with this life?' Biman is right; life's worth lies in loving life itself. She had, at certain point of life, lost much of this love for life.

Shanti comes running to her to break the news. 'Didi, they're perhaps impressed with Bina.'

'How did you deduce that?'

'They're asking her lots of questions. Had they not been impressed by her beauty, they would have looked glum and avoided further dialogue. I'm hoping that the marriage will be scheduled in the coming month of Aghran. There is a tradition of opulent wedding ceremonies in this household. There will be lots of fun and merry-making.'

'You seem to be in high spirits. Do you also wish to marry?' says Mandira jokingly.

'Nobody will marry me! Where's the money? My elder sister is yet to be married.'

'Haven't you fallen in love with any of the boys of your village? If you haven't yet, I suggest you should befriend someone of your choice and marry him. You don't need money then.'

Shanti, wide-eyed, says, 'Marriage without money! How is it possible?'

'Can't that boy Ananta, who often talks to you on the street, marry you?'

Curling her lips, Shanti retorts, 'Ananta! Do you know why he is not marrying? His father demands a huge sum as dowry.'

After the departure of the kinsmen of the would-be-bridegroom, the womenfolk are busy with the post-mortem of today's selection test.

As usual, the groom's representatives, before taking leave, have said that they'll let them know later about their decision. Bina's father and uncle will pay them a return visit. Then they'll raise the issue of dowry. But from their deportment, it's evident that Bina has passed the screening test, for she has given correct replies to most of their questions: 'What's the other name of Goddess Durga?'; 'When is Shivaratri brata observed?'; 'What kind of manure is used for coconut trees?'; 'Which side of the leg should be bound after a snake bite in the knee?'; 'Can potato jackets be cooked?' Bina knows the answers to all these questions. But they haven't asked anything about her musical or embroidery skills.

Mandira thinks to herself, that had she been in Bina's place, she'd have fared miserably in the test.

Some girls are rolling in laughter as they're narrating how the boy's father was scratching his moustache, or how the boy's aunt, obese and plum, looked ridiculous with her gaping mouth. Mandira is amazed at the power of observation of these girls. One of the girls is telling Bina, 'You should take a razor with you. Have you noticed the boy's toes? He has such long nails but doesn't bother to trim them.'

The would-be bridegroom reportedly didn't utter a single word. He was quiet throughout.

Hearing this, Mandira can't help saying, 'Not a single word? I hope he's not deaf and dumb.'

Mandira's comment causes an uneasy silence.

Bina's mother takes strong exception to Mandira's light-hearted but nevertheless unfavourable comment about the bridegroom.

'What an inauspicious remark on such a joyous occasion!' She looks at Mandira, reproachfully.

Mandira feels awfully embarrassed. How could she know that she shouldn't crack a joke about the groom? The boy's kinsmen posed a volley of questions to Bina but couldn't her parents ask a single question of the groom? Bina's father could have asked him something relating to his education or business. Perhaps, it's not the custom in conservative societies. Mandira realises that she should know a lot more about the society she is living in.

Bina's maternal aunt forthwith confirms to Mandira that there is no chance of the fellow being deaf and dumb, since he is a very good actor and recently played the role of Vidyasagar in the drama 'Lord Ramakrishna: the Incarnation of God', staged by their local club. But basically, Sukhendu, the would-be groom, is shy.

On her way home, it becomes difficult for Mandira to supress her laughter. What an enigma! The fellow who has played the role of a social reformist, as noble as Vidyasagar, will marry a girl with dowry. In fact, he has simply committed the dialogues to his memory without understanding the essence of the great character he has enacted on stage. Of course, one who plays the role of a villain on stage, need not necessarily lead a debauched life in real life!

At Bina's place, Mandira made some inappropriate comments. So she apprehends that Bina might not visit her further. But she comes to her house, the very next morning. She has brought a couple of sponge gourds for Mandira.

'Why on earth did you pluck them? They were hanging so beautifully from the mancha,' says a startled Mandira.

'Soon these flowers will be too ripe to eat. Tell Shanti to cook them with poppy seeds.' Then caressing her cheek with one of the fruits, she says, 'They are just like me. I can't be kept at home long lest I should get spoilt. So I must be gifted away to someone else ... the sooner, the better it is ... Isn't that so?'

Mandira is a bit surprised. 'Why are you saying this?' she asks, 'Aren't you willing to marry? But you seemed to be in an amiable mood. Don't you like Sukhendu?'

Nonchalantly, Bina replies, 'It matters little if I don't agree to my parents' proposal. I must get married off one day; or else my parents would make my life a living hell. Anyway, Sukhendu isn't a bad fellow.'

'Not a bad fellow! The person you are going to marry must impress you in all aspects. Otherwise, how can you spend your life with him? Do you like anybody else?'

'Didn't you see Chayan Ghose of Mamudpur last Saturday? He had come to attend the meeting. A handsome boy! I wish I married him! He knows me a little. We've talked on a couple of occasions. Once he took drinking water from my hand.'

'Then instead of keeping your desires to yourself, you should tell these things to your parents.'

'That wouldn't have helped. We've a caste barrier.'

'Do you think Chayan Ghose, who's a political and social activist, will approve of casteism?'

'He won't, but his family members will object. This is after all not your Europe.'

'Why do you go so far? Look around. In Calcutta, nobody pays heed to these things,' argues Mandira.

'Don't fool me, didi. I know that people in the cities with a few exceptions are also victims of caste prejudices like us. Don't I read the newspapers? How many of the matrimonial ads there mention that caste is not a barrier? Hardly five out of a hundred.'

'Still if you like Chayan Ghose, why should you marry Sukhendu?'

'Marriage is just a routine affair in a woman's life. I'll be more than happy if my husband is not blind or lame. Do you think my mother admires my father? Day in and day out, she heaps curses on him.'

Mandira is taken aback by Bina's philosophy of life. When Bina talks, she loses all her inhibitions. She loves to call a spade a spade. She lacks the depths of normal emotions like joy, sorrow and anger. She is incapable of intensely longing for something; she is mediocre in all respects.

'Well, so far has anyone from your village married against his or her parents' will, breaking the barriers of caste and creed?' asks Mandira.

'Yes, Nirmal Halder was in love with Basanti, the daughter of Shibtosh Das. One day, they were caught red-handed meeting at the desolate wasteland behind our house. Unfortunately, it was my father who spotted them there. A thorn had pierced Basanti's foot and Nirmal was pulling it out. Just then, my father collared him from behind and said, "I won't say anything to you, nor shall I get you thrashed by people. I just want you to promise that you'll never talk to Basanti again."'

'Did Nirmal agree to it?'

'Yes, he did and left the village to settle in Barasat.'

'No, Bina, I can't! For God's sake, don't make me listen to a story that ended thus.'

'Listen! There's more to this story. Nirmal was neither a coward nor a villain. He was bold and upright. He managed to get a job at Barasat and one fine morning Basanti eloped. Now, they're happily married with two children. But they never visit the village.'

'That's very good. At least, someone has paved the path for others.'

'So what? Had Nirmal refused to budge from the village, or had he at least kept in touch with the native people on a regular basis, then I think others would have been inspired by his courage. But he severed all ties with the village.'

'Bina, if Chayan Ghose proposes, will you elope with him?'

'Mandira di, please don't get yourself involved in these things. You will land in trouble.'

'I'll be in trouble! But why?'

Before Bina can reply, a bicycle halts on the courtyard. Sajjad Jahir alights from the bicycle and lifts a book over his head to draw Mandira's attention to it.

'Please come in,' says Mandira courteously.

Coming near the veranda, Sajjad says, 'You wanted to read a book on the Sunderbans. We don't have anything in our stock. But I've got this book from one of my friends. Will you please flip through it?'

'Yes, I'll read it. I hope you aren't in a hurry. Please come in. I'll make tea for you.'

Gesturing towards Bina, Sajjad says, 'Disgusted with Javed, she has stopped visiting our library. Now, if I sit here, I'm afraid, she'll be annoyed. It is best that I should go now, madam.'

'What reasoning!' says Bina spiritedly, 'Sajjad da, haven't you ever dropped in at our place for a cup of tea? My father has never disliked you. But nobody can tolerate Javed.'

Mandira hates being called 'madam'. She has told Sajjad a number of times not to address her thus. But he doesn't listen. Perhaps he doesn't know what to call her instead.

'Bina, give company to Sajjad. I'm coming back with tea.'

'It's better if you converse with him. Let me put the kettle on. But you'll brew the tea. Your magic touch makes it very special.'

Sitting on the chair, Sajjad lights a cigarette. Mandira hasn't smoked a cigarette until now. The passive smoking makes her long for one. But she will not smoke in the presence of the local people.

'A big factory is coming up near your house,' says Sajjad.

'Yes, I've heard of it. Lahiri Villa has already been sold. They want more land for it.'

'You came to live here in peace. If they set up a factory, you'll be troubled by all the construction related chaos,' Sajjad tries to point out to her.

Mandira smiles. 'It doesn't matter. I have not come here forever. I can also shift my residence. But don't you think that the factory will augur well for the development of the village? Concrete roads will be constructed, electricity will be supplied, locals will get employment.'

'But a large number of people will also come from outside. Prices of essential commodities will go up. A section of land losers will sink into poverty. Besides, industrialisation will automatically give rise to slums, spurious liquor dens, strikes, hullabaloo, police raids, etc.' Sajjad doesn't hide his apprehensions.

'You shouldn't be pessimistic to begin with. Industrialisation is essential. Agriculture alone can't feed everyone. Ancillary industries will spring up centering round the core factory. This will improve the socio-economic condition of the villagers. It's obvious that industries shouldn't be confined to urban areas only. It should gradually spread across the rural sectors.'

'Do you know madam, what factory is coming up here?'

'I don't know. But it isn't a glass factory. Something bigger than that.'

'It will be a fertiliser plant. They have named it the Sunderbans Fertiliser Limited. A joint venture of the state government and an influential entrepreneur.'

'Fertiliser plants are useful for our country. We have to import fertilisers from abroad. Now we can save foreign exchange.'

'But madam, I feel disturbed at the thought of a factory coming up in our village. I'm sure it won't augur well for the locals.'

'You're a great nature lover. You want to retain the pastoral beauty of your village. Isn't that so? But you must accept the inevitable changes. You can't shut out your village from the slow yet inevitable modernisation of rural Bengal.'

Still Sajjad looks thoughtful.

The water is boiling on the stove. Mandira goes inside to brew it. She comes back with a tray laden with teacups and some biscuits—local bakery products.

'Mandira di, you've made me a tea addict,' says Bina.

'To be frank,' says Sajjad timidly, 'I've taken the trouble of coming all the way to madam's house, ostensibly to deliver the book but really to have a sip of the inimitable taste of madam's tea. It's very expensive, isn't it?'

'Yes, it's from England. It's out and out foreign,' banters Mandira.

Both of them laugh heartily.

'It's a very simple process really. Pour the boiled milk through a sieve to remove the lumps. I've told this to Shanti several times but she can't remember the process. I get fed up when she adds sugar more than what I have repeatedly asked her to.'

Unmindfully, Sajjad says, 'I'm not sure, but I've read somewhere that before setting up a fertiliser plant, a proper survey of the land must be conducted. Doesn't the smoke emitted by it affect humans?'

'I'm ignorant on this subject,' replies Mandira.

'What factory was it in Bhopal where a large number of people died due to gas leakage?'

Mandira is startled. 'Oh yes, that was a very big fertiliser plant. But that was an accident. I hope, here they'll take precautions well in advance to avert a tragedy like Bhopal.'

'I'm also a layman on this issue. There's a science club at Dhalipara. They have lots of information. They can help us.'

'What did you say? A science club?'

'Yes, there has been a science club at Dhalipara over the past two years. They're doing a great job. They create awareness among the general public on matters of superstition, health and hygiene; they educate the folks about which snakes are poisonous and which are not through poster campaigns. Chayan Ghose of Mamudpur inspires the club members. He has also set up a club; they call themselves the 'Rationalists' Association'. He has on several occasions exposed the hoax, bluffs of the so-called sanyasis and fakirs. He's an educated man. I'm thinking of speaking to him.

Hearing Chayan Ghose's name, Mandira looks at Bina. Then she enthusiastically says, 'That's a very good idea. I'm also keen on talking to Chayan Ghose. Could you arrange a meeting with him?'

10

After incessant rain for two days, this evening is dry and hot. The sky is cloudy and the day is sultry. Rains make the days cool and refreshing; a shower at night is especially useful for a sound sleep. But tonight Mandira is tossing and turning in unbearable heat inside the mosquito net.

She has heard that rains have been sufficient this monsoon. The paddy fields are inundated. Floods are a perennial affair in these areas, damaging the farm lands. Harvests are raised once a year and once the crops fail they have to starve the year round. Mandira didn't have an idea about these things before coming to this village. The distance between the Sunderbans and Calcutta is hardly one hundred kilometres. Yet Calcuttans know nothing more about this part of Bengal other than the Royal Bengal Tigers of the Sunderbans.

The windows on both sides of the room are left open, yet no air is passing through it. Swarms of mosquitoes keep buzzing outside the mosquito net and Mandira is soaked in perspiration. She removes her outer robe.

At once she recalls her days in the Kensington apartment. It's an aristocratic neighbourhood in London. The Englishmen living there are under the impression that their English is laced with a particular accent of their own just as the Urdu-speaking population of Lucknow take pride in their own style of Urdu. No one in Kensington spoke without raising their eyebrows. Mandira had to sweat her brows to master the inarticulate pronunciation of 'r' at the end of several words. These refined Englishmen never sat at the breakfast table without wearing ties; even when watching TV alone in their drawing rooms in the evening, they wore lounge suits.

Soon after her marriage she was amazed by Tom's one particular habit. He never slept in sleeping suits at night. Interestingly enough he slept in his birthday suit. Straight from the bathroom he ran to his bed and dived under the quilt. He would compel Mandira to sleep like him. At first Mandira was reluctant to follow Tom's example. Though the bedroom was dark and private, yet she couldn't help feeling shy. Tom, however, believed in a particular theory of his own. According to his theory, it was not hygienic to live round-the-clock wearing clothes. Man is after all an animal. Does any other animal wear clothes like man?

Mandira followed Tom's example till Robin was around two years old.

In Western countries, children from their infancy are trained and encouraged to sleep all by themselves in a separate room. Nevertheless, in case they woke up in the middle of the night, Mandira would have to rush to their room. She had to change Liz's nappies time and again.

After a long time, coming to her house at Harrow on the Hill, Mandira had resumed the habit of sleeping without clothes. Tom's theory, she began to discover, was not totally wrong. Once she got accustomed to it, she enjoyed sound sleep.

In England the weather often turns very hot for a day or two in the months of July and August—almost like Calcutta. It becomes so sultry that one sweats while walking on the streets. But the mercury suddenly drops soon after a shower. There are no arrangements in houses to cool the rooms, if required. In place of air-conditioners, they have central heating systems. Some of the hotels and restaurants have made arrangements nowadays for fans to be used in summer months only.

Some winter nights, during snowfall outside, it so happened that Mandira woke up bathed in perspiration. Then she had to get up from bed to turn down the bathroom heater. How often she stood at the window without a shred of clothes on and had the novel experience of watching the snow falling!

Lying in bed, under the tin shed of her Sukhchar cottage, she reminisces about her days in London. She is feeling uncomfortable owing to the sweltering heat, yet in comparison to her life in London, she is not less happy here. During the later period of her life in London she had become a nonentity. She had no role to play in the social life there. But here, within a few months of her arrival, she has formed a strong attachment to its people and their well-being. She has been invited to a meeting to be held tomorrow.

Suddenly, she is alarmed by a strange clicking sound. She has often been told about thieves but till now she hasn't been confronted with one. The sound is repeated. Quietly she comes out of the mosquito net. Wearing the nightgown, the torch in hand, she opens the door noisily and calls out, 'Who's there?'

Someone rushes out of the kitchen. Mandira switches on the torch in the dark to find a boy, aged around twelve or thirteen ... Is he the thief? Or has he been sent by his seniors who might be lurking nearby? But how has he managed to enter the house? Mandira is baffled.

The boy tries to hide his face with his hands.

'Hey, who are you? Don't move a step from there,' Mandira shouts.

The boy cries aloud saying, 'Didi, oh didi!'

Shanti, who was sleeping in the storeroom, comes out hurriedly. Shielding the boy she piteously pleads, 'Didi, please pardon us, he's my younger brother.'

Mandira draws near the boy for a closer inspection. She finds his hands, face and clothes smeared with molasses. He was gulping down a meal of rice crispies covered in molasses when Mandira found him.

'Your brother? When did he come? Why didn't you tell me?'

'Just a while ago. I didn't tell you because you were sleeping. Our house has been flooded with rainwater. He has come to give me the news.'

Mandira, raising her eyebrows, says, 'But I didn't sleep.'

She wonders how the creature has entered the house. For safety she locks the main gate and keeps the keys in her custody.

On interrogation Shanti confesses that her brother has entered through the window, two bars of which are broken. Perhaps the boy had entered through it a couple of times before as well.

'He looks hungry. Why didn't you offer him a meal?'

Shanti is silent. Mandira feels disgusted with her. She feels like slapping her across the face. She has given every possible freedom to Shanti. She's quite at home to eat whatever she likes. Mandira doesn't keep any account of the storeroom. She never even takes Shanti to task. Though Mandira has tried hard to remove the distance between them, Shanti can never get rid of her inferiority complex. Her house has been flooded, her brother has come to deliver the news—so couldn't she wake up Mandira? Does Shanti consider her to be so inhuman? Has she presumed that Mandira will be angry? Perhaps the boy hasn't eaten anything today. That is why he has stolen the food. But why? Couldn't Shanti offer him anything to eat?

Mandira cannot tolerate this guilt-ridden mindset of these villagers.

The name of Shanti's brother is Biru. Even at this tender age he looks like a culprit, as though he has committed a sin by virtue of being born in a poor family.

'Here, how much of your house is under water?' asks Mandira.

'Up to the veranda.' Replies Biru.

'Where are your parents and other siblings?'

'In that home.'

If the water level rises further where will you go?'

Pat comes Shanti's reply, 'There has been no rain today. So the water won't rise any further. It'll rather come down now.'

It suddenly occurs to Mandira that as the rain has stopped, the water level won't rise further. Then why has Biru come running to her house at this hour of the night? He hasn't delivered any urgent piece of news, after all. Most probably pangs of hunger have brought him here.

She can't help punishing Shanti. This girl is too fond of sleeping. A lazy devil! So the ideal punishment will be to make her stay awake this night. Mandira commands, 'Go and light the stove. Cook rice, daal and mashed potato. You can't go to sleep tonight till your brother is fed.'

'He has already had a lot of rice crispies and molasses; he doesn't need anything more now,' Shanti tries to shirk the work.

'Do what I tell you,' Mandira snubs her, 'and mind it, tomorrow you must call Paban, the carpenter, to repair the broken rods of the window.'

Mandira comes back to her room and sits down by the window.

That is far better than the experience of tossing in bed. She is feeling out of sorts due to the hot weather but is happy that the abatement of rain will save the poor people's huts from being inundated.

On the table is lying an English book on the Bhopal Gas Tragedy. It is from Chayan Ghose's collection for her. She has read much of the book all through the evening.

Coming in close contact with Chayan Ghose, Mandira is quite impressed with his knowledge and outlook on life. Chayan has dispelled Mandira's prejudiced notion that only the weak, shy and inactive men live in villages and all the enterprising men migrate to towns. But people like Chayan and Sajjad also live in the village. Chayan is associated with an organisation called the Rationalist's Association, who instead of celebrating religious functions, are campaigning for the eradication of superstition.

Chayan Ghose tours across a score of villages in the neighbourhood to propagate his ideals. Besides, being related to a political party, he occasionally visits Calcutta. The only drawback is that he is without a fixed source of income. His family lives in dire straits yet he never grudges his unacknowledged social service.

Till today it was unknown to Mandira that the canal she used to cross by the wooden footbridge, on the way to the library, was known to the local people of Sukhchar as Kanaibenki's Khal.

This afternoon she along with Chayan Ghose, Sajjad Jahir and many others had taken a long walk along the edge of the canal. Bina was also with her. On a couple of occasions, Bina bumped into Chayan yet she couldn't find an opportunity to engage him in a conversation. Spellbound, she just kept staring at him. Basically Bina is outspoken and forthright but in the presence of Chayan she, as if, goes into a cocoon. She even went to the extent of confessing to Mandira that if Chayan ever proposed to her, she would elope with him without a second thought, let whatever be the consequences.

Chayan, however, seems to be apathetic to women in general. From his conversations, it is evident that he looks upon both men and women alike.

If one walks some distance along the edge of the Kanaibenki canal, one can reach Sathpukur sluice gate, the pathway to the Sunderbans. The waters of the Kanaibenki canal mingle with the water bodies of the Sunderbans. Now, the monsoon being in full swing, all water bodies there are overflowing. If ever the need arises to open the sluice gate, the adjacent villages will be inundated. They had gone up to that sluice gate to make an on-the-spot survey.

Climbing on top of the gate, Chayan was saying, 'We can somehow save the villages from the floods. But if the fertiliser plant comes up at Sukhchar, the surrounding villages will meet their doomsday. The process of destroying the Sunderbans will begin with it. Mandira di, I think you can imagine our predicament. Now, I think, it's high time we should join hands for a difficult journey ahead.'

Mandira wanted to clarify, 'I'm nobody. I'm an outsider. I'm just watching certain things and in the process trying to learn a bit. Nothing more than this.'

But they wouldn't listen. They keep urging her not to shy away. Instead she can provide them some impetus. Very often they almost forcefully take her along to attend their programmes.

Mandira never felt herself so indispensable before. Meanwhile things have gone far. The doubts raised by Sajjad have been confirmed by Chayan. The latter was saying that the Government of India has prepared a list of twenty such hazardous industries that would pose a threat to life. A fertiliser factory is one of them. Before giving the cue to set up a factory of this kind, an elaborate survey of the environment should be made. After the Bhopal Gas Tragedy, the authorities should have taken extra precautions.

An industrialist has hurriedly manipulated the higher authorities to obtain necessary permissions to set the wheels of the factory rolling. In Bengal, scores of factories have been shut down; the jute mills are meted out step-motherly treatment as they are considered out of fashion. Thousands of workers have gone jobless. In a situation like this, the government will quite obviously grab the lucrative offer from an entrepreneur to set up a new factory that can generate some employment opportunities. That is why the West Bengal Industrial Development Corporation has agreed to buy twenty-five per cent equity shares.

At first the factory was supposed to be set up at Mathurapur. But they wound up the plan since the ministry of environment didn't approve. The next proposed sites were Ghateswar and Raghunathpur but these sites too didn't click due to the objections of the local people. That is why the company is desperate to start the work covertly at Sukhchar. To their great advantage the land price is comparatively cheap here. They have already bought the old and deserted Lahiri Villa and its vacant land. Now they are trying to acquire some more land in phases.

Meanwhile Chayan has founded a body called Charbazaar Welfare Society. Very judiciously he has involved representatives from all political parties and religious groups. He is trying to convince them that despite their political and ideological differences, it is important to be united on an issue like this concerning people from all walks of life. The long-existing feuds between neighbouring groups based on religion, caste and creed have more or less transformed into wrangles of political ideologies. The CPI(M) is fairly strong in this area; there are also some strongholds of the SUCI. The Congress has not been washed away altogether. Besides, the Vishva Hindu Parishad, Muslim League, RSS and Jamate-Islami are also active in many areas. Chayan is intelligent enough to not become the president or secretary of the committee. He's just the convenor.

He tries to convince everybody that despite their political differences they should be united on a common issue like the construction of this factory. It's a local issue involving ten to twelve neighbouring villages. 'Take for instance,' he tries to illustrate his point, 'if the fish in one of the rivers of our area get poisoned for some reason, then it is our responsibility to tell the folks that they shouldn't consume that fish. Should we ever politicise such an issue?'

Mandira has often felt that Chayan is on a wild-goose chase for, though he may dream of bringing the CPM and Congress on the same platform, how can he think of aligning the Vishva Hindu Parishad with Jamate-Islami? But she is happy that she has been proved wrong. Even Bishnupada Halder of Mamudpur, who is an ardent Hindu and has been aggressively campaigning to change the name of Mamudpur into Mahadevpur, is supporting

Chayan on this fertiliser plant controversy. Javed and a couple of his friends, who are very loyal to Sajjad, also attend the meetings convened by Chayan. The local MLA, Susovan Roy and the president of the panchayat have extended their moral support to the movement.

As it is the rainy season now, it's not possible to hold a meeting in the open. So the meetings are normally held at the tea stall in the marketplace or in the library hall. Mandira these days has got somewhat accustomed to the tea served in glasses, wafting out the fume of smoke. In the meetings, she avoids speaking out; she has just lent her ears to them. Chayan and Sajjad have supplied her with several books and leaflets relating to pollution and environment from their science club.

Mandira tiptoes to the kitchen to inspect Shanti's progress. Rice is boiling and bubbling on the oven. Biru gapes at it, squatting on the floor. Shanti mixes the mashed potato with oil and spices. Biru's eyes are glistening at the prospect of a sumptuous dinner to be served soon.

'Wow! Didi, boiling rice has the sweetest scent in the world! Won't you take it off the oven? The rice is boiling over.' The kid seems to be unable to wait any longer.

He's getting impatient. Mandira withdraws herself silently from the spot. She hardly feels sleepy anymore. She stands at the window and looks out. The cloudy sky hampers the vision of a full moon. Nowadays, she keeps herself abreast of the auspicious dates of the Bengali almanac. Today is the fourteenth day of the dark half. At a little distance away, a frog is croaking piteously. Mandira has heard Shanti saying, 'This is the kind of scream that emanates from a frog when a snake preys on it.' Mandira, even to this day has not got over her snake phobia. Meanwhile, she has come upon snakes on two occasions. On one occasion, while walking along the side of the road, accompanied by Chayan, she saw a snake nonchalantly zigzagging across the ground. Mandira's blood froze at the sight of it. But Chayan ignored it saying, 'It's a *darhash* kind of snake, it's harmless.' Mandira's next encounter with a snake had taken place in the courtyard of Bina's house. That was, she was told, a Russell's viper, deadly venomous. Bina's father let it go unharmed by tapping his feet on the ground. After this incident whenever she went to Bina's house she felt goose bumps on her skin.

For quite some time now, Mandira has stayed away from Bina's house as Bina's father took strong exception to his daughter's hobnobbing with Mandira. He hasn't said anything directly to Mandira, but has scolded Bina. She, however, has decided that she won't ask Bina to stop coming to her house. Bina is an adult; she should decide for herself what would be good for her and what would not.

Mandira again moves towards the kitchen. Serving the meal to her brother, Shanti has also sat down with a tray of rice and potato. Anytime is mealtime for Shanti, whether she's hungry or not. The two siblings have sat on the ground facing each other, with a lantern placed between them. Their faces are beaming with delight. The sight draws tears to Mandira's eyes. She hasn't seen such a sweet yet cruel sight before. She has heard of the pitiable lot of the poor but it's hard, really hard to witness that in reality. A frugal meal of rice, daal and potatoes has made them so happy. Mandira can't imagine how human beings deprive fellow humans of this little bit of happiness.

Suddenly the sky seems to have turned dark. Does it portend more rains? No, Mandira won't like rains now.

Next day Chayan and Sajjad come to her house to take her to the meeting. She reluctantly goes with them. Some days ago, on behalf of the villagers, Mandira had drafted a letter of complaint to the Minister of the State for Environment. She had tried to convince the petitioners that a letter written in Bengali would certainly serve their purpose. But they wouldn't listen. They had tried to persuade Mandira by saying that they could get the letter typed out if it was drafted in English. Moreover, they felt that a handwritten letter would be thrown into the bin even before being read. Thus the typewritten letter, drafted by Mandira, was subscribed by some signatures in illegible handwriting and some thumb impressions and was placed before the appropriate authorities.

That letter has served the desired purpose. Today's meeting is going to be attended by two representatives from the company; the local SDO is coming to mediate on behalf of the government. So Mandira is specially requested to be at the meeting.

Both Sajjad and Chayan normally travel on their bicycles. But today, to give Mandira company on their way to the meeting, they're walking along the dusty road. 'You could buy a bicycle,' suggests Sajjad, 'and seeing you riding on it, the local girls will be inspired. Why don't you set an example for them?'

'But the problem is that I don't know how to ride a cycle.'

'You'll learn it in a couple of days,' says Chayan. 'These days in your European countries people prefer bicycles to avoid pollution caused by cars, don't they?'

Mandira smiles and asks, 'Do you read these things in newspapers?'

'Yes, we do. Why, am I not right?'

'I've seen students riding cycles but not others. They can't move an inch without cars.'

'They have a car in each family. In fact, some of them own more than one car. How do they breathe in an atmosphere so heavily polluted by the smoke belched out by a huge number of cars plying on the roads?' asks a curious Chayan.

'They don't allow cars guilty of air pollution to ply on the roads. Still pollution is a global phenomenon. They're, however, more concerned about industrial pollution,' explains Mandira.

'A day's visit to Calcutta leaves me gasping back home,' says Sajjad. 'When I wander the whole day in the city and wipe my face with a handkerchief I find a greasy layer of dust and oil settling all over the piece of cloth. It means that Calcutta's air is full of impurities like grime and carbon.'

As they pass by Bina's house, she rushes out of her home as though she has been waiting for them. Mandira hadn't sent any instructions for her. She is wearing a deep yellow sari, her face wreathed in smiles and wet hair hanging loose on her back.

This morning Shanti was saying that Bina's father and uncle had returned from Ulpur after finalising the negotiations for Bina's marriage. Now the bargain for the amount of cash, ornaments and other gifts is on the cards. After this the wedding preparations will start in full swing. At this stage, Bina will be forbidden from stepping out of home anymore.

So Mandira is astonished to see her joining them. 'You came!' she exclaims.

'Mandira di, why were you leaving me behind?' asks Bina reproachfully.

Sajjad doesn't look at Bina. Chayan ignores her presence. In continuation of the discussion, he says, 'Well, Mandira di, what was it that you were saying about the Green party in Germany? What kind of activities are they involved in?'

The wooden bridge on the canal has not been repaired yet. As the four people climb up on it, it threatens to cave in. Mandira is slightly scared. The canal water is overflowing the banks. She finds slight relief in the thought that she knows swimming.

Today's venue is the library hall. The representatives of the company and the administration have already turned up. In fact, it's a matter of utmost urgency for them to come to a settlement.

Some wooden benches and chairs have been arranged on one side of the hall for the guests and on the other side, a couple of straw mats have been spread on the floor. Javed is found busy fetching some extra chairs from outside.

This is Mandira's first meeting with the BDO. A young man, with a slim physique, he seems to have recently passed out of university. He's wearing a full sleeve shirt, evidently foreign-made. The officer's name is Dibyajyoti Mukherjee. Though a fresh entrant into the government service, his lips bear the signs of authority.

Seeing Mandira, the BDO greets her with folded hands, 'Good afternoon, Mrs Brockway. Please be seated on this side.'

Mandira feels most reluctant to act as the spokesperson of the local people. Besides Sajjad and Chayan, the local MLA and the panchayat president are scheduled to be present at this meeting.

However, she reciprocates his greetings and says, 'I would rather sit behind.' She is about to sit on the mat. Someone brings a chair for her. Sajjad requests her to occupy the chair. Mandira drags the chair close to the bookshelves.

On the bench beside the BDO, two gentlemen are sitting side by side. One of them, middle-aged, clad in a safari suit, is Dipak Roy Chowdhury, the chairman of the Sunderbans Fertiliser Limited. Next to him is sitting Biman. Lifting his one leg on the other and slightly bending, he sits leaning against the chair. In a suit, Biman looks like a perfect European. A cigarette is hanging from his lips. Even after the eye contact with Mandira he doesn't acknowledge her.

Mandira keeps staring at the BDO. He is very smart indeed! The young man's face takes after one of Mandira's classmates, Suranjan Mukherjee at Presidency College.

She won't be surprised if he happens to be Suranjan's son. The young officer seems to know a lot of things about Mandira. He even knows Mandira's former surname. She recalls Chayan saying that the local police station keeps track of Mandira's activities. Perhaps the higher authorities have instructed them to do this.

Before turning up at the meeting, Biman hadn't met Mandira. Perhaps he thought it prudent to maintain reticence about his acquaintance with her.

'We're going to start the meeting once the MLA arrives,' says the BDO. 'Before that let's get acquainted with one another. Chayan babu, one point: please choose around ten representatives. Let's not get the meeting hall unnecessarily crowded.'

Having counted his men, Chayan banters, 'If including me the number goes up to eleven, would you mind sir?'

Raising his hand, the BDO says, 'Oh, why should I? You must be with us, after all.'

'The MLA and the panchayat president are our representatives. But since you're the BDO, we look upon you as our man also,' says Chayan.

The BDO raises his eyebrows in appreciation of Chayan's presence of mind.

As they're getting acquainted with one another, Dipak Roy Chowdhury all at once turns to Mandira and asks, 'In which part of London did you live?'

This question, though irrelevant, has been asked with the intention of impressing those present there that he has been to London and that he is acquainted with the neighbouring places.

Biman is smoking one cigarette after another, without making any comment.

Dibyajyoti holds out his cigarette packet towards Mandira. Shaking her head she says, 'No, thanks.'

Biman's eyes remain fixed upon Mandira.

Dipak Roy Chowdhury holds out his cigarette packet before Sajjad and says, 'Keep this packet with you. I've lots more in stock.' Before Sajjad is able to say anything he throws the packet in his lap. Then he adds, 'We've arranged cold drinks for everybody; tell them to serve it right now.'

One of the men has been sent to fetch an ice box from the car. From it they pull out bottles of soft drinks in varying colours. Bottles are being opened generously. Lots of bubbles glisten around the bottles. Mandira politely declines the offer to take one.

Astonished, Dibyajyoti says, 'You won't even have cold drinks?'

Mandira is thinking of something else. She is tempted to ask him whether his father's name is Suranjan Mukherjee. But this kind of a personal question would be incongruous in the present situation.

In a soft tone, she replies, 'I don't consume bottled cold drinks.'

Smiling broadly Dibyajyoti says, 'I think you believe in natural food, don't you? Are you a vegetarian?'

'Not exactly. But I try my best to have fresh food. I don't have anything which is not essential for survival.'

'I've got the photocopy of your letter written to the pollution control board. Your English is excellent. Here few can write like you. I admire the precision and clarity of your expressions.'

With a smile Mandira asks, 'And what about the contents of the letter?'

He laughs aloud and says, 'Living in this village, do you really worry about pollution? Well, what can you and I do if the ozone layer in the stratosphere is being depleted?'

Mandira is painfully aware that all this small talk is a kind of show-off, intended to capture her attention and admiration. She feels embarrassed. Why are they giving so much importance to her? Simply because she's a woman? Or it might be that she hasn't yet managed to efface the stamp of urban sophistication from her countenance. Is it her fault? It is as though her foreign background is like a halo around her head.

Though the MLA and the panchayat president are yet to arrive, the organisers of today's meeting, Sajjad, Chayan and others, are present. So the representatives of the government and the company should carry on their dialogues with them, not with Mandira!

Bishnupada Halder, having gulped down two bottles of cold drinks, says in a voice mixed with impatience, 'Sir, the MLA hasn't turned up yet. Meanwhile, may I draw your attention to a serious issue? The influx of the Bangladeshi Hindus has again risen alarmingly. What are you doing about it? Haven't you yet reported the matter to the central government?'

Javed has been standing near the door. Hearing Bishnupada's remark, his eyes snarling in rage, he looks at Sajjad.

Chayan stands up; he wants to say something. Raising his hand Dibyajyoti interferes like a pucca bureaucrat, 'Please, please; don't raise an issue like this here. It's not a political meeting. By the way, Bishnupada babu if you wish you may register your misgivings to the SDPO on this issue. But today at this meeting we'll just discuss about the factory. I've come here only for two reasons. A company intends to buy land for building a factory. They'll pay a reasonable price. They'll acquire lands only from those farmers who're willing to sell their lands. No question of forcible acquisition.'

'But they're applying force. They're also cajoling people into giving up land,' says Javed with alacrity.

'Don't intrude into other people's speeches,' Dibyajyoti snaps at Javed. 'Has anybody lodged a complaint with the police against the alleged forceful acquisition of land? None. These are rumours. But it's a fact that the members of your Charbazaar Welfare Society are trying to persuade the farmers not to sell their lands. I've come on behalf of the government to explain to the people that it's illegal to prevent the willing farmers from selling their lands.

'Next on the agenda is your application on pollution. I'll come to this point later. The formal meeting will start soon after the arrival of the MLA.'

Just then a man sitting on the ground, demands, rather loudly, 'Why is he not coming? Will he come at all? Has he sent any message? How long should we keep on waiting for him?'

Sajjad and Chayan look at each other.

By this time some people have started expressing doubts over the intentions of the authorities. Both the MLA and the panchayat pradhans are the representatives of the government. How can they oppose the government in its stance on the factory? Are they being pressurised by the top brass?

Dibyajyoti is clever enough to read their thoughts. He says, 'We can always carry on with the meeting informally till they arrive. I think Mr Roy Chowdhury can brief you about the background of the factory.'

Dipak Roy Chowdhury, shaking his legs impatiently, turns towards Biman and looks at him hesitantly. Biman says, 'You speak on behalf of the factory authorities.'

Dipak Roy Chowdhury casting a glance all around fixes his gaze on Mandira and begins his address. He sounds a bit hoarse and tired too.

'I'm afraid there has been a misunderstanding from the very beginning. You're under the impression that we've come here to make huge profits. But that's not true. The Sunderbans is a neglected and underdeveloped region. The proposed factory is a part of the development strategy taken up by the government. Of course, I must admit that it's a commercial venture ... Well, without the commercial angle, nothing clicks these days. But the government too holds a stake in it. In fact, only after a lot of deliberations has the government sanctioned the plan.'

'Why isn't the government setting up an ice factory here?' asks Chayan. 'The cooperative societies engaged in fishery could have benefited from it. Besides, nowadays they're producing plenty of sugar and turnips that can be used for industrial alcohol. And medicines. We're more in need of a factory of that kind.'

Heaving a sigh, Dipak Roy Chowdhury replies, 'I can't say anything about an ice factory or industrial alcohol; I can only tell you about fertiliser. I can't understand why you people have a deep reservation about a fertiliser plant. Don't you need fertilisers for agriculture? In India we still have a shortage of fertilisers.'

'Yes, we definitely require fertilisers,' says Chayan, 'for it enhances the productivity of soil. But the fertiliser plant is a source of poisonous gas that kills humans. Moreover, the fertiliser produced from this plant will be sold elsewhere, like say, Burdwan, Hooghly where the peasants are affluent. They raise three crops a year. Our local farmers won't benefit from it.'

'Poisonous gas?' rebuffs Dipak Roy Chowdhury, 'who planted this misconception in your minds? Do you think the pollution control board gave us the necessary permission without considering the pros and cons of the matter? You've made poster campaigns citing the instance of the Bhopal Gas Tragedy. It's a far-fetched comparison. In Bhopal, it was a very large factory owned by a foreign company that hadn't taken adequate safety measures. That's why thousands died. But here we are going to set up a small plant to be owned by a Bengali entrepreneur. How is it possible that we'll have no concern for the welfare of our fellow countrymen? Besides, there are fertiliser plants of this type already in other parts of Bengal. Nobody opposes there. Your arguments are baseless. Mind it, we'll construct roads, ensure supply of electricity.'

Chayan again stands up to say something.

Dibyajyoti stops him, saying, 'Wait, wait, let Mr Roy Chowdhury finish first.'

Nevertheless, Chayan is determined to counter him. He says, 'You must argue point by point. Look Mr Roy Chowdhury, there are two more fertiliser plants in West Bengal—one in Rishra and the other one in Khardah. Sajjad and I had gone there. We've been told that those two plants have been declared hazardous for the environment. After the Bhopal Gas tragedy, twenty-five plants across the world had been identified as potentially dangerous. The two fertiliser plants in Bengal belong to this blacklist. We have the necessary documents with us. You can see them if you wish to. In fact, now it'll be a violation of law if a plant of this category is set up in the midst of human population.'

With a subtle smile of sarcasm hovering on his lips, Dipak Roy Chowdhury banters, 'Then we should set up a factory in the desert. But where in West Bengal can I find a desert, pray?'

The arguments and counter arguments cannot proceed further.

Suddenly an uproar can be heard outside. It is presumed, albeit incorrectly, that the MLA has turned up. But the commotion can be heard from a distance and gradually it's drawing near. Some people are shouting in rage. They have halted at the entrance of the library hall.

Sajjad, Chayan and some others rush out. Biman keeps on staring at Mandira. The present with its insistent demands have been left far behind as he surrenders himself to the beauty of his beloved.

An agitated Chayan comes back to tell the BDO, 'Sir, now you'll have to control them!'

'What's the matter? Who are they?' asks Dibyajyoti.

'Some peasants were working in the fields. The police went there and ousted them from their lands saying that their lands have been sold. Why should the police charge batons to drive them out?' asks Chayan excitedly.

'I know,' says Dipak Roy Chowdhury, 'some landowners living in Calcutta sold their lands directly to the company. The police were only vacating those lands. This is perfectly legitimate.'

'Never!' growls Chayan. 'You can't displace the sharecroppers; it's illegal. The landowners are taking advantage of the lot of the poor peasants. What will they eat? What kind of law is this? The BDO sahib is present here. May I ask you sir? Is the government really in favour of the have-nots?'

Dibyajyoti can't give a reply.

Javed comes back and shouts, 'The police are lashing out at them with batons. One of the protesters broke his hand.'

Outside there is mayhem as shouts, screams, wails and abuses rend the air. But Dipak Roy Chowdhury and his peers seem to be unperturbed. Perhaps they're well equipped with armed personnel. The BDO is looking slightly restive. He mumbles, 'The SDO must be informed.'

Mandira goes near the window. She peeps through it and sees some bare-bodied men smeared with mud, perhaps coming straight from the fields. With them also are some women and children. Mandira recognises Shanti's father and younger brother. They too have a small plot of land which they till as sharecroppers.

Mandira's eyes fall on Shanti's younger brother. What's that stain on his forehead? Blood? Could the police be so brutal that they thrashed a kid so mercilessly? Mandira is horrified. The boy, unmindful of his injury, is holding lumps of mud in both his hands and screaming in terrible rage.

Mandira says to herself, 'Rice, daal, boiled potato! They are trying to deprive the poor people of this basic frugal meal!'

The boy coming further towards the library starts throwing mud balls at the building.

11

Tonight at nine p.m. Biman has come to Mandira's house on foot. Perhaps he has parked the car in front of Lahiri Villa. His eyes suggest that he hasn't been drinking. On the veranda, Sajjad, Chayan, Javed, Balai, among others are engaged in a hot debate. Bina hasn't gone home yet. Her parents have sent the maidservant twice to call her home but she has snubbed her back. Mandira doesn't interfere; let Bina decide for herself whether she should go now or not.

They are chalking out their future plans to lodge their protest against police atrocities on the innocent villagers. Chayan is in favour of forming a women's squad which would lead the peaceful demonstration. The advantage being that the police will think twice before charging with batons without provocation.

As Bina is showing much enthusiasm about it, Chayan cannot but give much importance to her. With Biman's intrusion they break off in the middle of their discussion.

After a little pause, Mandira introduces Biman to the others saying, 'He's Biman, an old acquaintance of mine. In fact, he visited me before as well.'

That Mandira is apologetic is evident from her manner. Biman smiles meaningfully.

Chayan stands up to leave; the others follow suit.

Biman apologetically says, 'I'm sorry to have disturbed you. But you needn't go. I haven't come to talk about the factory; I've just come for a glass of drinking water.'

'That's okay. But I must leave now for it's going to rain again. I've a long way to go before I reach home.'

Mandira asks Sajjad to tarry a little but he also says he's in a hurry. Thereafter all of them leave one by one. Bina says, 'Chayan da, would you please accompany me to my house? It's so dark now.'

After their departure Biman says, 'Do they think that I, belonging to their enemy camp, have come to put a spanner in the works?'

'Oh, come on Biman! Why should you be our enemy? But at the meeting this afternoon you feigned as though you didn't know me.'

'You're after all the leader of their agitation. Hence I thought that I shouldn't let them know that we are acquainted with each other.'

'Damn your leader! I'm nobody. Now tell me, did you really come for water?'

'Yes, I'm awfully thirsty. I don't touch alcohol once a week. I know I can get boiled water here.'

Shanti's younger brother suffered a mild injury on his forehead after he was pushed onto the ground by the police. Shanti has taken a day's leave from Mandira. She has also taken her salary in advance to buy provisions. Mandira fetches a glass of water for Biman.

Biman empties the water down his throat.

Lighting a cigarette, Biman holds out the packet for Mandira, who after a little hesitation, mumbles, 'I don't smoke in public.'

'This is sheer hypocrisy,' says Biman. 'If you're a smoker then why should you mind smoking in public? Well, let's go inside and smoke.'

'No, it's hot inside. Wait a little, I'm coming in a minute,' says Mandira in a brusque tone.

Going inside the house, Mandira quickly opens a drawer and brings out her cigarette packet and lighter.

Then coming back to the veranda she flings out the cigarette packet and lighter.

'What the hell are you doing?' shouts Biman.

Without giving a reply, Mandira steps down on the veranda and picks up the lighter. This will be of some use later, she thinks. Then she kicks the almost full cigarette packet further away.

Meanwhile a fine rain has set in.

'Have I offended you, Mani?'

'It's not that, Biman. Rather I'm grateful to you for reminding me of the word 'hypocrisy'. I agree with you that one shouldn't smoke clandestinely. I had long been contemplating to give up smoking.'

'It's a great thing to give up smoking. I've also been trying to quit smoking but in vain. I think an anti-pollution campaigner like you shouldn't smoke.'

'Are you making fun of me?'

'Perhaps a bit. You see it rouses some inferiority complex when you see somebody else giving up smoking.'

'Then why don't you give it up at once?'

'Of course I will. But it will be a little too excessive if I give up right now because of your insistence.'

'Biman, will you please do me a favour?'

'What is it? Do you want me to fetch you something from Calcutta?'

'No. I'll give you a phone number. Please speak to my daughter in London on the phone. I'm so anxious for her.'

'Certainly. I shall talk to her on the phone. But have you decided to stay here for an indefinite period and carry on with your madness?'

'Do you call it madness?'

'What else? If the factory comes up in an undeveloped area like Sukhchar, thousands of people will be benefited. The government has given its approval to this proposal made by an industrialist. So you can't stop it under any circumstances.'

'Will they proceed further even if the local people are against the setting up of the factory?'

'It matters little whether the local people are willing or not. These rustics have little environmental awareness and health consciousness. How many of them boil their drinking water like you? They use the same pond for washing clothes, bathing their cattle and cooking their own food. They smoke dozens of bidis on empty stomachs, eat stale and spoilt food and don't even get rid of the fish that has been decomposed.'

'Do you imply that these people shouldn't be given a chance of educating themselves simply because they're too naive to be aware of their own welfare? Should more doses of poison be given to them simply because they are poor, ignorant and don't know any better?'

'But the SUCI supporters are misguiding the public. They spare no opportunity to promote anti-government drives. That Chayan Ghose must be a SUCI supporter.'

'That I can't say for sure, but he talks like a Marxist.'

'They're all Marxists nowadays. A little learning and then they all profess to be scholars with their own interpretations of Marxism,' scoffs Biman.

'Forget them. But what is your opinion, Biman? Don't you think that in a densely populated locality like this one, comprising as many as thirty-eight villages, with a population of around one lakh people, the plant will pose a serious health hazard?'

'Listen Mani, that's not my lookout. I neither belong to the government nor to the factory owners. My job is to construct the factory shed, buildings and other infrastructure as per the blueprint. I've no reservations regarding the venue. It could be in the Sunderbans or in the Himalayas. But personally, I support the government, for the factory will immensely benefit the local inhabitants.'

'How?'

'It's a twelve crore rupees project. At least one thousand local youths will get direct employment. Besides, it has a great potential for indirect means of employment.'

'Are you sure? Does a twelve crore rupees project have the potential to employ so many people? I'm afraid the company is wooing the public by making tall promises. You're well versed in statistics. Another important factor is that the technicians, skilled workers and top executives will invariably be recruited from outside.'

'If it really fails to employ one thousand people, I'm sure at least half of this promised figure will be engaged. This is not a matter of joke. Also a new township will come up in connection with the plant. New roads, library buildings, playgrounds, club house, etc., will be constructed. Even the place may be linked by rail lines.'

'Won't they build temples?' banters Mandira.

'Temples? Mani are you making fun of me?'

'Biman, did you draft the contents of the leaflet brought out by the company?'

'Now you must be seriously joking with me, Mani. I've told you categorically that I don't belong to the company. What I'm saying is the truth, to the best of my knowledge. Look, Mr Dipak Roy Chowdhury is a nice person. He's so unassuming! He was sitting on a wooden bench for so long in a library hall like that. It was not essential for him to come over here and soil his feet. He could have simply got his job done by influencing the people at the helm of affairs at Writers' Building. Yet he took the trouble of personally meeting the common people. It's really embarrassing for us that he has been sent back under police escort to Calcutta.'

'Well, I've nothing to say against Mr Dipak Roy Chowdhury. He may be a nice person. But it's a fact that he's hell-bent on acquiring one hundred and twenty bighas of land by any means for his factory, even at the cost of displacing the poor peasants. It's illegal to engage the police force to oust the sharecroppers. Do you think Writers' Building will approve of this?'

'What has happened today is extremely regrettable, I agree. The police have indulged in some kind of excess,' admits Biman.

'Biman, do you know that the company representatives are going door to door, late in the evenings, to tempt the villagers with lucrative offers? To acquire land, they are promising attractive compensation packages that include employment for one member of each of the displaced families. They have even assured some families that they would bear the wedding expenses of their daughters. The vice president of the company that day paid a visit to the temple and met the priest, Mr Amal Halder. Having performed the puja rituals like a perfect devotee, he offered a generous amount of donation for the temple. Then he went to the extent of saying, "Sir, the temple building is in a dilapidated condition. We'll be pleased to rebuild a beautiful temple house after the construction of the factory. Please tell the devotees coming to the temple to give up their lands as soon as possible for the factory."'

Hearing this Biman bursts into peels of laughter and says, 'The vice president, Mr Chakraborty is a smart guy.'

'Now I suppose he'll visit the mosque to win the hearts of the Muslim landowners!' says Mandira.

Biman leans forward and, resting his hand on Mandira's shoulder, says, 'Mani, if they can acquire the lands without delay, the company will be benefited. And we are all looking forward to quick land acquisition and construction of the factory. Shouldn't the company try its best to reach this target? Where lies their fault?'

Holding Biman's hand on her shoulder, Mandira says, 'Your fingers are so soft even today! Biman, you are in the construction business. But if you are asked to build a gas chamber for human slaughter will you agree to the proposal?'

Withdrawing his hand quickly, an excited Biman says, 'Your comparison has no relevance here. When you people talk about the Bhopal Gas disaster, you blow the whole thing out of proportion. Why don't you recall the Chernobyl disaster? Three to four countries adjacent to Russia were also totally exposed to its radioactive emissions. Still, did Russia shut down its plants? Accident risk factor is a part and parcel of modern civilisation.'

'Chernobyl is far away from our country whereas Bhopal is at our doorstep. That's why the thought of Bhopal comes to our mind so quickly,' defends Mandira.

'There's always a risk factor while starting up a new venture, so you have to take precautions to avert accidents.'

'Not just accidents! This fertiliser plant will pose a permanent health hazard to the people living nearby.'

'You people are obsessed with the catchword pollution, a term imported from the West.'

'I've not imported it to this place. In fact, I had a sketchy knowledge of it before. The people of Sukhchar have made me well informed.'

'But many in Calcutta are under the impression that a lady from England has come to Sukhchar to educate local youths about how to protect the environment.'

'Believe me, some boys here know better than me. Have you ever thought that this small village could boast of a science club? Do the babus of Calcutta know this?'

'Mani, you're an enigma to many people. They're in the dark about your actual interest and purpose of staying here. They were enquiring into your passport. Had you been a British passport holder, you would have been thrown out of this country long ago. Foreigners are not allowed to live in the Sunderbans as it's adjacent to the Bangladesh border. It's a sensitive area. However I have informed them that you still hold an Indian passport.'

'The Sunderbans may be a sensitive area but don't they know that it's also recognised as a biosphere?'

'Let it be, I don't want to know further. By the way, I've decided to build a bungalow for you on the riverbank.'

The proposal is so unexpected that Mandira, eyebrows raised, keeps staring at Biman for a few moments. Then she mumbles, 'Bungalow for me!'

'Yes, I've designed it myself. I hope it'll be as beautiful as the small cottages you can find in the English countryside. Mani, you never invited me to your London residence. I visited London at least four times on business trips. I had met you only once there; that too was a chance meeting at the party at Dr Sen's residence at Belsize Park. That day you didn't talk to me even perfunctorily. I was so hurt then that I couldn't forget it till date.'

'Perhaps having seen you I had become nervous that day. I was under the impression that you were very angry with me. I feared that if I spoke to you, you would turn your face away from me,' says Mandira.

Sighing deeply, Biman says, 'Mani, I've never done anything to dishonour you. I intensely longed for you but you always said, "No, the time is not ripe yet." I believed that the time would certainly come one day. So I agreed to wait. But in the meantime a very long period elapsed. Twenty-seven years! Life has taken us in completely different directions. Now any relation of that sort ... oh no ... Mani, I don't expect much from you now. I just want to drop in at your house occasionally and spend some time chatting with you ... I hope you won't mind my coming to your house now and then.'

'But Biman, if you wish to meet me, you can come at any time to this house also. What's the need of a new house then? I'm quite at home here.'

'You can't live long in peace here. I've selected the site for your bungalow. Tomorrow I'll take you down there for your approval.'

'Are you trying to bribe me with a new bungalow?'

'Oh no! Your house will also be demolished for the plant. Besides, when the construction work will begin at the Lahiri Villa site, you won't like the round-the-clock noise and commotion. I must look after your comforts.'

'That means you want me to relinquish this house, courtyard and garden? Do you want this piece of land also for your company?'

Hurt at these charges levelled by Mandira, Biman says, 'Mani, are you doubting my intentions? Frankly speaking, I've never come to you on behalf of the factory. I've only come to see you ... Whether you'll sell this property or not is absolutely your prerogative. What I intended of course was that along with the huge construction work to be done under my supervision, I would build a small bungalow for you, without any extra effort. It is my foremost desire to gift you a splendid bungalow on the peaceful riverbank!'

In a tone of affected alarm, Mandira says, 'I can't live alone on the riverbank! I've heard of the marauders coming in boats to plunder. This house is much better ... I've grown attached to the trees I planted here ...'

Unmindfully Biman says, 'My wife wants to meet you. She suspects that I'm so keen about this project only because of you.'

'Why don't you bring her here one day?'

'Rupa's presumptions are not incorrect. Initially I had taken a keen interest in the project with the desire of meeting you frequently. I had submitted the lowest bid in response to the tender call. Mani, the day I came to know that you have returned from abroad, I went on thinking of you. I can't help it. To me you're still as pretty as you were in your early twenties.'

'I had never been as pretty as you're trying to establish,' says Mandira with a smile. 'None other than a man in a drunken state ever praised my beauty. But now nobody will even do that, for I'm getting old.'

Mandira, rising from the chair, swathes her bosom and back with the free end of her sari and says, 'A cool breeze is blowing, portending another bout of heavy shower. By the way, are you not hungry, Biman? I'm hungry. Come let's share my dinner.'

Sighing deeply, Biman says, 'You want me to leave, don't you? Don't worry, I'm not going to put up here tonight; a room has been booked for me in the PWD bungalow.'

'Then have your dinner with me,' suggests Mandira.

'No, thanks. I skip my dinner once a week ... I can only drink coffee.'

With Mandira, Biman walks into the kitchen that contains a handful of utensils, a hearth and a kerosene stove. Standing on the threshold Biman comments, 'I can't imagine how this could be the kitchen of a British Member of Parliament's wife. No gas oven, no cooking range!'

'After coming here I've realised that one can easily live with the help of a few things only,' replies Mandira.

'When I had gone to see you off at the airport I had never thought in my wildest dreams that you would marry in seven or eight months of your departure. I was hurt, humiliated and even terribly angry with you. I took you for a selfish opportunist. You hooked a bright boy of an aristocratic British family. But now relinquishing everything you've retired to this obscure village to lead an unassuming, humble life. I'm still in the dark about why you've chosen this life.'

'This is also a kind of selfishness. I'm seeking my happiness.'

'Let me see what is it that you eat at night.'

'Tonight I'll have khichdi. Shanti cooked that for my lunch. I'll heat the remnants before eating. I'm basically a non-vegetarian. With khichdi I've some shrimp curry. Now let me first make your coffee. Biman, will you taste the khichdi?'

'I hate khichdi; Mani, I've to frequently come to Sukhchar for the construction work. It'll be nice if you cook special dishes for me.'

'But Biman, we've decided that we won't allow the plant to come up here.'

'You won't allow? I tell you, this is an exercise in futility. When the government is backing us, what will you, a handful of people, do against it? Soon after this the cadres of the ruling party will also join hands with the administration. The MLA, Susovan Roy is also leaning towards us. I suggest you to stay out of it.'

Lighting the stove and placing the kettle on it, Mandira says, 'Will you let me tell you why we're against the plant? Once you listen, I hope you'll also support us.'

'Oh sure, go on.'

"This fertiliser plant will manufacture superphosphate and sulphuric acid—am I right? The by-product of these substances are some poisonous fumes like sulphur dioxide, sulphate and fluorine. So this plant should be set up far away from human habitation. Air poisoned by sulphur dioxide causes bronchial troubles. Around five hundred people may be employed in the plant but their children will be infected with lung diseases. There is no health centre in the vicinity of this area. No one will die in two to six months but posterity will bear the brunt of its harmful consequences.'

Giving her a quizzical look Biman says, 'You were not a student of science; how did you learn all this?'

'It's not essential to study science to know all this. Newspapers and magazines these days regularly bring out reports and articles on these issues. There's more. The acids and other toxic wastes will flow through the open sewers and be disposed into the Kanaibenki canal which is sluiced out into the Sathpukur gate, just five kilometres away from here. All the water bodies of the Sunderbans will be poisoned imperilling the existence of aquatic animals, especially fish. Some fish can survive this toxic hazard but humans eating these fish run the risk of embracing slow but inevitable death ... Annihilation or run the risk of embracing slow but inevitable death ... If the fish start dying thousands of fishermen will be out of work. Your plant will absorb one thousand people but render thousands jobless.

'The tale of woes doesn't end here. Sulphur dioxide, fluorine mixed with air will bring about acid rain which is extremely harmful for the flora and fauna of the Sunderbans. The lands, mostly low-lying, are flooded every year. Apart from being exposed to saline water all the year round, the agricultural lands, further exposed to industrial chemical wastes, will turn unproductive and barren.'

Sipping coffee, Biman says, 'I take it for granted that all your apprehensions are justified. But do you think the plant authorities and the government haven't considered these hazards? How did the pollution control board and the ministry of environment sanction it? As far as I know, one crore rupees has been earmarked for pollution control. There's also a provision for a hospital.'

'One crore out of twelve crores—that means only eight percent?' says Mandira.

Biman almost chokes on his coffee. He can't but say, 'Oh, you're really quick! You're so good at arithmetic.'

'It's simple arithmetic. How much is spent out of the state budget for pollution control? The meagre amount allocated for it is actually spent in paying salary and planting some saplings, most of which die in a few days. When there's a shortfall in other departments, they make up by squeezing the pollution control budget. The reason being that people at the helm of affairs in this country don't take pollution control seriously. I know you'll build a hospital; but when? After you've played havoc with public health?'

'Amazing! Within a couple of months, after you returned to this country, you've learnt lots of things,' exclaims Biman.

'One is able to detect it in a better way when one comes from outside. You people have got used to it. Now you are not in a position to gauge how toxic the air is in Calcutta. But as soon as I got off the plane, I felt so uncomfortable while breathing. There was a burning sensation in my nose.'

'These are the ways of this country, Mani. We're all helpless.'

'A little while ago you were saying that the village folks know nothing about pollution. But I think that the urban population knows even less, and the ones who are aware, are indifferent. Otherwise why should heaps of garbage lie accumulated on the streets of Calcutta? Why do people use cars and other vehicles with backdated engines belching out dense black smoke? Why do the motorists in Calcutta honk electric horns randomly or puja revellers blare loudspeakers deafening their fellow citizens? The urban people, not the village folks adulterate food.'

'Mani, I think these arguments will lead us nowhere. What's the use of drawing comparisons with other nations? This is the way of life in our country. We must make the best of the given circumstances. At every step of life, there's a potential hazard of this or that kind. I still believe that this plant will herald more benefits than harms for the local people. The state government is backing this project not out of sheer financial profits. The development of the masses is their first priority.'

'Dipak Roy Chowdhury is acquainted with quite a few ministers, isn't he?' asks Mandira.

'Maybe but it's not a significant factor.'

'Nepotism is ubiquitous. In the past we couldn't get to know much about the internal affairs of the socialist countries. But now it's an open secret that they're also not immune to this. They too accept bribes. The sons, sons-in-law, friends of top-level politicians are given lucrative jobs, contracts. They, who are in power, show generosity. In this project, however, the state government also has an indirect purpose. It can employ one thousand people through this project. It means a vote bank. Like you many others are convinced that in a country like India, pollution is no big deal; rather it is inevitable. But I clearly remember one Mr Sengupta, a member of the pollution control board, saying, "If you want to make a factory like this free from hazards, you must allot at least twenty-five per cent of the total budget for pollution control. Still you can't be sure that you're fully safeguarded." I think he said this because of his own conscience. But later, under political pressure, he was compelled to gulp back his own spit.'

'Mani, your khichdi has been long waiting for you. A cold dinner is also a kind of pollution!'

'Oh sure, I'm going to eat it presently. As a matter of fact, I didn't talk at length on this issue with the others. I only told you.'

'While coming to your house, I was thinking that we wouldn't talk on this issue. You're my friend. There are scores of other subjects to share with you. But ...'

'Biman, are you not my friend?'

'I'm sorry I raised the issue first. You must be thinking I belong to the enemy camp.'

'Still, you're my friend.'

Suddenly Biman moves forward and impulsively embraces Mandira. Then caressing her back affectionately with his hands, he says in a melodramatic tone, 'Mani, Mani, Mani!'

However, in a moment affections evaporate; Biman holding Mandira's chin tries to place his lips on hers.

Mandira turns her face away, saying in a jocular vein, 'Today you're not in drunken state, then why are you trying to do this?'

He says in an impassioned tone, 'Mani, won't you love me a little?'

'Why a little? I love you a lot. There is no longer any need for physical reminders of how much I love you.'

'Isn't the time ripe yet?'

'Wait. Let me first marry someone. After that I will have an extramarital affair with you. Let me first prove equal to you in marital status.'

'You want to remarry?' asks Biman scornfully.

Laughing like a teenager, she says, 'I long to. But who'll marry an old dame like me?'

'I didn't realise that you wished to remarry. I'm sorry. You can remarry, for you're still attractive and look much younger than you really are. You're still covetable.'

'You men are under the impression that women rejoice at your comments that they look younger for their age,' she rebuffs.

'But it's a fact,' insists Biman, 'women are really happy to hear that they look young for their age. Tell a forty-year-old woman that she looks like a twenty-seven-year-old. Her face will beam with delight at the compliment. But you need not hide your age, for you're ever young.'

'You used the term covetable. This is the general attitude of all men towards women. Women have always been the victims of the appetites of men. Meanwhile I must satisfy my appetite for food.'

Saying this Mandira washes her hands in soap water and takes out a china tray for her dinner. Taking some khichdi and shrimp curry on the tray, she says, 'Come, let's sit on the veranda. I'll chat with you there while eating. To be frank, I don't like indulging in small talk about age or looks. Some people, immediately after greeting each other, start commenting, "Wow! You've become so obese!", "You're looking so handsome!", "You look young for your age!" It sounds uncivilised. Can't a woman grow in years? Shouldn't her glamour fade? If she doesn't suffer from any chronic disorder then there's no barring her from enjoying life.'

'Women in countries with cold climates enjoy better health than their counterparts in tropical countries. Women in their fifties look far younger than they really are,' observes Biman.

'But women there develop wrinkles prematurely on their faces,' points out Mandira.

Sitting next to Biman, Mandira has a portion of her meal. Then she says very softly, 'Biman, I would like to ask you a question to which I expect an honest reply.'

'How can I tell you lies, Mani?'

'Look, you have financial stake in this project. The contract involves a huge amount of money. You want me to withdraw from the agitation, do you not?'

'Of course, Mani. I want you to keep off from this agitation. That is because I love you and don't want to see you getting into any trouble.'

'If I, applying the same logic, ask you to stay away from this project which is detrimental to humanity and nature?'

'What logic! If I resign from this project someone else will grab it at once; the project won't be put off.'

'Still, I'll be glad to know that you're not in the project. Then it'll be easier for me to fight against the authorities.'

'At this stage it's not feasible for me to give up since I've already signed the contract papers. Besides, I have partners, one of whom is my brother-in-law, who looks after the finance. We've already invested a lump sum in it. Now on what grounds shall I move out of it?'

'I also have similar commitments. Take the case of Shanti, a poor girl who works in my house. Her father is a sharecropper. His farmland has been snatched away from him. They're too poor to even have a single proper meal a day. Now shouldn't I fight for the retrieval of that land? Take the case of Bina, who was once a lazy devil, without any constructive thinking. But now she has a philosophy of life, wants to know more about the world around her and takes an active role in the agitation. I've honoured the arguments put forward by Sajjad and Chayan on the adverse effects of a fertiliser plant. Now if I pull out of this movement, my conscience will trouble me for the rest of my life.'

'I'm telling you again, Mani, they're making a mountain out of a molehill. The company will take precautions against pollution. Besides, what will you, a handful of so-called environmentalists do against the combined force of the factory owners and government? It's an exercise in futility.'

'Still we must try our best to keep our environment pollution free. There should be a beginning, however small it may be. A couple of movements of this kind in Kerala and Andhra Pradesh have reaped dividends very recently. The chief minister of Orissa had to wind up a similar project in view of a strong mass protest.'

'Where can one find open land in West Bengal?' asks Biman. 'Do you at least admit that there is a need of a fertiliser plant in our state?'

'Yes I do. But I also think that people don't need sulphur dioxide poison.'

Biman sighs and says, 'Now I should leave ... if I have to ... Tonight I have to myself drive all the way to the bungalow since my driver is not with me.'

Mandira is feeling very sleepy as she couldn't sleep properly the previous night. She is about to yawn but checks it. It's indecent to yawn in front of someone in Western society.

From the manner in which Biman is wearing his socks it's evident that he's reluctant to leave Mandira's home and go to the bungalow.

'Why are you staying back tonight at Sukhchar? Are you eager to see what happens tomorrow? We'll gherao the police station.'

Disgruntled, Biman bursts out, 'Yes, yes, you'll be in the procession and I'll be standing on the opposite side. It was written in our destiny.'

Laughing out loud, Mandira says, 'In our student life we walked side by side in the same procession on many occasions. Twenty-seven years elapsed since then.'

'Our life's journey took us in different directions. The vision of our youthful days to build a new social order has been shattered. Did you ever imagine that even in socialist countries draconian measures could be taken to crush the youths fighting for democracy, human rights and justice? Rubbish! I never supported capitalism; I hate dictatorship. The onslaught of corruption has made the fabric of democracy unstable. Socialism too is guilty of nepotism, autocracy, despotism and tyranny. Can you tell me for sure which system is ideal?' asks Biman in an impassioned tone.

'My mind is too small to tackle all the problems of the world. I'm just preoccupied with the problems of my immediate surroundings,' says Mandira.

'Your domestic help is on leave today. Are you not scared of staying alone?' asks Biman after he finishes wearing his shoes.

'It has been long since I've got accustomed to living alone. And if I shout for help, neighbours will rush to my help here.'

'Must I get back to the bungalow tonight? Can't I stay back at your home? What if you offer me shelter for a night?'

Resting her hand on his arm, Mandira says, 'No Biman, it's not high time yet.'

Extremely upset, he says, 'If the time is not ripe yet, then when will it be? Before that I'll die of old age! It's me who is always begging favours of you, but you never wanted anything from me.'

Then he hurriedly walks out and suddenly halts. He comes back to Mandira and says, 'Let the factory go to hell! Let money, wealth and personal interests go astray! Mani, I really care for you. Everything in my life will become meaningless if something happens to you. Mani, please take care; don't rush into anything on the spur of the moment.'

12

Mandira has enjoyed a sound sleep as the night became cool and refreshing after the showers.

She wakes up to behold a bright and sunny morning. The rains have stopped; the wet smell of the earth is being borne aloft through the air. A pair of Indian nightingales are sitting on the branches of a pomelo tree. From her bed Mandira can see them singing in full-throated passion. A buzzing hornet is flying all over the room. She is not scared of it, since she knows it won't sting unless provoked.

She stands by the window. She didn't anticipate the surprise waiting for her. Her eyes fall on a large rainbow in the sky. What a lovely sight! Can a morning be better than this? She becomes as merry as a kid. She recalls the lines she had read long ago: 'My heart leaps when I behold a rainbow in the sky!' Having muttered the lines twice she remembers another song that had been very popular in the early 1960s: 'There's a gold mine in the sky far away/ We will find it, you and I some sweet day ...' All of a sudden she cannot help recalling the Tagore song: *Ei to tomar alok dhenu surjya tara dole dole ... charao maha gagan tale ...* (Yonder shines your herd of the sun and the stars/ Where dost thou sit and play thy flute/ As they graze under the majestic firmament ...)

The singing nightingales keep springing up from one branch to another. While watching the sweet creatures, all of a sudden Robin's face flashes in front of her eyes. She used to affectionately call him Bulbuli (the Bengali name of a nightingale). Tom used to call him 'Robin Goodfellow'. Later when he grew up to discover that Robin was actually the name of a goblin in a fairy tale, he would throw about his arms and legs protesting, 'No-o-daddy, I'm not a good fellow!'

It has been long since she heard her children's voice. Do they remember their mother? She must write to them. They could be hurt by their mother's long silence.

The rainbow has slowly vanished into the sky. Today the sky is a resplendent blue. The trees and plants have been washed and cleansed by the night-long showers. What a splendid sight: a cluster of deep, yellow marigolds!

Mandira goes into the bathroom to brush her teeth. Her eyes fall on the wall. She must fix up a shelf on the wall to keep the toiletries. She opens the windows. After washing some clothes, she will have her lunch and set out for the meeting at the school playground.

While moving towards the veranda, she sees Shanti sitting outside. She's dozing, leaning against a column. She couldn't enter the house as the door was locked. Mandira fetches the keys to open the door. 'How long have you been waiting there? Why didn't you knock at the door?'

'I did but you didn't hear.'

Mandira is a bit embarrassed. She says, 'Really I had a sound sleep last night. Now put the kettle on for tea.'

Shanti looks behind. A well-built man is standing at a corner of the courtyard.

The man is Ghanashyam, Bina's father. He is clad in a dhoti and a blue shirt, holding a bundle of bindweeds in one hand.

After meeting Mandira's eye, he gravely says, 'I've come to talk to you about something urgent.'

'Please come and sit down on the veranda. I'm coming back after washing my mouth from the tubewell.'

Ghanashyam advances a little but doesn't sit.

Coming back from the tubewell, Mandira asks him, 'I hope you'll take tea? Shanti, boil more water.'

'No, thanks. I don't have tea,' says Ghanashyam.

With folded hands he says politely, 'Didi, please release my daughter.'

Mandira is somewhat flabbergasted. She says, 'Are you talking about Bina? She's not here. She went home yesterday evening.'

Ghanashyam, altering his tone subtly, repeats, 'Release my daughter.'

This time Mandira gets the drift of his statement. She has been in a buoyant mood since morning, but now her temper has slowly begun to rise in Ghanashyam's presence. The man could have come later.

'I haven't held up your daughter,' says Mandira.

'Her marriage has been fixed up. Now do you think she should remain as wayward and shameless as before?'

Mandira remains silent.

'Your house is a meeting place of different types of people including Muslims. I don't want my daughter to flirt with them,' says Ghanashyam quite rudely.

'You may say this to your daughter. I don't force her to come here.'

'You must forbid her to come to your house,' he shouts.

'Ghanashyam babu, you can't dictate things to me. It's my prerogative to decide who'll come to my house and who'll not. You have no right to interfere. What you can do at best is to ask her not to come to my house any more.'

Ghanashyam lights a bidi and says, 'I've told her several times but she doesn't listen. I know what attracts her. I've been reported that in your house they indulge in vulgar revelry and debauchery. This must not be allowed to continue in our village.'

Wearing the same smiling expression, Mandira replies, 'You've been misguided. No one indulges in any kind of vulgarity here. Some youths meet in my house to discuss about the welfare of the village. You're unnecessarily worried for your daughter. Believe me, she hasn't done anything wrong.'

'Who the hell are you to think of our welfare? Do you think we are in dire straits? Make your tall talks in your towns ... in Calcutta.'

Mandira looks straight into his eyes while remaining very still.

Raising his finger he says, 'How dare you be so impudent with me? Don't forget, I can throw you out of the village any day.'

Without losing her patience she replies, 'You're trying to frighten me; I take strong exception to your threats. What you're doing is against the law.'

Ghanashyam, raising his voice further, shouts, 'I don't care a damn for your law. Law is ... my foot! I can oust you from your homestead. Your house will be on fire. If you want to save your skin, get lost from here. The sooner will be the better for you.'

Mandira stands staring at him. She is too hard a nut to crack. It's very difficult to scare her off. Threats make her more obstinate.

In the same quiet tone, she says, 'I won't go anywhere. You can't harm me in the slightest possible way. And if you do anything rash, you'll have to serve imprisonment, though I don't want this either.'

Flying into a rage, he shouts back, 'What? You are threatening me of imprisonment? Were you not a woman ...'

'Ghanashyam babu, you're out of your senses now. Please go home,' says Mandira.

Having cast one last scorching look at Mandira, he turns back and walks away quickly.

Shanti was hiding behind the door. Now she whispers into Mandira's ears, 'Didi, you shouldn't have provoked him. He's a hot-tempered mastaan. They even have a gun!'

Now, seeing Shanti, Mandira gives vent to her pent-up anger. 'Haven't you boiled the water yet? I've not yet had a cup of tea since morning!' she says to Shanti rather brusquely.

'The water is boiling! Just like your temper, didi!' Shanti banters.

Mandira cannot help laughing. Then she says, 'Fetch the kettle, cups, etc., here.'

Having brought the things, Shanti says, 'The man was threatening you with dire consequences. Yet you did not budge an inch from your stance! He had once cracked the heads of two people trying to loot his fishery.'

'Why should I be scared? You people are basically cowards. You die of fear, which is the root of your misery. You have seen what happens here. Tell me, do you think we indulge in shady activities?'

'If he really sets your house on fire?'

'Pooh! It's an empty threat.'

'Ah didi, what should be done with the bundle of bindweed that the man has left behind in rage?'

'Go to his place and return it to him.'

'If he vents his temper on me?'

'Then can't you give him a fitting rebuff? They are encouraged because you suffer the insults quietly'

Oh didi, you're too naive to understand the consequences of such an act of audacity on my part. If I try to argue with him he will not only thrash me but give a drubbing to my father also ... My father occasionally gets some odd jobs at his fish depot.'

'Okay, then you need not go. Keep it aside. Meanwhile if nobody comes to take it back, then cook it for our lunch. Why should we waste it?'

In order to forget the nasty episode, that threatens to mar the rest of her day, Mandira has taken a long time to bathe today.

Biman's thought flashes through her mind. He is chivalrous, just like an Englishman. Again Mandira knew some Britons who were rather uncivil. Behind the mask of courtesy and civility they hide their ferocious natures.

Biman hugged her twice last night. The gap of twenty-seven years no longer seems to be a huge one. Mandira liked the warmth of his embrace. As though, Biman's chest is a nice refuge. But she can never belittle herself before his wife.

Ghanashyam's threats hardly seem worth the bother to Mandira. But will Bina be the target of her father's rage? Now along with the campaigns against the fertiliser project, she should also fight for the emancipation of girls like Bina. When parents impose their will upon these girls, should it not be treated as a disguised form of domestic violence and violation of human rights?

After a simple meal of rice, daal, bindweed mush and boiled eggs, Mandira tells Shanti, 'Come, let's leave for the procession.'

Shanti says, 'Should we leave the house unguarded? If Bina di's father sets the house on fire?'

'I've threatened to send him to jail; he won't dare to do anything further.'

Locking the front door they set out. Clouds are again gathering in the sky. The atmosphere all around is in shadows. Won't the rains stop this year? The eastern sky is overcast with dark clouds.

The school building is situated on an elevated spot of land. In times of flood, some families take shelter in this building. Due to this year's flood some houses at Dhalipara were flooded. The affected residents had taken shelter in the school building. The classes remained suspended. The twenty or twenty-five people who had taken shelter in this building returned home yesterday.

The procession is about to set off at one-thirty p.m. but the attendance is still thin. Some children are found hollering around while a handful of adults are squatting at a corner of the field. The villagers have gone to the paddy fields or river for fishing. They're not in a position to forsake a day's income and take part in the procession.

It's an uphill task to explain the health hazards of a fertiliser plant to these simple folks. They're too naive to distinguish between the common smoke produced from the burning of charcoals and the sulphur dioxide gas emitted from the fertiliser plants.

The harmful effects of pollution on the future generations, to be caused by the fertiliser plant or poisoning of fish, is always subservient to the lucrative offers of employment in the upcoming industries. However, yesterday's police excesses, to repress the agitators, have enhanced the popularity of the Charbazaar Welfare Society. Many landowners of Sukhchar now live in Calcutta and their lands are cultivated by sharecroppers. The sharecroppers know that the government has given them the right to cultivate the land. Even if the land is sold they won't be deprived of that particular right. Meanwhile the rumour has spread across the region that the industrialists, in collusion with the government and police, have begun to oust the sharecroppers. This is very bad news for them. Nobody knows who will get a job in future and who will not. But right now it's going to spell disaster for the sharecroppers. Again, if cultivation comes to a halt, the landless labourers will also be jobless. So the sharecroppers and the landless peasants have started to join today's protest march.

Under the guidance of Chayan Ghose some young boys are writing posters. Mandira cannot find Sajjad there.

Unless there's an assemblage of at least one hundred people they can't make much of the procession. So they have to wait some time more. Heaven forbid there should be rainfall again.

Climbing onto the veranda, Mandira is inspecting the posters, four of which are written in Bengali and two in English. English has these days made its inroads into the remote villages of Bengal. Perhaps the persons carrying the posters won't know the meaning of what is written on the posters. English is essential for the government officials. 'Pollution is no solution!', 'Save forests of Sunderban!' Once it occurs to Mandira that she should tell them to add 'the' before Sunderban and 's' after Sunderban. For a long time she worked as a copy editor. If she ever happens to come across a misspelt word or even a slightly wrong usage of language she always feels an irresistible urge to correct it. But she changes her mind. Forget it! What is the need of perfect English in a remote village? Let the government officials realise that today's protest march is not merely provoked by a lady who has returned from abroad; rather this is the outcome of the spontaneous outburst of the village folks.

One of the Bengali slogans is very beautiful. It says, 'Not only food for the hungry, we also want free air, free from poison.' The phrase 'free from poison' could have been deleted. The expression 'free air' itself is ironical. Well, let it be what it is.

Squatting down beside Chayan, she asks, 'When do you want to start the procession?'

'Oh my God, you've sat there! The place is smeared with ink ... your sari will ... please wait, they'll soon fetch a chair from inside,' says a concerned Chayan.

'It's alright, you needn't be so formal with me,' says Mandira in a hushed tone. 'By the way, how can you hope to start a procession with such a thin attendance?'

'I've sent a few boys to gather some more people. Without a couple of hundreds, we can't make any impact. I've heard that many officers have arrived from Calcutta. A huge number of police personnel have been deployed. They have also brought CPM party cadres from other places. Look how the MLA, Susovan Roy, has ditched us.'

'Chayan, are you a supporter of SUCI?' Mandira asks.

'Why this strange question?'

'Oh, just for the sake of curiosity. Many are under the impression that the SUCI is organising this agitation against the Left Front government.'

'I have never been a SUCI cadre. Everyone knows me as a committed CPM cadre. I've even campaigned for Susovan Roy during the elections. But of late I don't feel drawn to class struggles, revolutionary ideals and elections. Instead I love to work for the eradication of religious fundamentalism, superstition and casteism from society and creating health awareness among masses. I feel these things should have a prior claim over everything else in a country like ours.'

'But are not these things more difficult to tackle than politics itself?'

'Of course, and therefore more challenging as well. Many political leaders in Calcutta suffer from a sense of complacency that West Bengal, unlike many other states of India, is not plagued by the evils of communalism and caste prejudices. They're unaware that communal parties like VHP and RSS have already spread their tentacles to the remote areas of the state. The Muslim League and Jamate-Islami are not lagging behind. Riots may erupt at the slightest provocation. You may be aware of the Katra Mosque episode in Murshidabad.

'Innocent lives were lost there for no reason. The idea of revolution is a mirage until religious fanaticism is driven out of our society. Once upon a time the word "revolution" was associated with a romantic halo, but now things have undergone a radical change.

'But one good sign, Mandira di, is that both the Hindus and Muslims are equally affected by the land acquisition stance of the government against the sharecroppers. That's why our strategy is that we'll never allow the government to acquire land from the farmers and sell it to the factory owners.'

'Where's Sajjad?'

I'm also worried about his delay ... he should have been here already.' Saying this Chayan calls aloud, 'Javed, come here.'

Javed is sitting alone, aloof from the others present there. He looks like a black statue; squatting in a corner and keeping a safe distance from the rest of the people, he is peeling the hard skin off a sugarcane with his teeth.

Chayan says, 'This is Javed who ekes out his living by fishing, though his father is a small farmer. The small piece of land owned by his father has also been acquired by the company.'

Javed says that he met Sajjad in the morning. He has come here only because Sajjad had requested him to attend the gathering.

'Will you please go and see why is he late?' says Mandira to Javed.

He looks at her. His eyes are scarred with red spots and his face betrays repressed anger.

In a rather harsh tone he replies, 'Brother Sajjad knows his responsibility. He'll arrive on time.'

'Still you could ride on your bicycle to make a quick round and see if you can find him,' insists Mandira.

'I don't have a bicycle.'

'Where are the girls? Bina was saying that she would bring them ...' says Chayan.

'Oh, Bina won't be coming,' says Mandira.

No sooner has she said this that Bina comes running towards them. Her hair dishevelled, the free end of her sari flying in the air, against the backdrop of dark clouds she looks like a character from a film.

In a low tone Mandira explains to Chayan, 'Her father is strongly against his daughter stepping out of home to take part in these activities. Will it be right on our part to encourage Bina? Her father will create trouble for us.'

Pooh-poohing Bina's father, Chayan says, 'I don't care for him. You better talk to Bina to be sure whether she has the guts to come with us defying her father. By the by, the SDO is now in the local police station. We'll go and hand him the memorandum. The police may resort to lathi charge to disperse us.'

Javed spits contemptuously on the ground.

'I couldn't call anybody ... but I've come!' says Bina panting desperately.

Her daughter Liz would also have behaved similarly if she were here in Bina's position. In fact, intrinsically individuals do not vary much from one another, Mandira thinks to herself.

'What will you do alone? You should have called many other women,' Chayan reproaches Bina.

'Why, there are two of us—Mandira di and myself.'

'Now we need some more womenfolk. Go quickly to Daspara once before we start the procession. See if you can garner some supporters there. We still have some time in hand,' says Chayan.

'The poor girl! Let her take some rest first.'

Bina casting a glance at Chayan runs off at once.

Chayan asks Javed to fetch a glass of water for him. Javed having brought two glasses of water, offers one to Mandira.

Mandira is a bit surprised. 'I didn't want it,' she says.

'You won't take it?'

Mandira shakes her head. In fact she feels revulsion at the sight of the tin glasses used by scores of people. Who knows whether they are clean or not? Moreover she drinks boiled water only.

With controlled fury, Javed throws the water out of the glass onto the ground.

A little later a jeep stops in front of the school gate. Sajjad is sitting inside. A middle-aged man alighting from the jeep comes near Chayan and greets him and Mandira with a smile.

The man is not known to Mandira. Chayan introduces him to her saying, 'He's our local officer-in-charge, Bhaktipada babu.

'What's the matter Bhaktipada babu? Have you arrested Sajjad?'

With a beaming smile the OC says, 'Oh! What are you saying? As a matter of fact the SDO wants to speak to him once. You're also requested to come, Chayan babu.'

'We're going to meet him shortly to place a memorandum,' says Chayan.

'Yes, but before that he wants to speak to you in private. It's urgent. He knows you personally.'

'I don't think I have anything personal to discuss with him right now. I intend to speak to him in the presence of others only.'

Keeping his hand on Chayan's shoulder, the officer tries to cajole him into going with him.

'Are you going to arrest me, if I don't come with you?' Asks Chayan firmly.

The officer bursts into a laughter that reeks of affectation. 'What are you saying, brother! I've just come to escort you to a friendly talk with the SDO. Sajjad sahib is also going with you. It won't be long.'

Turning to Mandira, Chayan says, 'Now I can see that I must go. Meanwhile you should carry on with the preparations for the procession.'

From the jeep Sajjad is staring at Mandira. He looks disturbed. His wrinkled forehead indicates that he is anxious to speak to her. But the latter is in a fix whether she should approach Sajjad. She feels snubbed by the police officer's nonchalant attitude.

Javed at once jumps from the veranda and runs towards the jeep. He asks in an anxious tone, 'Brother, why are you sitting in the police jeep?'

A constable from inside the jeep howls at him, 'Get the hell out of here.'

Nobody can hear what Sajjad is trying to say from inside the jeep.

Soon the jeep speeds away with Chayan.

A distraught Bishnupada Halder of Mamudpur demands, 'Madam, why did you let the police take away Chayan? What right do they have to do this?'

A sense of guilt overpowers Mandira. But would the police have listened to her pleas? Nobody on earth has the slightest suspicion that they have arrested Chayan. They could have at best jointly lodged a protest.

'Why didn't you people say anything?' asks Mandira.

'We thought that since you were in front you would obviously protest,' replies Bishnupada Halder.

Thereafter they get themselves embroiled in a kind of debate and heated discussion that continues for an hour or so. They are undecided about whether today's programme can be carried out or not. In the absence of Sajjad and Chayan, who is there to lead the agitators? Meanwhile one or two people, who have been to the vicinity of the police station, come back with the news that the SDO has left long ago and Sajjad and Chayan have not been released yet. There is no way also for Mandira to confirm the news.

Bina comes back accompanied by seven to eight women protesters from Daspara. The procession should start right now—many of them are of this opinion. They say, 'If we put off today's agenda, it will lose credibility in the eyes of the common protesters. We should immediately march towards the police station and mount pressure on the administration to release Chayan and Sajjad.'

Mandira is in a dilemma. She is being urged by the folks to lead the procession. But she is also haunted by her outsider image. Should it be proper for someone coming from outside to instigate the local people against the administration? Mandira had been abroad for a long time. Her opponents will cash in on this loophole against her.

The sky is overcast with dark clouds, accompanied by thunderstorms, though the rain hasn't started yet. About ninety men and women have assembled today. None of them is in a spirit to go back home.

At long last Mandira agrees to lead the procession. It's difficult for her to turn a deaf ear to the persistent pleas of a crowd of protest marchers.

Fighting shy of her reclusive nature, Mandira raises her voice: 'Friends, brothers and sisters, we'll now march towards the police station and press for the release of Chayan and Sajjad. If they don't listen to us we'll gherao the police station. But I would like to make it a point that our agitation will all along remain peaceful. None of us will let out a holler nor try to tussle with the police, for in that case we'll lose in the unequal fight. Please try to remain unfazed at the sight of the cops.'

The women have been asked to lead the march. Bina is followed by Mandira. Bina and another comrade hold aloft the red festoon of the Charbazaar Welfare Society.

While walking in the procession, Mandira is overcome by strange feelings. It occurs to her that she has been walking on a land, billion miles away from Kensington apartment or the residence of Harrow on the Hill. It is as though this is a different planet. Even when she lived in Calcutta in her early youth, never did she feel such an affinity with her country, its people and their lives.

Sheer curiosity brings some householders out of the thresholds of their houses to glare at the procession passing by them. Someone from the procession over-enthusiastically calls out, 'Come on brothers and join us.' None, however, seem to have responded to his call.

In a conscious state of mind Bengalis perhaps cannot keep mum for long. Defying Mandira's instructions, someone raises the slogan: 'We want the release of Chayan Ghose and Sajjad! We are not going to tolerate the tyranny of the police!! We are against the setting up of a factory that'll kill human beings!!!'

Now Mandira doesn't feel right about stopping them. She is, after all, not their leader.

Bina apologetically says, 'Everyone can't read the posters. That's why they're shouting slogans ...'

'Bina, didn't your father stop you today from coming here?'

Giggling, she replies, 'Father had shut me in a room but mother opened the door. I told my mother that if he beats me again, I'll pour kerosene on my body and set myself on fire.'

'Your father beats you?'

'He beat me yesterday night. Coming from your house this morning also he beat me up. Mandira di, had your father beaten you what would you have done?'

'How can I say? My father never raised his hand on me. In fact, no one has ever raised a hand on me.'

'Nevertheless think of a situation like this: You were born in a village like me ... you didn't study much ... let alone the question of going abroad ... your father shuts you in a room all day. What would you have done?'

'I would never have thought of setting myself on fire. I would have walked out of my home and gone away to a far-off place never to be disclosed to him.'

'If they don't release Chayan da, I'll also stay in the lock-up. Will they torture him?'

'God knows. The OC was very courteous then.'

'That they do but when they get you inside the lock-up, they torture you to death.'

'But Chayan is not an offender after all,' points out Mandira.

The road is muddy. Mandira treads on cowdung. She is the only woman wearing shoes in the procession. The others are effortlessly striding barefooted. She feels nausea at the thought of her rubber sandals being plastered with animal excrement. She can't wash her feet now. Instead of cowdung, London streets are exposed to dog's excrement in the early morning hours as people take their pet dogs out for walks in the streets. Once she had stepped on canine droppings. As she was then very close to her residence, she got rid of the shoes on the spot and came back home barefooted.

But here she dare not do that since the broken pieces of glass, dry bones and oyster shells have made the road treacherous. So she keeps on walking in the soiled shoes.

Approaching Battala crossing they find a crowd occupying the road. Apart from three to four policemen, the crowd mostly comprises well-dressed men, perhaps brought from outside by the proposed factory owners. From the manner in which they are blocking the road, it's evident that they won't allow the procession to move beyond Battala.

Expecting Biman to be present in the crowd, Mandira strains her eyes to locate him but can't. She is not sure whether he is inside one of the vehicles parked behind the crowd.

What next? In the absence of Chayan, Sajjad and a formidable leadership, what is going to be the fate of the agitation? They should have anticipated this beforehand. It won't be wise for them to try to penetrate through the baton-wielding policemen lest it should result in a clash.

Mandira's face is creased with wrinkles borne out of anxiety and bewilderment. Again should the protesters disperse in fear of the cops, it would be a herculean task to assemble them in the near future.

She is reluctant to lead the agitation. But all her female comrades are eagerly looking upon her. So it's not a moment for vacillating.

She raises her voice to address her comrades: 'Please squat on the ground. None of you should flee from here. Like them we'll also block the road.'

In spite of her appeal, a couple of women run towards the opposite direction. Many men also have started fleeing. At this point Mandira realises the need for one or two more leaders to boost the sagging morale of the confused lot. Some kids are shouting slogans: 'We don't want a human slaughterhouse in the name of a plant! Stop police atrocities on innocent people!'

At once someone pelts brickbats at the police.

'Who's pelting bricks? Quietly sit down on the ground,' Mandira commands.

But more missiles are being hurled at the police. Someone says, 'We aren't throwing stones. Some people, not belonging to us, are doing this.'

This has created a pandemonium since the demonstrators are apprehending the worst as they find themselves hemmed in by their opponents from the back and the front. Most of the agitators are running pell-mell, either to the left or right, crashing through the undergrowth. Bina tries her best to resist the fleeing girls but fails. The cops are advancing towards them.

Mandira immediately decides to stay where she is. She will not fizzle out so quickly.

The policemen, holding their batons like crossbars, push the demonstrators away. They, however, avoid hurting any person; they just aim at keeping the agitators off. Interestingly enough, they have avoided Mandira.

A young police officer approaches Mandira and says very politely, 'Madam, please come with us.'

'Where to? Are you arresting me?'

'Oh no! We want to remove you from this unpleasant situation for your own safety; come inside the car, please!'

'No, I won't come with you.'

Suddenly Mandira's attention is diverted by an uproar. She turns to the right to find to her horror, Javed being dragged by two constables. One of them is holding him by his hair while the other is lashing him with the baton and hurling filthy abuses.

Mandira cannot fathom why they have singled out Javed for such merciless treatment. Is it the fallout of an old grudge? Someone from the crowd shouts, 'Hit him more, leave that blackguard half dead!'

Mandira tries to run towards Javed. Right then two girls come forward and hold Mandira tightly on both sides. One of them with a coquettish smile says, 'Didi, please sit in the car.'

Who are they? Police? Party comrades? Mandira is in the dark.

She tries to extricate her hands from their vice-like grip. The girls, still smiling, hold her tightly. She doesn't like the idea of applying force.

'What on earth are you trying to do with me? Leave me alone. I won't come with you!'

Still holding her tightly the girls move her a little away from there.

By this time, beaten black and blue, Javed has fallen to the ground. Still he springs up and pushes a cop onto the ground. Then he picks up a brickbat. Another cop, raising the baton over his head, shouts at him, 'You scoundrel, you bloody mollah!' The young officer brings out the revolver from his waist pocket.

One of the two girls whispers into Mandira's ears, 'You'll talk to the SDO, won't you? Then what are you waiting for here? Come, let's go.' They push Mandira out of the spot while she keeps pleading, 'Don't kill the poor fellow! Please spare him!'

Having flung the brick, Javed turns round and leaps into a bush. One of the cops chases him like a greyhound. Mandira can't see what happens next as she has already been thrust into the jeep. She can't even get an opportunity to give any instruction to Bina or Shanti. The procession is completely ransacked. She feels utterly helpless and decides to lodge a protest with a high-ranking official such as the SDO. If she luckily meets Sajjad and Chayan there, she will gain more gumption.

She is made to sit at the back of the jeep, guarded by the two girls.

Now large drops of rain come pelting down.

13

Mandira is standing at an unknown place.

On one side of the asphalted road, stands a huge peepul tree and a bog lies on the other side. After a heavy shower, the road bears a deserted look. All around being dark, she fails to locate any hut or shanty nearby.

She is burning in rage and humiliation. But she can't do anything. The police jeep, instead of taking her to the SDO, aimlessly went round in circles through this or that way in the rain.

She is not sure whether those two girls were cops or just party cadres. They were trying to convince her that the work at the project site had already made much headway, hence it was a futile attempt on their part to try to halt the progress of the fertiliser factory. Rather, it would have tarnished Sukhchar's image had an educated, respectable lady like Mandira been accidentally hurt in the fiasco.

She was obstinately silent in their presence, determined to call on the SDO and get her point across to him only.

After roaming around aimlessly for one and a half hours, the jeep halted here. The young police officer, sitting beside the driver, jerked his head out of the window and said, 'Now get down here and go home.'

A shiver ran down her spine at that moment. She had heard in Europe how the police in India would set a prisoner free in a lonely, desolate place and ask him to flee. When the man would take to his heels, they'd shoot him down. The next day's report would be: 'One dies in police encounter.'

With that apprehension deeply rooted in her mind, she asked, 'Now, will you kill me?'

The young officer burst into laughter. 'Oh no! How can you even think of such an absurd thing, madam? Why should I kill you? You're a respectable lady. Have any of us misbehaved with you? For your safety, we just removed you from the troubled spot.'

'Why didn't you allow me to meet the SDO?'

'The SDO has gone away to Calcutta to attend an urgent meeting. Neither the SDO nor the DM is available today.'

One of the girls said, 'Didi, you'll get your bus from here. You won't face any trouble reaching home. We are heading in the opposite direction, otherwise, we could have given you a lift.'

Soon they reversed their jeep and sped away leaving Mandira stranded under this peepul tree.

Since then Mandira has been standing at a stretch. Till now not a single bus has passed by.

Resorting to lies, the police removed Mandira from the procession, ostensibly to safeguard her from being injured. Was it the contrivance of the police? Also, is Biman involved in this plan? If it is so, she will never see his face again.

Mandira's left foot is still smeared with cowdung, her sari is spattered with muck water, but she is paying no heed to it. She is concentrating with an iron will on one single point: she must wield her pen to write to the chief minister, editors of national dailies and highlight the Sukhchar issue. She must teach a lesson to people like Biman and Dipak Roy Chowdhury. They must learn that mass movements can't be suppressed by coercive powers of the police. Since she has already soiled her feet, she'll never acknowledge defeat so quickly without a fight.

Meanwhile, she has seen no vehicles, except two lorries passing by. After the rain has stopped, a couple of cyclists have started plying. One of them stops to cast a scrutinising glance at Mandira standing under a tree and then rides past. The poor fellow must have been startled at the bizarre sight—an attractive, respectable lady standing there; it's really like a hallucination.

A bullock cart is seen coming at a snail's pace; there is no trace of a bus. Buses on most of the routes in these areas stop plying by sunset. Mandira doesn't know in which direction she must go to reach Sukhchar. Whom should she ask now? She is paralysed with fear.

A cycle-rickshaw van going past Mandira, halts at a little distance.

'Will you come?' asks the van puller.

Mandira very gratefully asks the man, 'Will you take me to Sukhchar?'

'Sukhchar? That's a long way from here. I'm not going in that direction.' Saying this the man resumes cycling. But at once, he stops to say, 'I can drop you off at Kumorpara crossing; from there you'll get the van to Sukhchar.'

Without a shed, square in shape, these cycle-rickshaw vans are used for carrying goods as well as passengers. This is Mandira's maiden ride on this bizarre country cart. The passengers have to sit on it by dangling their legs. She is feeling uncomfortable as the van is springing up on the potholes in pitch darkness. She is tightly grabbing the wooden planks, yet is time and again on the verge of losing balance and lunging forward or backward by the sudden jumps on the bumpy road.

'You were standing alone there; it's not safe. The place is known as Dakatepara, a common haunt for robbers,' the van puller says.

'You've done me a great favour. Could I have got a bus from there?'

'The last bus has left at six p.m. Whose house did you come to visit here?'

'I've lost my way,' says Mandira.

Without showing further inquisitiveness, the man suddenly starts singing aloud:

Had God possessed eyes
The pious would have never been sad.
Obviously He would have been considerate.
Had the sugarcane trees borne fruits
How sweet would have the fruits been
And then would have increased His glories.

It's a folk song which Mandira would have enjoyed in normal circumstances; but now her mind is boiling in rage. She is soliloquising with the voice of her own psyche. Again she imagines that she is conversing with her ex-husband, who as it were is raising his finger and mocking her, 'Is this your freedom? Indians are yet to be independent. They don't know the meaning of fundamental rights. The police take them away at their own sweet will to harass, to heckle, paying no heed to human rights. You don't know where you're threading your way through mud, dirty water, pitfalls ... this van puller can easily kill you as you travel across dark, desolate paddy fields.' She replies, 'This is an insignificant chapter of my life. I haven't thrown in the towel yet, Tom. I might have been held by the police for the time being, but the villagers value me, honour my views. I've found a way of linking my humble existence with the stream of life in this country. In England, I had nothing really, to call my own. This van puller won't harm me, for look, he's singing in pure ecstasy. Those who sing with such joy in their hearts can never be criminals.'

Biman had warned her against danger. Mandira doesn't care for any danger. She'll certainly reach Sukhchar. Tomorrow she'll send off letters to different places. She will hone her powers of expression in English; the newspapers will be obliged to publish her letters. The urban populace is unaware about many incidents of riots, violence, bloodshed, police atrocities taking place in the rural areas. Unless a man is murdered, it makes no news. Chayan Ghose, who regularly scans newspapers, has said that no news has so far been published in any newspaper on the Sukhchar movement or about the high-handedness of the fertiliser plant authorities.

Kumorpara crossing is like a small marketplace, though most of the shops now have their shutters down. With three or four passengers, a solitary van is waiting to take off. Mandira occupies a seat in it, that too after a great deal of pleading. Though the van won't go up to Sukhchar, it will drop her off on the main road.

Altogether seven passengers have been taken on that van; Mandira is the only woman passenger. She has had to sit in a huddle with strangers with unpleasant body odours, but none of her co-passengers shows the slightest curiosity about her.

After an hour's ride, the van halts at another crossing. The puller says, 'Didi, please walk straight along that road to the right, go past the Shiva temple, take a left turn and you'll find your way to Sukhchar. It's not far away from here.' Her shoe is torn; but she will never walk barefoot. She keeps on walking.

There's no arrangement of streetlights in these areas. It's pitch dark all around. Even though there have been heavy bouts of shower for days on end, the sky is still overcast with clouds. Due to this the road has been broken in many places; Mandira is stumbling repeatedly. The shoe gets torn further; but she won't get rid of it and walk barefoot. So she keeps walking unsteadily wearing that torn shoe.

She has heard of notorious robbers prowling in these areas but nobody has attacked her today. She is travelling alone so late at night; undoubtedly she is frightened but she has had safe passage so far. Having spotted the Shiva temple, Mandira heaves a sigh of relief; she knows this place.

Having walked along the road on the left and crossed the Battala, she is surprised to find no trace of the events that took place here this afternoon. The place is as dark as any other place. Except the chirping of crickets, the entire land is plunged in silence. Why did the police stop the procession of villagers who wanted to meet the SDO? It is a fundamental democratic right of the people to send a deputation. Did they kill Javed? They ultimately singled him out! They were desperate to kill him; was it because he was a strong and sturdy fellow who was hobnobbing with the Muslim fanatics? But Javed didn't join the procession with that particular identity. When they were beating him, Mandira couldn't help him as the two girls were holding her back. At least had she been once able to extend her hand in sympathy to Javed!

Where did they take Chayan and Sajjad? On what grounds did they arrest them though the procession had not started yet? Can they detain them without proper grounds? In the rural areas the police make a mockery of the law of the land.

What's the time now? The entire village seems to have gone to bed.

Stepping on the courtyard of her house, she heaves a sigh of relief. Also, she is greatly astonished. The police released her at an unknown place far away from home. The place, they say is called Dakatepara. Yet she didn't have to stave off any danger. At least she has come back home unharmed.

Twice she calls out to Shanti.

Getting no reply she realises that Shanti is not there. The door is locked. Now Mandira remembers that she took the key with her; how could Shanti have entered the house?

Fishing out the key from her handbag, she opens the front door. Before entering the house, she washes her feet at the tubewell. She throws the shoes away. If there's no water in the bathroom, she will have to bathe by the tubewell. Now she doesn't wear a wristwatch, so coming inside the room she looks for the torchlight to see the table clock. Had she taken the torchlight today, it would have been of great use. She'll never repeat the mistake in future. The time is eleven p.m. by the table clock, yet the village seems to have been engulfed in a pall of silence. Shouldn't she find out whether Bina is safe or not? Had Shanti been here, she could have sent her to Bina's house. She herself is not in the mood to go to her house at this hour of the night.

Lighting the stove she prepares tea. Now she begins to feel quite refreshed. Her brain doesn't function if she doesn't get a cup of tea in the afternoon. After tea she pines for a cigarette. Oh no, she has quit smoking.

Now she'll have to take a bath. After that, she'll draft some angry letters to the home secretary, chief minister, editors of English dailies, Press Trust of India. She'll also write to Philip Larkins, the Delhi correspondent of *London Times* and whom Mandira once met. Publicity through

European media works like magic and rouses the central government from its slumber. She is also contemplating to contact Amnesty International. She will not give up.

But soon after taking a bath, cleansing her whole body with soap water and removing all the mud and dirt, she feels exhausted. She doesn't feel like drafting the letters now. The tube light has almost run out of battery. Instead of keeping the lantern on, she decides to procrastinate the business of drafting letters for the next day. And foregoing her supper, she bolts the door and goes to bed.

Soon she falls asleep.

Around three hours later, a rattling sound rouses her from sleep. It sounds like heavy metal falling on the floor. Mandira is still under the spell of a drowsy numbness. Is it real or is she dreaming? The sound is repeated, and now at a higher pitch, alarming her. It can't be a thief, for they don't make such a ruckus while breaking into a house. It must be a cat. The kitchen window must have been left open by mistake. She has always been allergic to cats. She gets up to shoo it away before it licks up food in the kitchen. With the torch in one hand, she opens the door. Hardly has she stepped out, when someone hits her hard on her shoulder with a heavy bar. Having let out a piercing scream, Mandira falls with a thud on the ground while the torch falls from her hand.

For a couple of minutes she remains unconscious. When she dimly regains her senses, she finds herself gagged, laid fully on her back with her arms pinioned. She experiences unbearable pain all over her body but is unable to shout.

As Mandira shakes her head with all her might, the assailant slaps her repeatedly. Then throttling her with one hand, he begins to tear open her blouse. Like a savage brute, he bites one of her breasts, his breath as hot as a furnace.

Mandira realises that she is being murdered ... she is finding it increasingly difficult to breathe. Try as she might she can't extricate herself from the beast trying to strip her below the abdomen and rape her. She can't lift her leg to kick him as he is sitting firmly on her thighs. He is wildly biting, scratching and mauling her but she is determined not to give in till she dies. She senses that she is choking to death.

Before she fully loses her senses again, the assailant suddenly leaves her and hurries towards the kitchen. Mandira is aware of what is going on but she is devoid of the strength to rise.

Will the man stage a comeback and kill her? She tries to crawl towards her bedroom; but she can't even breathe properly. She feels an excruciating pain in her neck. Perhaps the veins and ducts have been torn.

The man doesn't return; neither does she hear any untoward sound again. A dog barking outside shatters the silence. As though a bit relieved, she becomes unconscious for the second time. At last she feels that she is dying, really dying.

14

The intruder was not an ordinary burglar. He hadn't stolen anything. He had just come to outrage Mandira's modesty.

Before making a hasty retreat he had left behind a towel and a crowbar. Had Mandira not voluntarily opened the door, he would have certainly broken it open. Even if she had shouted for help, there was little chance of any neighbour hearing the cry or rushing to her rescue. The villain had taken the risk of accomplishing his heinous crime within the shortest possible time.

Though the broken window has not been repaired yet, the intruder had no knowledge about it before he broke into the house. He broke two more rods with the help of the crowbar. It proves that he had come prepared to break the window and barge into the house.

Had he intended to kill Mandira? The crowbar had been aimed at her head but the fatal blow missed its target and struck on her hair only. She has sustained a mild injury on her head. Thank God, the skull has not been cracked. He had throttled Mandira's throat but couldn't hold on till she could be choked to death. He couldn't even rape her; in his excitement he must have had a premature ejaculation. Did he run away in haste because of that?

It is not so easy to die. Mandira gets back to her senses a little later.

She is writhing in pain all over her body. The blackguard has left his mark on several places which are now extremely painful. Somehow she removes the gag from her mouth. Lying for some time more she tries to rise slowly.

She enters the bathroom and sprinkles water all over her face and mouth, thereby coming to her senses properly. From the kitchen she takes a glass of water to drink. She experiences a sharp pain as water passes down her throat.

The bathroom has run short of water. She should at once fetch water from the tubewell and cleanse her body of dirt and hate.

All at once, she feels so depressed that she doesn't go out to fetch water. She doesn't even apply medicine on her wounds. She is alive, true, but she feels as though everything in her life has come to an end.

She somehow comes tottering towards her bed and lies in it. Tears are raining down her eyes.

Why didn't the man kill her? What will she do with her life now?

She has been polluted, tainted. She no longer has the right to think about the pollution in the environment, for she herself has been corrupted.

She hasn't lost her sexual desires. Yet she practised celibacy all through these years. She was ready to offer everything to a person who would truly love her. She didn't let Biman touch her because his longing for her was a combination of the romantic memory of the past and the lust of the present. She often felt tempted to respond to Biman's overtures, yet she restrained herself. But today? A beast has destroyed everything.

Oh no, it was not a beast. Beasts are not rapists. They mate with mutual consent. Man falsely defames them.

Man makes man's most beautiful experience ugly. A section of people try to meet their sexual hunger by raping women. But they get nothing out of it. They do not realise that this pleasure cannot be forced out of a woman. That scoundrel, too, didn't get anything, except that he ended up poisoning her body.

She has lost the very purpose of staying on in this village. And why should she even stay alive anymore? All her dreams of freedom have been shattered. No one will let a single woman live independently!

She can engage bodyguards for her security but that would be out of keeping with a village life. No, she must now leave this place for good. She had always thought of maintaining friendly terms with the villagers. She was careful not to be accused of snobbery. Through an ordinary lifestyle she wanted to be one among them.

Had that scoundrel been sent by someone? The factory authorities? In that case Biman may have had an inkling about it beforehand. Has he betrayed her ...? He was talking about danger repeatedly. Oh no, he can't stoop so low. He is an honourable man. Besides, he's still under the romantic spell of Mandira's love. He'll never allow her to be ravished at the hands of a rapist.

Then was the man sent by the police? The police had deserted her in the dark at Dakatepara. Only they knew that she was at her home that night. Mandira has heard of many incidents where the police has committed similar atrocities against civilians in this country.

Or was the assailant Bina's father, Ghanashyam? Only this very morning he was threatening her with dire consequences.

He might have seen the light in Mandira's house. The man was very stout and sturdy. He must be hanged to death! But will she be able to send him to the gallows? Who is going to lend credence to her allegations? He had said that he didn't care for the law. It would be very difficult for her to prove that he was a criminal.

Exhausted and utterly depressed, Mandira falls asleep some time later.

Next day, early in the morning, she is obliged to get up when Shanti knocks at the door. She opens the door to let Shanti come in and goes back to bed again.

In her characteristic way Shanti goes on prattling about the previous day's events. 'Oh didi, when did you come back? I was told that you had gone off to the town. I was under the impression that you wouldn't be back in the night. You were lucky to be escorted in a police jeep, but you don't know how all hell broke loose here.'

Mandira turns over on her side, not wishing to hear what Shanti is narrating.

'Wait, let me first make tea for you. Then I'll tell you in detail.' Saying this she goes towards the kitchen. But soon she comes back running. She is looking terribly excited. Wide-eyed, flailing her arms in the air, she breaks the news, 'Oh didi, I found the kitchen window broken, the utensils scattered all over the floor. It was a burglary! Strange! You didn't hear anything?'

Mandira remains silent.

After this Shanti runs from one corner to another to make a survey of the post-theft situation. Having failed to get any clue, she comes back to Mandira to know whether cash, valuables like ornaments have been stolen or not.

Disgusted, Mandira replies coldly, 'No, nothing has been stolen.'

A little later Shanti comes back with tea.

Though the traumatic experience of the previous night has made her apathetic to life, she can't refuse her morning tea. Leaning her back against the raised pillow on the bed, she begins to drink tea.

Everyday Shanti has tea with Mandira. Today also, Shanti is sipping her tea noisily while squatting on the floor. She resumes her reporting of the previous day's events.

'Yesterday many of them blamed you. When the police were clubbing our men with lathis, you simply slipped away from the spot in a police van, without showing any concern for those people. I, however, tried to convince them that my didi must have gone to attend an urgent piece of business for which, I had seen with my own eyes, two young ladies had come to call her. But none of them was willing to pay any heed to my explanation. Rather they scoffed at me. Even Bina was saying, "Mandira di fled like a coward! Fie!"'

Mandira keeps staring at Shanti.

Now the mist of confusion clears. The simple equation is that the two ladies had been engaged for the express purpose of sending a wrong signal to the public —that they already knew Mandira and that she was leaving the troubled spot voluntarily. The task for the police became easier since the village folks hadn't seen any women cops before.

Shanti goes on, 'The police told us "Your didimoni has got the hell out of here. Sajjad and Chayan also haven't come back. So why are you fools shouting for nothing? Scoot! Go home!"

'Oh didi, do tell me who came to call you. Why did you go away with them?'

Mandira still remains silent.

'Frightened, I had taken flight well in advance,' recounts Shanti. 'Luckily I was not hurt. But the police lashed at Javed mercilessly. Those who were pelting stones were also severely beaten up by the police. It was a bloody battle. People were running helter-skelter to escape from being hurt. The local Muslims are awfully incensed. They are alleging that the police singled them out. The Hindus, they say, were deliberately spared.'

Mandira, having finished the tea, lies down and covers her face with the thin wrapper. She feels close to tears.

Shanti draws near Mandira to say, 'Why, what's the matter with you, didi? Are you not well?'

Then removing the wrapper from Mandira's face, she places her hand on her forehead.

'But I don't think that you have fever. Then are you down with a stomach-ache?'

'You can go home, Shanti. I'm terribly upset now,' says Mandira.

'Well, I would rather suggest you to keep on lying in bed some time more. Meanwhile let me make a quick visit to the bazaar. Okay?'

After Shanti's departure, Mandira lies with her face down and sobs her heart out. She has never wept like this before. She has now wept buckets, but nothing can alleviate the burden of her grief-stricken heart.

A savage attacked her, made her impure. She is yet to change her clothes, wash her body. She is bearing the scars of hate all over her. She is determined not to get up from bed again.

The previous night she had walked all that way to reach home. It was a solitary walk, yet none intercepted her on the way. It was a singular sight in the countryside to come across a sophisticated woman walking alone. It wouldn't have been unusual had she been kidnapped and raped in a lonely village path like that. But the passers-by behaved gently with her. In contrast, the intruder was reckless. He broke into the house through the window; he wouldn't have hesitated to break open the door and rape her, had the situation demanded so. He just left behind a towel and a crowbar—not enough to prove his crime.

The protest march turned out to be a total failure. They had cunningly removed Sajjad and Chayan in anticipation, as they did with Mandira as well. Then by pulverising a derailed procession they proved how futile the movement was. That is why they didn't let the procession reach the SDO. The villagers were made to understand that a handful of over-enthusiasts were instigating them for no rhyme or reason against a combined force of the government, police and the company, and that no sooner did they sense danger they got the hell out of the troubled spot. The upshot of all this being, the factory will be set up and no one can stop it from coming up.

Perhaps Sajjad and Chayan were released late in the evening. They were not arrested; they were just summoned for some dialogues with the authorities. So the police can't be blamed. Possibly a rumour might have been spread by this time that Sajjad and Chayan had been treated with a sumptuous dinner during their meeting with the police authorities, while their comrades were screaming in pain.

Sajjad and Chayan had an excuse—they had been compelled to go with the police. But Mandira? She was removed by two young ladies, who gave the impression of being very close to Mandira. So the common people took it for granted that she had voluntarily left with them. Being after all an outsider, she always ran the risk of snapping the fragile thread of trust reposed by the naive villagers in her.

In spite of staying in England for so many years, she was treated as an outsider there. And here, in her own country, she is not better off.

From the market Shanti comes back armed with more information.

'Ah didi, you're still lolling in bed? Won't you wash your mouth, have a bath?'

'No, you may cook your own meal. I won't eat anything today.'

'Understood. Today you'll just drink tea and nothing else. So let me put the kettle on the stove.'

Mandira accepts the second cup of tea without protest. The hot brew is working like medicine in her body. While changing sides she feels acute pain all over.

Shanti resumes her tale once again.

At the market she has heard that Javed didn't succumb to his injuries. He had fled from the spot. The Muslims are furious. They are accusing the police of siding with the Hindus. A section of the Hindus allege that the Muslims threw stones at the police first. They were the root of all trouble. The police had to resort to lathi charge on being provoked by them. The arguments and counter-arguments have given rise to a serious feud between the two communities. The simmering tension is palpable. Chayan Ghose has tried to intervene but he has been whacked on to the ground by some of them.

Shanti further says that another procession of people carrying red flags have been organised this morning. They are clamouring for the setting up of the factory, which they believe would benefit the locals. The sharecroppers, giving up their lands, will be compensated. The MLA and the panchayat president are present at the market to persuade the people ...

Mandira all at once screams at her, 'What the hell are you chattering for? Get out from my house!'

Completely taken aback, Shanti exclaims, 'My goodness! Why on earth are you scolding me, pray? Where do you mean me to go?'

'Wherever you wish to go. But get out of my sight. Don't come back to my room.' As soon as Shanti walks out of the room, Mandira sinks her teeth into the pillow and keeps biting it desperately. She goes on tossing and turning in bed. She is overcome with an uncontrollable rage and fury. An unbearable pain seems to rend her heart.

She doesn't know what she should do with her life now. Must she embrace death? But how?

She longs to rend her throat with terrifying cries. She feels a frantic urge to spring out of bed ... to run headlong to the pond and jump into it.

Her whole body writhing, twisting in pain, she calls out in an almost choked voice, 'Ma, ma, ma!'

She craves and yearns to return to her long-lost mother. Only she could offer solace to Mandira at this hour.

An hour or so later, Shanti has a peek into her room and then quietly tiptoes inside.

An exhausted Mandira is lying with her eyes closed. She is awake, her whole body trembling.

In a very mild tone, Shanti calls her, 'Didi, oh didi!'

After being called a few times, Mandira opens her puffed up, reddened eyes. Her cheeks are tear-stained.

'Didi, Chayan da has come to meet you.'

'Tell him that I can't meet him. I'm unwell.'

Still Shanti nervously asks, 'Should I call him once into the room?'

Glaring at her and gnashing her teeth, Mandira screams, 'I said I can't! Didn't I? Shut the door. Get lost from here.'

Nevertheless Chayan is standing at the door. Without entering the room, he says, 'Mandira di, are you sick? Did the police inflict any torture on you?'

Turning her face away, Mandira replies, 'No!'

Anxiously Chayan pleads, 'Tell us the truth. We'll take serious exception to any unfair treatment meted out to you. I'll meet the district magistrate, complain to the superintendant of police.'

'I'm alright. You may go now.'

'I know you're upset by yesterday's incident. This is part of our life yet we must not give up. Yesterday the police outwitted us. But we must renew our struggle. I've chalked out a couple of new plans.'

Turning towards him, with her eyes burning in rage, Mandira curtly says, 'Why are you pestering me like this? I don't want to listen to your new plans. I'm least interested in your village. Tomorrow I'll leave this place for good.'

Staring at her in stunned silence, Chayan says, 'You will leave? Won't you come back again?'

'If you think I've come to live here forever, you're mistaken. Why should I rot in this ugly, pathetic village? No, I don't wish to stay here any longer.'

'You'll leave ... really?' Asks a puzzled Chayan.

'Yes, yes, what I've said is the truth. I'm going to leave your village.'

Chayan mumbles, 'Well, even if you go away, can I ask for some help from you? Would you please draft a few letters in English? Well, not now ... I may come later, if you please.'

'No, you needn't come back. I don't want to involve myself further in any affair of your village. To me it matters little whether a fertiliser factory comes up in your village or not. I'm after all not going to live here.'

'You have changed your mind abruptly. That day Biman babu had come ... Did he influence you to change your mind? He's an old acquaintance of yours.'

Being deliberately vicious, Mandira bursts out, 'Yes, Biman babu is my friend. Influenced by him I'm going away. Now I want you to be off. Go away, I'll sleep now.'

As soon as Chayan shifts from the door, Mandira gets down from the bed and bolts it. Coming back to the bed, she again starts tossing and twisting and rolling, her eyes flooded with tears. She is being tormented with an excruciating anguish resulting from the thought that she is unable to tell others how she has been ravaged, polluted. And she has not been polluted by the poisonous gas of a factory; it was a man who poisoned her. What will she do by trying to save the environment from pollution? Now, being rotten and decomposed, she herself is going to meet her end.

In the afternoon Shanti calls Mandira twice or thrice but she can't make her budge an inch from the bed, nor eat anything. Shanti, however, cooks for herself and after lunch whiles away the time by sitting sprawling on the veranda.

Late in the afternoon Sajjad, accompanied by two or three others, drop in. On hearing that Mandira is out of sorts, both physically and emotionally, Sajjad himself forbids Shanti from calling her out.

Shanti relates the tale of the attempted burglary to Sajjad and shows him the crowbar and the towel left by the thief. Shanti knows if she offers tea to the guests without Mandira's permission, the latter wouldn't mind. So she says, 'Sajjad da, let me make tea for you.' Sajjad agrees but doesn't wait till the water boils. He leaves all of a sudden.

From noon through evening, Mandira spends the time by partly sleeping and partly remaining awake and the rest weeping buckets. When she is slightly composed, she comes out of her room to tell Shanti, 'Fetch water into the bathroom.'

While bathing, Mandira makes up her mind to leave Sukhchar immediately after recovering a little. Her legs are still trembling violently, she feels severe pain in her neck. If she has to end her life, she should do that in a civilised society, by swallowing sleeping pills. If she dies here, God knows what will be the fate of her mortal frame at the hands of the locals.

Also she decides not to live in Calcutta. She will rather go back to London. All her Indian experiments are over for good. She repents the fact that she hoped to rediscover life's zest in a country with which she snapped her ties wilfully as long as twenty-seven years ago.

If she gets back to London, perhaps she will stop being suicidal—she thinks. Rape is an abominable crime in that country but nobody hates a rape victim there. If one's wife is unfortunately raped, her husband sympathises with her. If a rabid dog bites a woman, does her husband desert her?

Nobody in England will have a whiff of Mandira's mishap. That scoundrel last night couldn't rape her. It was just a clumsy attempt at rape. But she is now constantly being tormented by a sense of humiliation.

Being a well-wisher of this village, she has innocently involved herself in some social activities. Yet how could someone from this same village slap her, hit her on the head with a crowbar, and after stripping her, bite her all over her body, though she hasn't harmed a soul in the village? This ungrateful locality now seems to be a fiendish place in her eyes.

Though she will leave this place for good, she won't sell the house and the plot of land adjacent to it. She can forego the little bit of money that she might get from the sale of the homestead. The property will belong to her forever and she will never let the Sunderbans Fertiliser Company acquire it. That will be her revenge.

Mandira doesn't eat anything tonight as well. She only has a cup of tea before going to sleep.

In the next two days also she doesn't leave Sukhchar. At first she is looking forward to recuperating from the trauma she has undergone. She now feels so dizzy that she is unable to balance herself and fears she may fall down if she tries to walk on the road. By this time she has taken the decision to go back to London and meet her children before calling it a day. For speedy recovery she has started eating properly again.

In these two days nobody has visited her. Not even Bina. The latter must have found out that Mandira has insulted Chayan before driving him out of her home. She is ostracised by the villagers. Has the rumour spread in the meantime that she has been working on behalf of the police?

On the third day, Shanti, coming back from the bazaar, brings the news of another meeting to be held on the school playground in the evening. The meeting is not organised by Chayan's group; on the contrary it is a government-sponsored meeting to be attended by the SDO personally. People belonging to both the Hindu and Muslim communities have been invited. She has seen the party workers, with red flags in hand, roaming through the marketplace blaring loudspeakers to inform the public of the meeting to be held at five-thirty.

Mandira shows little curiosity about that. Today she is feeling much better. So she is sitting on a cane chair on the veranda—this after three long days of keeping indoors.

Very affectionately she is staring at the sandhyamalati, red China rose and green chilli plants in the courtyard. She has developed a deep attachment to these plants. In London one cannot come across sandhyamalatis and red China rose plants, though one can buy plenty of Indian marigold and chillies from the market. Still, she'll never come back to India!

Though she doesn't hear the sound of a car engine, she sees Biman at the gate. He is accompanied by that young BDO, Dibyajyoti.

With a smiling face, Biman hastily walks to Mandira and stretching out his hand, says, 'Congratulations! You win!'

Then dropping himself in the chair next to her, Biman continues, 'Mani, three cheers for your victory! You must have heard the news, haven't you?'

Mandira looks at him indifferently.

Shanti is standing nearby. Turning to her Biman says, 'Make some tea; hurry up, for I can't wait longer.'

Then turning to Mandira he says, 'What's the matter, Mani? Why are you silent? Haven't you heard the news?'

Still Mandira remains quiet.

Lighting a cigarette Biman says, 'I hope you haven't resumed smoking, have you? Very good. Now I'll also say no to smoking. Listen Mani, your wish is going to be fulfilled. The Sunderbans Fertiliser Limited and the West Bengal government have jointly taken the decision of shifting the venue of the plant. The fertiliser plant is coming up in North Bengal, not here. They have found a vast stretch of wasteland, far from human habitation. So nobody will raise any objection there. Mani, you may remember what I told you before—that it matters little to me whether the plant comes up in the Sunderbans or the Himalayas. It's all the same to me. I'm just happy to think that ultimately they have honoured your viewpoint. Are you not happy?'

Mandira's face remains inscrutable. She is reluctant to utter a single word.

He goes on, 'Dibyajyoti has come to make a special request to you. The other day you were unaware of his actual identity. You remember Suranjan, your classmate at Presidency college, eh? Dibyajyoti is his son. He's a very bright fellow. He's also appeared for the UPSC examination this year.'

Dibyajyoti draws up a chair and sits beside her with utmost respect. Today his deportment is different because of the reference. That day's insolent, sly and diplomatic officer today looks polite and submissive.

He says, 'The government has taken your demands into consideration. The day before yesterday, the contents of your letter, written to the ministers and the pollution control board, was discussed at length by our DM and the district officers. Point by point, you've splendidly backed up your arguments. If the toxic wastes flow into rivers, or there's an acid rain, the flora and fauna of the Sunderbans will definitely be imperilled. It cannot be disputed. The sulphur dioxide fumes, to be honest, cause bronchial troubles in humans. The government has finally agreed to these points of yours.'

'Ah, come on Dibyajyoti, don't give Mani the whole credit for the success,' Biman jokes. 'As a matter of fact, very few ministers or people at the top had the idea that a fertiliser plant could be as hazardous as a plant manufacturing acid or explosives. Even I was in the dark. Many have the misconception that fertiliser is something benign, innocent. Besides, well, Dibyajyoti should I cite the other reasons?

'There's another reason why the government has agreed to relocate the venue. It has realised that its hasty decision to acquire land by displacing the sharecroppers, has placed it in an awkward situation. If the news spreads that the West Bengal government, which is the champion of the Bargadar system, has ousted the poor sharecroppers from their lands, it'll make the ruling party lose more votes than what it would have gained from a handful of beneficiaries of the fertiliser plant. If the rest of India gets to know that, in collusion with the factory owners, the state government is throwing the sharecroppers out of their lands, that'll be very bad publicity for the ruling party. The CPI(M) cadres have realised that. On the other hand, the Congress party will cash in on it. That's why the top brass of the state government has rushed to change the location of the factory. The new location is on a wasteland in North Bengal; naturally there's no hassle of land acquisition there.'

'We're all happy now,' adds Dibyajyoti. 'Today I can tell you officially, I'm also dead set against anything that causes pollution. Anyway, all's well that ends well ... You've also reaped the fruits of your efforts.'

Taking a sip of the tea, Biman exclaims, 'What's the matter with you, Mani? Why are you silent? Are you not happy with this?'

Quietly Mandira says, 'I'm soon going to stop living in this village. I'll go away from here.'

Almost jumping out of the chair, Biman shouts, 'Finally! Very good! I've been asking you from the very beginning to settle in Calcutta. I'll help you buy a flat in Salt Lake ... Occasionally you can make pleasure trips to the countryside ... that will be enough. Come to North Bengal ... there you'll view the majestic forests in the backdrop of snow-peaked mountains—beautiful! I'm so fond of North Bengal! The very sight of mountains delights me.'

Dibyajyoti says, 'I've come to make a special request to you. At today's meeting we're officially going to announce our decision. The DM will preside over the meeting and the SDO will be present as the chief guest. And we want you as our special guest. Well, I'm just a small fry ... it's a request that I'm making on behalf of the DM. You'll just have to say a few words on behalf of the villagers.'

With folded hands, Mandira replies, 'Impossible! I can't go. I'm ill.'

'Why, what's wrong with you, Mani?' Demands Biman very anxiously.

'Nothing as such. I'm just not feeling well.'

'The TV, All India Radio are coming to cover the meeting,' says Biman, 'and along with the one-sided government announcement, you could have also put forward your point of view. So why don't you come?'

Mandira reacts vehemently, 'I don't belong to this village. I'm not even going to live here in the near future. Why should I address the meeting?'

'Because everyone will listen to what you'll say. You've after all returned from abroad. Being an educated lady you naturally stand out by miles in this village. This could also be an opportunity for you to use the meeting as a platform for airing your views on environmental hazards through radio and television channels,' argues Biman.

Shaking her head firmly, Mandira says, 'I'm not going to your meeting. I've no more views about pollution control measures. And I've no further interest in rural affairs either. I don't want to know anything nor do I want to make anyone understand anything. Is that clear? Now leave me alone.'

Quite rattled, Biman enquires, 'Mani, what is bothering you? You are behaving in a strange fashion ...'

Gnashing her teeth, Mandira moans, 'Get the hell out of here!'

At once Dibyajyoti gets up. He is in overall charge of the meeting. So he must turn up at the venue well in advance, even before the other officials. Besides he is quite reluctant to tolerate the tantrums of a middle-aged woman; it matters little whether she was his father's college mate or somebody else. The DM's request! It's a blatant lie. He has actually been importuned by Biman to offer the special guest's chair to this lady. Now it becomes abundantly clear to him that she is a nutcase.

Placing his hand on Mandira's head, Biman says, 'Mani, I'm sorry, very sorry that I couldn't understand that you're unwell. Alright, you needn't go to the meeting. Take rest. I'm coming back to you after the meeting. Mani, I leave you to your air and water, unpolluted and pure.'

Once Biman leaves, Mandira remains seated gripping her head tightly between her hands for quite a while.

The thought that now leaves her pondering is: why has the government become so generous all at once? Perhaps there is some mystery lurking below the surface. Whatever it may be, the protesters shall certainly rejoice at the announcement. The mist of misunderstanding will be dispelled for the time being. Biman said he will get back to her after the meeting. Chayan, Sajjad and their comrades will rush to her and celebrate the victory.

Mandira won't meet a single one of them. This victory is not her victory.

A little later, lifting her head she asks, 'Shanti, when does the last bus leave for Calcutta?'

'At six-thirty.'

Getting up, she says, 'I'm packing up. I'll leave for Calcutta today. I'm not coming back.'

Breaking into sobs, Shanti says, 'Didi, will you really leave us for good?'

Hugging Shanti very closely to her bosom, Mandira says, 'I know you love me. You're the only person who hasn't deserted me. Through these days, I scolded you so much. Yes Shanti, I'm going away. But this house belongs to me. I'll give you the keys. You may live here, even with your parents.' Then all at once Mandira bursts into sobs and adds, 'All the best! All the best!'

Mandira hadn't intended to show her weakness before Shanti. But she couldn't contain her emotions. This country, its people no longer hold any interest for her. But she, indeed, feels bad about leaving Shanti. This girl has been slowly changing her attitude to life, learning to know the world better, but Mandira now has lost all her powers to help her.

She has not cried for someone else like this for a long time.

15

Shanti has come to the bus stand to see off Mandira. She has only a suitcase with her. From a little distance away on the school playground she can hear the loudspeaker blaring fiery speeches thundered by the MLA, Susovan Roy. His eloquence seems to rend the sky.

It's six thirty-two p.m. The express bus is yet to arrive. Flights of twittering birds are homing towards the sprawling tree nearby. Their sweet tunes have filled the air. Reaching Calcutta today, Mandira will put up at a hotel instead of Sankar da's residence.

Suddenly Sajjad is seen dismounting from his cycle a little away from Mandira. He walks up to Shanti. Mandira casts a sidelong glance at him but doesn't say a word. Sajjad, too, doesn't greet her.

All three of them stand in silence waiting for the bus. Shanti, with her head bowed, is still secretly weeping for Mandira. At the same time her childish heart is curious about the goings on in the school playground.

The headlights of the advancing bus can now be seen from a distance. The road is pitch dark. The bus will take five to seven minutes more to arrive at Mandira's stop.

Turning to Shanti, Sajjad says, 'Shanti, you may go now; I'll see madam off.'

Shanti looks at Mandira.

'Please go Shanti. Don't worry. I am here,' says Sajjad forcefully.

Shanti goes up to Mandira to touch her feet and take her blessings. Mandira in a choked voice says, 'I'll write to you. You must reply in your own handwriting.'

Shanti crosses the road ... still Mandira doesn't bother to acknowledge Sajjad's presence.

'The bus has arrived. So you're going?' Sajjad breaks the ice.

Mandira doesn't reply. She has decided to sever all her ties with these people. She shall not change her mind now.

All at once Sajjad leans down on the ground and, enfolding Mandira's feet in his hands, breaks into a heart-rending cry, 'Didi, forgive us! Have mercy on us!'

Embarrassed, Mandira tries to free herself from Sajjad's clasp and exclaims in disgust, 'What is this nonsense? Leave me alone. And why are you not rejoicing at your victory, pray?'

'Please listen to me just once,' Sajjad pleads, 'we ...'

'I don't want to listen to you at all,' says Mandira point-blank, 'and what on earth are you doing here? Go to the meeting and deliver your speech.'

'I won't go to the meeting ... I can't think of the meeting without you.'

'I'm an outsider; I've nothing to do with your village. Now let me go, the bus is coming.'

Sajjad without budging says, 'I know why you're leaving us. I know everything. Fie on us! What an ugly curse has befallen us! I don't know how I should beg your pardon, didi; let me hold your feet in apology on behalf of him. Please punish me if you want to—kick me, give me whatever punishment you intend to give.'

'"On behalf of him!" What do you mean by "him"?' asks Mandira raising her eyebrows.

'If you wish you can send him to jail. That bastard deserves to be imprisoned. His ears and nose should be severed. That day he had gone off his head.'

'Who are you talking about?'

'He has confessed everything to me. That day I saw the towel and the crowbar in your house. The stuff belongs to him.'

'But who is he?'

'That means you haven't recognised the culprit! I thought that you recognised him but wanted to maintain silence. But I can't forgive this heinous crime ... I can't rest until I slay that blackguard.'

'I want to know who that man was.'

'Are you sure that you don't know? That day he was behaving like an insane ... like a rabid dog ... Javed!'

Mandira is terribly startled but can't speak for some moments. Then she says slowly, 'Javed? That makes a lot of difference. I never thought of him!'

Mandira pulls up Sajjad. Tears are rolling down his cheeks and he is unable to look straight into her eyes. In the meanwhile, the bus has arrived while they're standing like statues. After a couple of minutes, the conductor signals it to move on.

'Javed!' she murmurs.

'I couldn't sleep two nights,' goes on Sajjad, 'what an unpardonable sin! If I were not able to personally meet you and apologise before you were gone, I would have burnt in regret for the rest of my life.'

'Did he admit to his guilt?'

'Yes he did. I would have lashed him to death, had my wife not been there to stop me. He was screaming in pain at my feet like a dog from hell. He confessed how he smashed the bars of your window with the crowbar, broke into your house and tried to kill you after raping you.'

'He seems to be full of vengeance against me. Why? Have I ever harmed him?'

'He's under the impression that you despise him. You don't like to speak to him. You won't drink water fetched by him. That day he was singled out of the crowd and beaten severely by the police. He was hounded out of the bushes, perhaps to be killed. He's basically a hot-tempered, impulsive fellow; people scorn and shun him; nobody gives him a job. He's getting fanatical by the day as the Hindus can't tolerate him. This has made him an avowed Hindu-hater.'

'Didn't I take water from him? Oh yes, that day he had offered me a glass of water which I politely refused as I was not at all thirsty.'

'That has made him assume that you also hate him. That day, in spite of being the leader of the procession, you didn't protest when he was being thrashed by the police; rather you sped away in a car.'

'I see! Everyone thought that I deliberately left with the police.'

'No, I don't hold their views. I know what the truth is. I know that those were low tactics employed by the police. But how can that fool of a Javed understand this? Like a hunted dog he ran from this place to that, growling in rage. He found it hard to control his wrath against the Hindus. As you're their representative, he grew desperate enough to ...'

'Where's he now?'

'His crime is unpardonable. He must be punished. Didi, if you wish, I'll kill him before your eyes and bundle his body into the river. None will have the slightest inkling. And no one will shed a single drop of tear for that rascal. He has no wife or children who might have wept for him!'

'Where's Javed now?'

'He was intending to flee to Bangladesh, crossing the border, but I have held him up in a place. If his kinsmen get wind of his crime, they'll tear him into pieces. You're like a goddess to us; everybody respects you so much ... Oh, I can't imagine the magnitude of his crime! Javed's sin is our sin also. Come, let us tell everything to the DM and SDO who're incidentally present at Sukhchar today.'

'Do you have a cigarette?' asks Mandira irrelevantly.

Astonished, Sajjad keeps staring at Mandira's face for a few seconds. He has never seen her smoking before. Slowly he brings out a packet and a matchbox from his pocket.

Mandira has given up smoking but now she badly needs a puff. She lights one and puffs ravenously. Her whole body keeps trembling. Javed's name has figured so unexpectedly that she feels at quite a loss. She never harmed him, nor did she represent the Hindu community, for she never propagated any religious ideology. Then why did he bear a grudge against her?

'The bus has gone,' says Sajjad, 'come, let's go to the DM to report the whole thing to him, and hand over Javed to the police.'

'Are you sure it's Javed?'

'Yes, and he has confessed to his guilt; he says he lost his sanity that night ...'

'I want to see him once.'

'Do you want to punish him yourself? He'll be pinioned down and thrown at your feet; I'll see to that.'

'I want to see Javed once and, of course, alone,' demands Mandira.

Sajjad, bewildered, keeps looking at Mandira, as though he can see a very powerful weapon in her hand; as though this woman is like Goddess Durga, the incarnation of good about to triumph over evil.

He speaks in a hushed tone, 'Will you come? I assure you that no one will dare harm you further. You may mete out any punishment to Javed.'

'I'll stay back this night only. Let's move along a different route to avoid being watched by the people at the meeting ground.'

Lifting Mandira's suitcase in one hand, Sajjad moves along the narrow dyke across the paddy fields. He is holding his bicycle with the other hand. Both his hands being engaged this way, he is walking awkwardly, but he doesn't mind that. He goes on saying, 'In a country plagued with religious bigotry and fanaticism, it's a curse to live as a member of the minority community ... it's really a cursed existence! Many presume that our condition is better than that of the Hindus in Bangladesh. We're just alive but without dignity.'

Mandira isn't listening to Sajjad. The paddy fields in the rainy season are vulnerable to snakes coming out of their hiding places in search of harvest mice. Today she seems to have completely forgotten that. She is walking through the mud and slush, quite mindless of her immediate surroundings.

They walk past the Kanaibenki canal; Sajjad stands before a hut. He unlocks the door and brings out Javed. Two others, who were smoking bidis behind the hut, also come and stand beside them.

On seeing Mandira, Javed falls at her feet and starts grovelling on the ground.

Turning to Sajjad, Mandira says, 'Tell him to rise.'

Sajjad at once, holding Javed by his hair, slaps him across the face. Gnashing his teeth he shouts, 'Look who you have harmed, you bastard!'

Javed can't look into Mandira's eyes; he covers his face with his hands.

One of the men standing nearby brings out a knife, saying, 'Do you want me to chop that bastard into pieces? He'll ruin us. If the news of his heinous deed spreads across the Hindu neighbourhood, they'll set our houses on fire. We'll be choked out and shot like pigs by the police.'

Mandira looks around scanning her immediate surroundings. It has not rained today. In the distance, the sky is dimly illuminated by the last rays of the setting sun. The vast expanse across the canal lies desolately before her. There is not a living creature in sight.

'I would like to speak to Javed in private,' says Mandira. 'Shall we go this way? I don't want anyone to follow us. You must wait until we come back.'

'Can I accompany you?' asks Sajjad.

'Nobody else,' insists Mandira.

Sajjad stares at the others. The knife-wielding man pushes Javed from behind and says, 'Look, you damned dog, you must go with madam. Listen to what she says. Tacitly accept whatever punishment she gives you. If need be you must lay down your life for the sake of her honour. If you try to do anything untoward, mind it, you'll be hacked to death. I shall first keep your father hostage here. If you try to flee, I'll cut his throat.'

'Remember,' says Sajjad, 'honour is more precious than life. Don't land your kinsmen in further peril.'

Both of them keep walking by the side of the canal. A little later they can't see the hut any more. Here and there lie scattered bushy undergrowths; they're heading towards the Sathpukur gate.

Javed is speechless; he doesn't even cast a glance at Mandira. After getting past a thick bush she halts. Her sandals are smeared with mud. She gets rid of them. The ground she's walking on is covered with wet grass.

Javed also stops and stands looking around. Bringing out the torch from her handbag, Mandira scans the area. They're standing between the edge of the canal and the paddy fields that have already been sown with seeds. A few stars have come out twinkling in the sky.

Mandira focuses the torch quickly all over Javed's body. He's wearing a greasy grey half pant and a vest. His face is unshaven and his hair is in need of the service of a comb. His arms and chest are moulded as though in wrought iron while his shoulders seem to be a little raised; perhaps he's frightfully alert. He's unable to gauge her intentions.

Slowly Mandira says, 'That day you were intent on killing me, were you not? Had you hit me with the crowbar a little more forcefully, I would not have been here now to speak to you.'

Javed is standing with his head bowed low, so his eyes are not visible to Mandira.

'Are you a man or a coward? You broke into my house when I was alone. Then why did you hit me straightaway instead of first trying to talk to me? Why didn't you bother to ask me why I had gone away with the police? How could you be such a coward? Didn't your hands tremble before attacking a woman on her head with a crowbar?'

He is as if struck dumb.

'Are you dumb? Can't you talk?' Mandira asks reprovingly. 'You're afraid I'll punish you. What sort of punishment do you expect from me? If I cut off your arms, with which you attempted to taint my honour, do you think that will be punishment enough for you?'

He stretches out both his hands towards her.

'I've never hurt any human being before. You may go now,' she says.

He draws his fists close to her.

'I assure you that no one will harm you. You may go wherever you like,' she reiterates.

Finding him silent still, she queries, 'How far is the Bangladesh border from here? If you desire you may go there also. Here, I'll wait until you go out of our range of vision. So, run away. I'll tell them not to disclose anything to your father. You're not happy in this country. Now go and see how you feel there. I was also not happy with the country I was living in. So I came to this land. You may go; I guarantee you that you won't be chased.'

Javed this time tries to say something, but he ends up making some undecipherable sounds only.

Gripping one of his hands she says earnestly, 'You needn't speak much. Just tell me one thing: you harboured a grudge against me; but did you not love me at all?'

Casting a quick look at Mandira, he bows his head. His countenance suggests that he longs to say something but doesn't know how to react to a situation like this.

'I'm so senior to you in years; there were several other Hindu women. Nevertheless why did you target me?'

He shakes his head very fast. He's quite clearly at a loss as to what to say.

Mandira, shifting a little from the wet grass, drops her handbag on the ground first and then sits beside it. She mutters to herself, 'I wish I were dead that day. Now I don't know what I should do with myself.'

Kneeling down before Mandira, he lays his hand on her feet, intending to beg apology.

'Javed, I don't want to die. Why should I die? Death terminates everything.' While saying this she can't suppress her sobs. She can't contain herself today.

Placing his head at Mandira's feet, he also bursts into wails.

Both weep together for some time.

A gentle breeze is blowing over the paddy fields. Glowworms are flying around them. Suddenly they hear a strange sound coming from the canal water.

'You used to occasionally stare at me with a strange expression. I couldn't read the meaning of your stare. But Javed, to be very frank, I used to often think about you though I didn't ever talk to you frankly. Even you never sought to speak properly with me, did you? But both of us longed to know each other better, didn't we?'

She raises his chin with one of her hands and says, 'You're really handsome. You have large eyes, deep eyebrows, a dark complexion—yet why do you always look so angry? I don't like angry people.'

Javed is still weeping with his head bowed low. Tears are trickling down his cheeks.

'We misunderstood each other, Javed,' says Mandira. 'Your anger had totally enwrapped you. Yet you fascinated me. Had you not done what you did and had I left this place in the normal course, even then I would have remembered you forever. Your anger actually masquerades your sentiments. I've never seen a sentimental man like you before.'

All at once Mandira bursts into laughter. With the sweet playfulness of a teenager she adds, 'I've grown in years but I'm not old, Javed!'

Lifting up one of his hands, she places it on her neck and as she slowly draws it towards her breast, a startled Javed at once tries to remove it. Mandira tightly holds his hand and presses it to her breast. 'Yes. It's the same touch. I've recognised it.'

She touches his lips playfully and says, 'Javed, do look at me tenderly. What did you want from me that night?'

Then removing the free end of her sari, she unbuttons her blouse.

With a measured, unhurried rhythm, she makes his hand stroke her left breast and then asks, 'Last time you had hurt me. You were angry at my body, even though you should have been tender and placed your head over my breasts like a baby. Let me teach you how there may yet be some gratification for us both.'

Now Javed looks intently at Mandira and his dazed eyes sparkle.

'Hold me tightly in your arms, Javed,' Mandira whispers pleadingly, 'let me lie on your chest. I want so much to love ...'

Mandira gets rid of her sari and lies flat on the grass. She pulls him closer and runs her feverish fingers through his hair. She draws her mouth close to his and gives herself up to a kiss that she wishes would never end.

Tom had once said to her, 'Isn't it somewhat ironic that *Kamasutra* (Erotica) was written in India, because from all that I've read, it seems that all you women do is lie still while the man dominates the proceedings. When was it decided that it is entirely the man's responsibility to take care of the business? The woman must take the initiative, or else the very notion of pleasure is no more than a ridiculous myth. Kiss the man. Indulge in some foreplay. Learn the art, Mani. Learn for your own sake.'

Mandira feels herself floating like an errant planet free of its orbit, away from caste, creed or religion. She is no longer a mother, wife, or even a stubborn emblem of emancipation. The veils have been ripped apart, and she stands unabashed in the glorious nakedness of womanhood.

16

An airbus touches down at the Dum Dum Airport. A young couple alight from it. The young lady is wearing a printed gown and a thin white cap; a blue overcoat is hanging from her hand. Her face is beaming in ecstasy. The man is clad in a heavy grey suit, wearing a pair of gold-rimmed spectacles resembling half moons.

While alighting from the plane the young lady says with utter amazement, 'I'd heard that India would be very hot ... that the climate in Calcutta is unpleasant. But it's actually a far cry from that.'

'Darling,' says the man, 'this is January, the coldest month of the year. Rather it's relatively hot here.'

'Not at all! It's very nice, cool and comfortable here. What glorious sunshine! Didn't I tell you before that you would never have any trouble here?'

'I have been to this country before, though Calcutta was not in my itinerary then.'

An elderly American couple is walking beside them.

'Are you bound for Kathmandu? Then you must wait a couple of hours in this hideous airport,' says the American gentleman.

'No, not to Kathmandu,' she says. 'We have come to Calcutta.'

'Calcutta?' frowns the American gentleman. 'But why? The city has nothing to offer. If you drink a single drop of water here, you'll suffer from stomach disorders. The tour operators and travel agents forbid foreigners from visiting Calcutta.'

The young lady bursts into peels of laughter.

The man, feeling a little embarrassed, says, 'Actually I've been invited to deliver two lectures at a seminar here.'

'Wish you good luck then,' says the American gentleman. 'I hope you have brought anti-malarial drugs? Be sure to drink only sealed mineral water. Otherwise have beer instead of water to quench your thirst.'

The American lady mutters, 'I hope this airport has decent toilets!'

Saying this, they walk towards the transit lounge. The British couple take another path. The immigration and customs formalities are over without hassles. The officials have showered them with a lot of attention, since they're white-skinned and the crowd is thin.

As they come out, they see a man standing with the placard: 'Mr and Mrs Robert Roth, welcome to Calcutta.'

Seeing the placard, the young man heaves a sigh of relief. It seems he is not as smart and confident as other European fellows of his age; he seems rather nervous and diffident. Without any help from a guide he'll feel helpless.

The Bengali man, in an unusually flattering tone, says, 'I've come to receive you on behalf of the British Council. I'm Nirmal Kar.'

'How do you do, Mr Kar?' says Robert. 'Nice to meet you ... this is Elizabeth, my wife.'

She shakes her head saying, 'Glad to meet you. Carr is also a British title; Bob, do you remember Arnold Carr, one of your friends?'

The Bengali guide leads them towards the car that is waiting for them. He volunteers to push their trolley.

'I expected the airport to be much bigger and busier than what I see; after all it's the second largest metropolis of the British Empire,' says Elizabeth.

'Forget about those days,' her husband whispers. 'Don't talk about these things now. They may be hurt by your comments. I've noticed in Delhi that they're very touchy about these issues, even to this day.'

While travelling in the car, Robert chalks out the next two days' programme.

Nirmal Kar hesitantly asks, 'Excuse me, but are you related to Philip Roth?'

'Which Philip Roth?' asks Robert in amazement.

'The novelist. I've read *Goodbye Columbus* and *Letting Go* by Philip Roth. He is one of my favourite authors.'

Amazed, Robert turns to look at his wife. As if he is trying to say that—look, thousands of miles away from England, a nondescript Indian knows so much about a lesser-known American author. He feels a bit jealous, for he himself is a poet with two published volumes, yet this man has not heard of him.

He says, 'Philip Roth is an American. I'm not related to him, nor have I read any of his books.'

Elizabeth impishly exclaims, 'This is amazing! You're working with the British Council and you're a fan of American authors! Now tell me how you got this English-sounding title.'

Nirmal knows that there are plenty of Rathas in Orissa. Just as Doss and Ray are common surnames in England, Das and Roy are common titles in India. But he doesn't say anything. He just smiles at them.

In the car, Elizabeth suddenly starts behaving like a restless teenager; she shouts, 'Stop the car! See that holy cow. Bob, do give me the camera. I'll take a snap.'

Yes, just at the entrance of the VIP road, is standing a sturdy, robust-looking bull. The vehicles are wriggling by him but the totem stands unperturbed. Elizabeth takes a few snapshots and then says, 'I think the holy cows aren't disturbed.'

'In fact,' says Nirmal, 'you can see plenty of holy cows in Benaras. They block the lanes and alleys but nobody disturbs them. Do you have any plan to go to Benaras?'

'To see the holy cows? No, we would like to see the Royal Bengal Tiger.'

Ignoring Nirmal, the couple now veer their conversation towards pollution. Which of the two cities—Calcutta or London—is more polluted? They have a heated exchange of arguments over it. Elizabeth, being very obstinate, will never give in. She says, 'Unlike Calcutta you can never have a glimpse of an open sky in London, due to the poor visibility there. And the most important thing is that in Calcutta you don't have to wrap yourself up in heavy coats even in January.'

Nirmal intrudes in the conversation. 'London is far more beautiful. I had once been there. The green patches on the outskirts of the city are so refreshingly lovely!'

They are passing along the Eastern bypass. A stinking smell forces Robert to pull out the handkerchief from his pocket. 'This much!' says Elizabeth, puffing up her nostrils, 'It could be worse!'

As they enter the heart of the city, Robert is astonished at the sight of the teeming millions. 'My God, look at the masses of people! I wonder how the traffic moves here.'

'They're all liars,' says Elizabeth. 'I've read in the newspapers that this city is full of teeming millions. But where? It's just an overcrowded city. Bob, don't you think it's even better than Madrid or Rome?'

Robert just smiles.

The traffic is standing still at the Park Circus crossing. Elizabeth keeps looking at her wristwatch time and again. After a while, the car begins to move at a snail's pace.

'Just seven minutes,' says Elizabeth. 'In London the wait could have been longer.'

Robert is slightly afraid of his wife and therefore does not dare utter a word of protest. But from his countenance it is evident that he doesn't like the city at all.

They are accommodated at a three-star hotel. Nirmal leaves saying that he will be back at three o'clock in the afternoon.

The room is agreeable. But as soon as Robert gets rid of his shoes, he starts sneezing. He's allergic to dust.

Lifting one corner of the carpet he shows his wife how the floor under the carpet is covered with dust.

Elizabeth says, 'Wherever you go, in any hotel, in any part of the world, you'll find the same thing. In fact, you'll get the wrong end of the stick if you judge a country by the standard of its hotels. Layers of dust beneath the carpet are common everywhere!'

Saying this she stands at the window and removes the curtains. A common landscape of a city—nothing extraordinary. A very busy thoroughfare is running between rows of buildings—of unequal height and shape.

They have their lunch in the suite. The menu comprises both continental and mughlai delicacies.

Robert's digestive system is weak. So he has avoided the mughlai cuisine. Instead he has dined on clear soup and chicken roast. Half-heartedly he swallows the contents fearing food poisoning and mutters to himself, 'Stale food.'

Elizabeth says, 'Look, I'm having mouthwatering dishes—peas pulau, paneer masala, fish curry and papad. Daddy was so fond of papad, you know! This is real Indian curry—so different from what we eat in London. You should taste the local cuisine when travelling abroad. I'll choose your menu for tonight's dinner.'

'Alright dear, I'll try it out if you say so,' says Robert, slightly reluctantly.

'Don't you like this city ... unlike those Americans?' persists Elizabeth.

'I love it darling; in fact, I love it more because you love it.'

At the British Council Robert will deliver a couple of lectures on two consecutive afternoons. The topic of the first day is contemporary poetry. Then he is scheduled to visit a newspaper office. The next day's lecture is about the vocation of poets and journalism. Then he is supposed to attend a get-together with some intellectuals. In fact, he is not a distinguished guest here. This is his private visit to India and the invitations he has got from the British Council are the fruits of his own initiatives.

Elizabeth accompanies Robert to the British Council. But she doesn't go to the newspaper office; she goes out shopping. Nirmal Kar acts as her guide. At New Market she feels claustrophobic and comes out of there soon. At the state cottage industries emporium, she is disappointed as she doesn't get what she is specifically looking for. She is looking for an article, batik print on silk, which she once had spotted in an Indian shop in London. A beautiful dress material! But she can't find it here. Strange! The Indian silk and batik print, which she has seen in London, is not available in India!

'Please come tomorrow,' says the man at the store to Nirmal, 'we'll see if it's in the stock at the godown.'

Elizabeth has been scanning the stores for a pair of terracotta horses to decorate her home. There are several of them on display but none of them conform to the size she is looking for. Finally she finds a pair of her choice in the same store but unfortunately one of them has a broken ear. She has always been very fastidious about these things. 'Don't you have another pair of the same size?' she asks the man.

'Come tomorrow, I'll try to get one for you,' replies the man.

Though a bit disappointed, Elizabeth buys plenty of imitation ornaments such as brass rings, stone necklaces, etc. She wants to gift them to her friends.

After two lectures in Calcutta, Robert will go to New Delhi five days later. There he will attend a seminar to be hosted by the British Council. Before him two more important guests will deliver their lectures at New Delhi. So he has to wait out five days before his turn comes.

At night Robert says, 'Come dear, let's go to Kashmir. I cannot rest without seeing snowfall in January.'

'Kashmir! Why?' frowns Elizabeth. 'The landscape of Kashmir is much akin to that of Switzerland. But what about the Sunderbans? Have you forgotten the commitment of visiting Sunderbans? The beauty of the Sunderbans sanctuary is said to have no parallel.'

'Oh sure, we must have a glimpse of it,' replies Robert.

Next day they ask Nirmal Kar about it. Can't they visit Sunderbans in a rented car? Or will they have to hire a boat?

Having pondered on it for a while, Nirmal says, 'By car you can go near the Sunderbans. But you need a special permit to visit it.'

'Special visa for the Sunderbans?' asks Robert.

'Not visa. For foreigners visiting the Sunderbans, a special permit is mandatory,' reiterates Nirmal.

Then he banters, 'During your rule for over two centuries, you had imposed so many restrictions on us; shouldn't we now take a little revenge?'

'Don't ask us to atone for the actions of our ancestors. The British of the present era are different from the colonisers of yester years,' defends Robert.

'From where can we get it, Mr Kar? asks Elizabeth, adding, 'Come, lets go there right now for it.'

They arrive at the concerned department at the Writers' Building.

The clerk-in-charge at that department is chewing paan and looking into a file very attentively. He lifts his head once but doesn't bother to show much concern for the visitors. Evidently he is accustomed to visitors like Robert and Elizabeth frequenting his office.

Nirmal says, 'Look, they want to visit the Sunderbans.'

'Fill up the forms,' says the clerk.

'Where can we get the forms from?'

'Balai, do fetch the forms for the Sunderbans.'

Then looking up, he tries to be civil, 'Please take a seat. It'll take a little bit of time. Meanwhile I've some other business to attend to.'

There's only one chair. Robert beckons his wife to it. But Elizabeth doesn't sit. She just stands holding the chair.

'Balai, do fetch more chairs,' says the clerk.

Instead of obliging him, Balai says, 'Where is the form? All are finished. I told you before to requisition them. Didn't I?'

Now the clerk opens his drawer to see if there is any there. Then shrugging his shoulder, he says, 'No, we have run out of forms. *Kaal ashben* (come tomorrow); I shall try to get one for you.'

Helplessly Nirmal looks at the couple.

'*Kalas ben*—what does it mean? In fact, I've heard this phrase before ... *kalas ben* ...?' asks Elizabeth naively.

Laughing, an embarrassed Nirmal says, 'It's *kaal ashben*; he's asking us to come again tomorrow.'

'I want it today. How do you say that in Bengali?' Elizabeth has heard from David Andrews that Bengalis have a great weakness for their mother tongue. They melt considerably if they hear one or two Bengali phrases uttered by foreigners.

Elizabeth says in broken Bengali, 'I want it today. I love Calcutta. My mummy is a Bengali lady. I'm half Bengali.'

The clerk now looks at Elizabeth in astonishment. How can this golden-haired, blue-eyed memsahib be the daughter of a Bengali lady?

With utmost respect he says, 'Sit down madam, please sit down.'

By this time many others in the office, taking an abrupt break from their work, throng the table to see this unusual kind of lady. She is a pucca memsahib in spite of having a Bengali mother. She speaks Bengali as well. One of the officials hanging around her takes a personal initiative to get a crumpled form from the drawer, which they had searched earlier. Everything gets done in ten minutes.

Shaking the clerk's hand, Elizabeth says, 'Thank you, thank you, Mr Kalas ben!'

With the form in hand, she triumphantly comes out of the office and says, 'Let's go to the Sunderbans.'

Nirmal volunteers to accompany them. 'It's a very big area. Where do you want to put up at night? We must book the tourist lodge well in advance.'

'I hope you've heard the name of Mandira Brockway?' asks Elizabeth.

Nirmal gets a little flabbergasted. Is she a noted person? Should he have known her? But he hasn't found a Mandira Brockway in his office records. So he asks, 'Is she British?'

Elizabeth is a little disappointed. She was under the impression that anyone in Calcutta would know her mother by name. She is after all the ex-wife of a very powerful British MP.

She, however, says, 'Mandira Brockway is my mother. A great lady.'

'Can't we get back from the Sunderbans tonight?' mumbles Robert.

'We are going there in search of mom. We don't know her address. At first we've to go to a village, called Sukhchar. There we've to meet a gentleman ... I can't pronounce his name; it's written in my diary.'

Nirmal looks at the diary and says, 'Chayan Ghose. Well it won't be difficult to locate the man.'

It takes two and a half hours to reach Sukhchar. But they can't find Chayan Ghose there. He is now a resident of Mamudpur, some distance away from Sukhchar.

It's three o'clock in the afternoon. The sun is blazing hot. They have not had their lunch yet. There are some roadside eateries, but Robert has strong reservations about dining there. He's carrying boiled drinking water. Stopping the car on the road, Elizabeth has drunk plenty of coconut water and bought a bunch of ripe bananas from the roadside stalls. According to her, Nature cooks food without spice and adulteration. Everyone, including Nirmal, have had to quench their thirst and hunger only with those things.

The road up to Sukhchar is somewhat passable. But after Sukhchar it's badly broken. The car is constantly bumping up and down. With the help of the local people they trace Chayan Ghose's residence in a narrow lane at Mamudpur ... With much difficulty the car enters the alley.

A person like Chayan Ghose is not supposed to be home at this hour. But he has been down with fever for the last two days.

Hearing the sound of a car engine, Chayan Ghose comes out. Thinly built, with long hair, he is wearing a pyjama and a vest.

Instead of Nirmal, Elizabeth herself comes forward, saying, 'Good afternoon. Do you speak English?'

'A little bit. What can I do for you?' asks Chayan self-consciously.

Fishing out a letter from her bag, Elizabeth says, 'My mother's name is Mandira Brockway. Now she might have changed her title. Formerly she was Mandira Dutta. I've come to meet her. Can you tell us where she stays now?'

Shaking his head, he says in a despondent tone, 'No.'

'You don't know my mother! Strange! She wrote about you in one of her letters to me,' says a shocked Elizabeth.

'I knew her once,' says Chayan, 'but now I don't know where she is. I'm not in touch with her.'

'But I received this letter two months back. She had written that she was suffering from a death phobia. Is she alive?' says Elizabeth.

'I don't know,' replies Chayan.

In a stern voice, Elizabeth says, 'Strange! You knew my mother who lived in or around this place. But you're claiming that you don't know whether she is alive or not.'

By this time, Chayan has got over his initial shock of meeting a foreign couple. He stares at the young lady resplendent in her bright skirt. What do these people think of us? thinks Chayan—they look upon us as their loyal subjects, even now!

He also rebuffs in a brusque tone, 'I knew her. But that does not necessarily mean that I have to keep track of her activities on a daily basis. I don't know whether she is alive or not.'

Saying this he mends his speech at once. 'I'm sorry. I shouldn't have said that. I'm sure she is alive. If she were not alive I would have heard of it, of course. She must be somewhere around this region.'

'I intend to find her. Would you please help me?' asks Elizabeth.

'No, it's not possible for me. I would suggest you to go to Sajjad sahib at Sukhchar. He can guide you better than me.'

Nirmal writes down Sajjad's name. They get into the car but as soon as the engine starts, Chayan rushes towards them, saying, 'Sajjad is ill; I'm afraid he can't help you now. Better I come with you.'

Chayan's countenance bears a dejected look. He is as though shocked to meet Elizabeth and Robert and is accompanying them only out of sheer courtesy.

Chayan is sitting beside Nirmal on the front seat.

'What do you do, Mr Ghose? Are you a teacher?' asks Robert. He is perhaps under the impression that in Bengal teachers alone can speak English.

Chayan smiles and then turning to Nirmal says in Bengali that he is unemployed. Nirmal tells them in English, 'Look, he is one of the many millions of unemployed youths in Bengal. He just sits at home doing nothing productive.'

The car has halted on the bank of the river Raymangal. Some mechanised boats are waiting for the passengers. They will now leave the car and cruise across the river in a boat. But Chayan looks hesitant.

Impatiently, Elizabeth asks, 'Which side?'

'Are you willing to cross the river and go to that side?' asks Chayan.

'Of course,' says Elizabeth, 'both Bob and I know swimming; we're not scared of a boat journey.'

Chayan knows that swimming won't be of much help, for the river is infested with crocodiles. But he doesn't say anything. Now it being winter there is little chance of a storm but his mind is preoccupied with other kinds of apprehensions.

'Do you just want to know whether she's alive or do you also want to meet her? If it is the former, then I can just gather the information from the boatmen,' says Chayan.

'No, we of course want to meet mom,' says Elizabeth.

'Are you prepared to face what you'll see?' Chayan has a grave expression on his face now.

Elizabeth is startled by this particular remark. 'Why, what has happened to my mother?' she asks anxiously.

Chayan keeps quiet for a while. Then, after a little bit of hesitation, he changes his tone and says, 'In fact, I don't know exactly what has happened to her. Let's go now and see.'

As soon as the boat starts cruising Elizabeth claps her hands like a child, saying, 'Very modern! It's a wooden country boat. Is it not ingenious, Bob?'

'Indeed!' replies Robert, 'and soon they'll fit a motor with a bullock cart as well.'

'Look Bob, how splendidly blue the sky is!' screams Elizabeth in sheer joy.

'I'm fond of rivers. I admit that this place is really beautiful. But I hope the Royal Bengal Tiger won't spring upon me,' says Robert.

The rivers and canals here are like city streets. The rivers and their tributaries form the backwaters of the sea. The sides are lined with bushes of dwarfish trees. The boats are packed with passengers like sardines. The scent of briny water is borne on the air.

Taking help from the local boatmen, and after sailing for about one and a half hours, they spot a large-sized boat on the silted bed of the river. From a distance they recognise a woman, in a greyish sari with red borders, sitting in the middle of the boat.

Chayan's heart aches in grief. He had almost forgotten Mandira. She had really hurt him. On the day of her departure she had not even bothered to meet him once. Didn't she understand that Chayan worshipped and adored her like a goddess? And that there was a deep love in that adoration?

As they draw near, they see Mandira sitting cross-legged on the board. On the other side of the boat, a strongly built man, holding the rope tied to the net, is staring at the water. Mandira is arranging the betel nut container. She looks suspiciously at the boat full of strangers. The colour of her sunburnt face resembles that of the local soil.

Elizabeth, standing on the boat, throws up her arms and shouts, 'Mummy!' 'Mummy!'

Mandira stands up and, in an impassioned tone, cries back, 'Lizzi, my darling, you've really come at last!'

As if both of them will jump into the river.

'We should rather stay back here; we shouldn't intervene between them,' Chayan says to Nirmal.

Liz, jumping into the next boat, embraces her mother and plants kisses on both her cheeks. Mandira's eyes are full of tears and she stands speechless.

Some moments later Liz says, beckoning to Robert, 'Mom, he is my husband, Bob. At long last we have got married. We did a most out of fashion thing ... Bob's father was insisting a lot.'

'I'm so glad to see you ... I can't imagine how you took the trouble of coming all the way to meet me,' says Mandira to Robert.

'I have been longing to meet you. You are a very daring lady. I shall write a story on you in our newspaper. We didn't face any discomfort in coming here. Lovely countryside!' says Robert.

'How are you all? How is Robin? Is he alright?' asks Mandira anxiously.

'Robin is fine. He has conveyed his congrats to you. Why don't you write to him? I think you should write to him immediately.'

'And your father?'

'Daddy is busy as ever. We talk on the phone sometimes. Linda is no longer daddy's secretary. A new girl has been appointed in her place. Daddy is dating a new girlfriend these days. The fact is that he does not like to be steady with somebody for long. He prefers a no-strings-attached relationship. By the way, where is our stepfather? Won't you introduce us to him?'

Javed is unwinding the net on the other side of the boat. Some fish are caught in it. He pours the catch inside the boat and lights a bidi.

'Javed, please come this way; look, my daughter and son-in-law have come. You don't believe that I have a grown-up daughter. Now see for yourself. My son is even older than her.'

Just wearing a lungi below his bare chest, dripping wet, Javed is standing leaning on the covering of the houseboat.

Robert stretches out his hand saying, 'Hello! I'm Robert Roth. Glad to meet you.'

'He knows a little bit of English but hesitates to speak. In fact, he is basically reserved. Javed, say hello to them.' Mandira prompts him.

Javed offers a shy smile and says 'Hello.'

He's very handsome, Mom; I must appreciate your taste. How do you live in this boat!' says Liz.

'Yes dear, we live in this boat. What's the need of a homestead? We are quite happy here. Javed catches fish and I cook. Everyday I go to the market to sell it. I keep accounts. In the evenings we sail on the river and sing together. He sings so well ...'

'In your letter you had written you were apprehensive of some danger befalling you. You had written that you might die any day; what was it?' asks a concerned Liz.

'Yes, initially there were many attempts to kill us. They were so hostile to us ...'

'Why? Why were they hostile to you? What was your fault? Did you ever harm anybody?'

'No darling, our fault lies in marrying in spite of a considerable age gap between us. Besides, there's a religious barrier too. The people here are obsessed with matters of religion and caste. Robbers had attacked twice. They had once seriously wounded me with a dagger. I was saved only because Javed had fought them away like James Bond.'

'Oh, he looks like a black James Bond! Mom, you have really taken a very good decision. If you can spend your whole life this way, what's wrong in it? You can also venture out into the ocean one day, if he's with you,' says an elated Liz.

'I don't know whether I can spend my whole life this way, yet I'll enjoy happy days as long as I'm destined to. Then, when I'll grow old and Javed, still young, will marry someone younger and prettier, I'll go away somewhere else.'

Saying this she turns to Javed and fondly teases him, 'So Javed, won't you desert me to marry someone else?'

Without replying, Javed hands the half-burnt bidi from his lips to Mandira.

She puffs at it as Liz and Robert stand gaping at her.

Throwing out the bidi into the water, Mandira says, 'Come, let's have tea. I couldn't get rid of this particular habit. I can't help without a pretty good brand of tea. Won't you stay the night with me? You can leave your boat. I'll cook fresh fish and rice for you. We are accustomed to spicy curry but for you I'll prepare a simple preparation. I hope you'll enjoy the taste of steamed rice and fresh fish curry.'

All at once Javed shouts, 'Chayan da, won't you come to our boat?'

Chayan was looking the other way. He shakes his head. He hasn't forgiven Javed till today. The sight of him makes Chayan burn in envy. So he wants to forget both of them.

A little later Javed comes to the other boat with cups of tea for Chayan and the others. Mandira comes down on the sandbanks accompanying Liz and Robert. Normally, the place is not visited by tigers but it is notorious for snakes. However, the chance of being bitten by a snake is rare in winter.

Suddenly Mandira's eyes fall on Chayan, sitting in the other boat. In fact, she has been overwhelmed by the presence of her daughter and son-in-law; so she doesn't notice him initially. She's grateful to him for guiding Robert and Liz safely to her.

'Chayan, Chayan, why are you sitting there? Come here. I have lots of things to talk about.'

Chayan turns his face away from her. He maintains his reticence.

'Mr Ghose, she is calling you,' says Nirmal. The boatman says, 'Sir, madam is calling you.'

So Chayan has no other alternative but to get down on the sandbank and meet her.

'How are you all—Bina, Shanti at Sukhchar?' asks Mandira with a smile revealing her lips stained with betel leaf juice.

In a glum voice, Chayan replies, 'I'm not sure but have heard that Bina was married off and went out of Sukhchar.'

'Oh! My God! Bina has finally married that man! But she was telling me that she was in love with someone else. She had to yield to her parents' pressures in the end. By the way, what are you doing now?'

'Nothing,' replies Chayan.

Robert comments, 'It's really amazing. This gentleman knows English, yet does not do anything for a living.'

Mandira flies to his defence, 'Who says that Chayan doesn't do anything? He is a very good social worker. He runs a science club, a rational association in the village. He has been working hard day and night to free village folks from the clutches of superstition. I have seen very few people as enterprising as Chayan.'

'He has helped us a lot,' adds Liz.

'Is Sajjad still running the library?' asks Mandira. 'I hope there was no further trouble related to the Babri Masjid–Ramjanmabhoomi controversy at Sukhchar. I heard some outsiders had come to ...'

All at once, Chayan says in a sharp tone, 'You have no right to ask me all this. You fled from our village. You instigated a whole lot of village youths and then fled to serve your self interests.'

'Are you also annoyed with me?' asks Mandira, gently laying her hand on Chayan's shoulder. 'You couldn't accept our relationship?'

Moving a little away from her, Chayan says, 'It matters little whether I accept or not; but when people slander you, we cannot protest. We were able to unite them for a good cause; we could have made further progress with them ... but you nipped everything in the bud.'

'But I'm an outsider. Suppose somebody came to murder me in the dead of night, would anyone have come to rescue me?' asks Mandira heaving a deep sigh.

'Is that why you've engaged a bodyguard to live on the river with you? What did you get from Javed? Only sex?' says Chayan, almost screaming now.

Liz bursts into laughter, 'Why do people take sex so lightly? Is it not possible to leave everything for sex?'

Turning to her, Mandira says in a quiet tone, 'No, not just sex, I've discovered a human being in Javed.'

'You call Javed a human being! You couldn't find anyone else to live with?' Chayan can't suppress his bitterness. He loses his patience and walking up to his boat, jumps into it.

Mandira keeps staring into the distance for a while.

Liz says, 'The man seems to be very angry with you.'

'They're all angry with me. They just couldn't accept it. So what if I carry out an experiment with my own life? Must everybody conform to age-old customs and traditions?'

'Mom, I suggest you shouldn't listen to them.'

The light at the fag end of the evening is softly hued. Flights of exotic geese are flying in the sky. The riverbed is crisscrossed with innumerable golden streaks. Tiny red crabs scurry into holes at the sound of footsteps.

Mandira and Liz are walking side by side across the sandbank. Robert is busy with his camera, taking snapshots and muttering lines from his own poems. A new poem has come to his mind.

'Keep visiting my residence in London occasionally. When I'll die, you shall inherit it. But right now I don't intend to sell it.'

'Mom, don't you miss London?'

'Of course! Besides, I miss you all so much! How I often long to meet you. It has been such a long time since I visited the theatres, read a new book or saw a Meryl Streep movie. The yearning for things that were once favourite doesn't wane overnight. Again you can't get a lot of things that you want. For the sake of some of your heart's decisions, you have to sacrifice a great deal. I used to often feel claustrophobic when I lived in solitude in London. Here I'm far from being lonely, rather too preoccupied. Sometimes I think that Javed and I have been banished to an island; here we have found each other so deeply. Again we can also return to mainstream society at our sweet will any day.'

'May I ask you one question?' asks Robert. 'Can you erase your cultural levels altogether? You spent a greater part of your life amongst educated, sophisticated and urban intellectuals. But I wonder, how can you possibly live with an uneducated person for sex alone?'

'Javed is not uneducated,' Mandira counters.

'Is that so?' says Robert mockingly.

'Who do you think should be called educated? I think one who is an expert in a particular subject. You can't believe, Bob, how well Javed knows by heart the ins and outs of the rivers, seas, skies and climates. Even by touching the waters, he can forecast the weather. Once he was extremely violent, wild, rather fierce; now coming in close communion with nature, he has got rid of his wild, bestial passions. Each day, little by little, I happen to know this man better than the previous day. Knowing a man really well—isn't that an achievement of sorts?'

In a light-hearted spirit, Liz says, 'Bob, can't we too live like them in a boat? You'll pick up the art of fishing from Mom's friend.'

'God forbid!' says Robert, 'I don't like the idea at all. And what about my lectures scheduled to be delivered in New Delhi?'

'No dear, I know you will be bored if you stay here for more than a day or two,' says Mandira.

'Mom, I'm proud of you. The majority of middle-aged women lead very ordinary, prosaic lives. But you have a philosophy of life, an independent and youthful bent of mind, thumbing your nose at conventions.'

'I don't have any well-defined philosophy of life. Life itself is a fathomless mystery to me. We're puppets in the hands of destiny. I don't know where I'm ultimately destined to be. But basically what makes me happy is that I don't run after it. I'm content with what I have got. I'm not haunted by the past, nor do I speculate about the future.'

'I'm relieved to know that you're fine and happy. If it were not so, I would have compelled you to return to London,' says Liz.

'Yes, I'm happy. I have a partner who just wants me; what could be more gratifying than this for me? Moreover, I have been able to erase all traces of hatred and malice from his mind—don't you think that is a great achievement? I don't know how long I shall continue to be blessed with this kind of joy. Still, however ephemeral it might be, I must say it's invaluable. Without this unfettered joy my life would have been incomplete. Look at the skies—they are so unblemished here; the air is uncontaminated; our daily meals are laced with a hearty appetite. I don't want to forsake all this to live elsewhere.'

Both of them keep strolling silently. Silence sometimes has the power of bridging the gap between individuals.

They walk up to the other end of the sandbank. The river is gradually swelling because of the brawling high tide. The western sky has turned kaleidoscopic. Dipping her feet in the water, Mandira says, 'How wonderful is the experience of being alive! Isn't it Liz?'

Like a kid, Liz sinks her head in her mother's lap; caressing her daughter, Mandira repeats, 'How wonderful is it to be alive!'

Acknowledgements

Sujal Bhattacharya for such a lucid and well-written translation.

Shurit Doss and Monimoy Dasgupta, for a write-up which provided me with certain facts regarding the Sunderbans Fertiliser factory.

Nirmal Kanti Bhattacharjee for his involvement and support.

Bikash Niyogi and Tultul Niyogi of Niyogi Books for their exceptional help and encouragement.

Sucharita Ghosh, my editor, for her kind understanding throughout the process.